A TREASURE FOUND

Jessica held the book for a moment, studying the cover. Then she opened it. Tentatively she held the book open with her thumb and forefinger, and gave it a little shake. A thin white packet fell to the floor.

With one mind, they knelt to pick it up, their hands colliding on the folded, sealed paper. Then they sat down together on the floor, their backs against the shelves, their heads touching, to examine it in the circle of light cast by the lamp.

"My mother's hand." Jessica's hand trembled as she pointed to the first line scrawled on the front: "If you are truly honorable and truly love me, Godfrey, you will put this back unopened." And her father's: "Annette: If you ever again question my honor or my love, I will show you this."

It was an eerie moment, this dialogue between lovers long-dead, and John sensed that Jessica was close to tears. It seemed natural, imperative in fact, to take her face in his hand and bend to kiss her—a distraction from sorrow for her, from desperate curiosity for him.

And inevitably it became more than a distraction. Her lips parted under his—no, this was no green girl, he thought, closing his eyes and letting the paper drop so he could pull her closer. It was so very sweet, the taste, the feel of her, the radiant moment in the darkness . . .

ZEBRA'S REGENCY ROMANCES
DAZZLE AND DELIGHT

Poetic Justice

Alicia Rasley

ZEBRA BOOKS
KENSINGTON PUBLISHING CORP.

This book is dedicated to my writing friends in the Indiana RWA and the Romex board of the GEnie computer network, especially Lynn Kerstàn, who gave me the key to the Shakespeare puzzle, and Danelle Harmon, who suggested I flog John.

ZEBRA BOOKS are published by

Kensington Publishing Corp.
850 Third Avenue
New York, NY 10022

First Printing: June, 1994

Printed in the United States of America

By the time his shipmates arrived panting, daggers drawn, the light was gone entirely and the dock was slippery with blood. Two of the bandits had fled; the third lay unconscious on the dock. John loosed his death grip on the saddlebag, let his first mate take it, let his steward peel his fingers from around the knife and put it away. He nudged the bandit with his foot. "Tell your employer," he said, then paused to drag in a breath, "that I passed that test too."

Chapter Two

May 25, 1818

Sir, he hath never fed of the dainties
that are bred in a book.
He hath not eat paper, as it were;
he hath not drunk ink.

Love's Labor Lost IV, ii.

I have spent most of my life like this, Jessica Seton thought, sitting here on this settee, waiting for two men to determine the rest of my life. It was an exaggeration, of course, if a forgiveable one. Long ago she had waited here in the hallway while a solicitor read her father's will to her uncle, and three years ago when a colonel from the Horse Guards came with news from Waterloo.

Now another afternoon of anxiety and dread. Impatient suddenly, she slipped off her shoes and in her stockinged feet crossed to the door that shut her out of her uncle's study. She rested her temple against the cool wood and held her breath. She could hear nothing but a low rumble of voices. Consigning convention to perdition, she reached for the knob. But it turned under her fingers, and she stepped back quickly as Damien Blake emerged.

She could tell from his brooding face that his suit, like the others, had been unsuccessful. She grabbed his hand and pulled him into the drawing room, closing the door behind her and leaning back on it, near despair. "He said no, didn't he?"

Damien was a poet, and measured his words for sound and sense before he spoke them. "That is so." Two beats, and then rest of the line. "He will not give his consent."

"Did he tell you why?"

Damien inclined his head to the side, considered this. He was a radical also, and so etched irony into his next verse. "A man granted such authority need have no reason to use it."

Jessica closed her eyes for a moment and gathered her tattered temper back together. "Did you try to persuade him?"

"Persuade him?" The radical vanished, and the marquess's son regained control of Damien's features. "Certainly not."

"Damien, you didn't—oh, what *did* you say, then, if you didn't try to change his mind?"

Suddenly he swept her into his arms, protective and ardent at once. "I told him that true love needed no consent, and we would marry without it."

"You didn't really say that," One look up at his proud noble face told her he did. She wrenched herself free of him. "Oh, Damien, this isn't *Romeo and Juliet!* We *can't* marry without his consent."

Damien withdrew sulkily to the couch, assuming a picturesque pose with head back and arms flung out. In the dusty sunlight he shone like an Elgin Marble. "You are of age. I am of age. We can marry tomorrow, if we desire. No man can gainsay us."

"*That* man can gainsay my inheritance. Damien, if you would just have tried to convince him that you care enough—"

'It should be self-evident."

That this was true did not make it right. She halted her pacing in front of the couch and regarded him with exasperation. "Probably my uncle thinks that the perfect suitor would argue his case."

"Probably," Damien suggested, ironic again, "he thinks no one is the perfect suitor. No one yet living, that is." He reached out his hand to hers, and drew her to sit beside him. "As far as your uncle is concerned, you were meant to marry his son. His son's best friend is no substitute. And neither, I wager, is anyone else."

As he spoke this home truth, he regarded her sympathetically and opened his arms in invitation. But with her uncle just across the hall, she didn't take advantage of this to seek comfort, instead rising again to pace, her stockinged feet sliding across the oak floor. Comfort wasn't what she wanted, at any rate. She wanted—control. Control over her life, her fate—her inheritance.

"It isn't fair."

"What isn't fair is that you deny yourself to suit him."

"I am not denying myself to suit him. It is in my father's will, that I must marry with his consent, or lose my inheritance."

"Jessica, what is it you want, me or the inheritance?"

It was too obvious to say aloud. But Damien was waiting, sitting up, leaning forward, as if he didn't know the answer.

"Both."

"Both? Both? Equally?"

It was not, she was supposed to realize, the answer he

wanted. But it was the only one she had. And, she thought with renewed anger, he should accept that. "I have lived all my life thinking—*knowing*—that I was to have the Parham Collection. I am not going to give it up, not while I still have a chance."

"And if you marry me now, without your uncle's consent, you will lose it forever."

Relieved that he understood, she nodded.

But Damien was Damien, and she should have known that whatever else he understood, it wasn't the value of the Parham Collection. "Well, love is worth the sacrifice of it, I think. And you should think so too."

A sacrifice for love. It was a poetic sentiment, and with half her heart she longed for the man who made it. The other half, however, was reserved for the collection her parents had left her—or would have left her, had they known how much she would sacrifice for it.

Damien observed her stubborn silence for a moment, then rose, his jaw taut but his hand open and extended towards her. "I can promise you a pleasant, worthy life, in recompense for giving up the collection. You won't have the old books, but you will be my helpmeet as I write new books." When she only frowned and looked at his hand, he withdrew it and bowed. "I shan't try to persuade you, but my offer remains open. If you decide you want to marry me, you may send a note to my lodge in the Cotswolds. I am preparing a book of pastorals, and need more of nature than I find here in London."

As he departed, Jessica considered suggesting that he might *sacrifice* his communing with nature to help her change her uncle's mind. But she knew she wouldn't be able to strip the sarcasm from her voice. Indeed, even the careful "Do have a good holiday" she called after him fairly dripped with irony.

She watched over the staircase till Damien was almost out the door, and then called after him, "I hope the flies are biting and the fish aren't!"

Men. They were so eloquent in calling for sacrifice, as long as the sacrifice was being done *for* them and not *by* them. Uncle Emory was just the same, expecting her to sacrifice both marriage and the collection—and for what? To ease his conscience, that was all.

She retrieved her shoes from under the hall settee, but by the time she had slipped them back on she was still too angry to confront her uncle. So she had to wait outside his study door, breathing deep until the passion seeped away. Only then could she greet him with a level voice and the polite inquiry, "Have you a moment to talk, Uncle?"

Lord Parham looked up from the papers at his desk. His eyes still held a martial light from the battle—not that Damien had put up much of a fight. She took the seat across from him, and took a moment to compose her angry thoughts into civil words. Her aunt and uncle were kindly people, but they expected filial deference, especially from the niece they had raised these last half-dozen years. She would earn no points by shouting and stamping her feet, no matter how much she might like to do so.

A statement of fact seemed the most inoffensive opening. "Uncle, Damien tells me that you refused his suit."

"Yes, I did."

"He didn't say why, though."

"Hmm, I imagine he didn't."

Lord Parham shuffled the pages on his desk, took one out, studied it significantly, and dropped it on top of the blotter. Without craning her neck, she couldn't read the lines, but she could see that the message was written in elaborate old-fashioned cursive. "Another poison-pen note, I suppose. Uncle, you have known Damien all his life. Surely you won't believe some vicious gossip that claims he is unworthy."

"I went to the trouble of checking this information, and found it accurate. Indeed, the young man as much as admitted that he was an opium-eater and kept a mistress in Richmond Park."

It would be just like Damien, Jessica thought, to set his mistress up in some picturesque but inconvenient place like Richmond. The poor girl must have perished from the isolation. "He isn't an opium-eater. He told me he tried a bit of the hookah on his grand tour of the East, but didn't like it. And as for the mistress, why, all the young men have them. They're like high-perch phaetons—just a fashionable item for the young beau." Jessica wasn't actually quite so nonchalant about Damien's fashionable item, but her uncle brought out the cynic in her. "Once we are properly engaged, he will give her up, if he hasn't already."

"He is a rackety young man, you can't deny it."

"He is a perfectly pleasant young man, and a very good poet," Jessica retorted, "and he will settle down well when we marry."

"When you marry?"

Lord Parham fixed her with a stern gaze, and, with a sigh, she looked away. *"If* we marry." Then, in despair, she cried, "Oh, Uncle, I thought this one you would approve. This is *Damien.* You know him, you know his family, he took a first at Oxford, he has a respectable fortune, he hasn't any insane great-uncles, he doesn't beat his servants, he doesn't gamble—how can I do better?"

"You have done better."

His face was bleak. Trevor again. Always. Involuntarily she glanced up at the miniature of her cousin on the bookshelf. Trevor had been a true Seton, as Jessica was, slender and blonde and delicate of feature. The sight of him in the scarlet and gold infantry uniform never failed to disorient her—he had been the unlikeliest of soldiers. He had been, however, the most dutiful of sons.

But now was no time for recriminations. Carefully she softened her tone. "I know, uncle. I was meant for Trevor. But he is gone. And—and I shan't find his like, you know that. But I have had many fine suitors, and you haven't considered one of them worthy, even though—" bitterness crept into her voice, no matter how she tried to prevent it. "Even though each of them managed to win a bride after you dismissed them for me."

"Well, that's it, isn't it?" Parham was triumphant, as if she had given him the trump card. "They couldn't have loved you very well, as they were so quick to find another. And you—how many 'fine suitors' have you brought before me? A half dozen, at least! If you felt the least real devotion to any of them, you wouldn't have entertained the next. Or you would have ignored my disapproval."

"Surely that's not what you want! For me to marry a man out of hand? Without your consent?"

"No. That is not what I want." Lord Parham added significantly, "But perhaps that is what *you* should want."

But then—then I would lose the collection. It seemed so simple to her, but she realized despairingly that her uncle, like Damien, didn't understand. True love, that's what he meant she should feel. But since he had got it fixed in his head that she could feel true love only for Trevor, she could hardly win by professing undying devotion for another. She couldn't win at all, not with her uncle making the rules.

Falteringly, she said, looking down at her clasped

hands, "I fear I haven't such high standards any longer. I want to marry, and have children, of course. But I don't seek a perfect husband. A pleasant man, with an even temper and worthy pursuits, is enough for me. He needn't even care so much for the collection, as Trevor did, for I am eager to take that on myself. Just—just a good man, whom I can respect, and who will respect me. You know I have never been very romantic, Uncle."

But her humble admission didn't move him. "That's as it may be. But you'll have to do better than Damien Blake, to expect my approval."

Jessica gave way to panic. "Then *tell* me! Just tell me! Name the man you will approve, and if he will have me, I will—" She swallowed back her rash promise, and when she could speak again, she added in a low voice, "My twenty-third birthday is but two months away. I cannot wait very longer to find one you approve."

Lord Parham had the grace to look guilty just for a moment, but then his brow cleared and he resumed his Old Testament patriarchal expression. "Perhaps if you thought less about the collection and more about your duties, I would have greater respect for your judgment in these matters."

"Duties? I will perform whatever duties you require, if you will only—"

"Your aunt told me you refused to accompany her to Parham Hall yesterday, because you had made an appointment to visit Montagu House. She was most distressed and couldn't understand your decision."

Jessica was naturally outspoken, and might, at an earlier age, have retorted that perusing Henry VII's land grants at the British Museum seemed a better use of her time than laying flowers on a grave and watching Aunt Martha weep. But she had learned that her aunt and uncle did not appreciate such candor. "We had just been out there on Trevor's birthday. And we will be going again on the eighteenth next—" June eighteen would be the third anniversary of the battle of Waterloo, a day the Setons spent, like the families of the other fallen heroes, in subdued commemoration. Her uncle shook his head sadly, and Jessica sighed, knowing that he didn't consider that sufficient.

"I will try not to upset Aunt Martha again. But Uncle, please consider that Trevor would never have wanted the collection to pass out of the family."

That it was a mistake, she knew before the words were out of her mouth. Her uncle's expression shuttered, and he seized the letter that indicted Damien Blake and stuffed it back into a folio. He didn't look up as he said coldly, "The collection won't pass out of the family. It will merely go in a trust, administered by the family attorneys, and managed by the curator your father appointed before his death."

"Alfred Wiley." She couldn't keep the distaste from her voice. "If Father saw how he 'manages' the library, he might have changed his mind."

But her uncle was no intellectual, and seldom set foot in the library. He only knew what he had heard about Wiley—most of it, she was sure, from Wiley himself. "He is the kingdom's leading Bacon scholar, and the library has an extensive Bacon holding. Besides," he added brusquely, "that was your father's wish."

"My father's wish was that I inherit the library!"

"Only if you married Trevor. He wanted Trevor to have it, as he had no son of his own."

"No! If that is what he had wanted, he would have left it to Trevor alone!"

But there was a cold obstinacy at the center of her uncle, one that she glimpsed only when she tried to defy him. "He expected you to marry Trevor. That is why he gave me consent power over your marriage. He never meant for you to marry another."

"But he didn't know that Trevor would become a soldier—how could he have expected that? Or that we wouldn't have a chance to marry? Uncle, my father *loved* me. He would never have meant the sort of future you intend for me—no husband, no children, not even the collection! Trevor is dead and yet I—"

"That's enough! You have said enough!"

Her uncle rose, scattering papers across the desk. His anger was so palpable, blazing across the study like a flame, that she couldn't catch her breath to finish her sentence. Instead she sat silent, still, as her uncle stood over her. "You don't need to tell me my son is dead! Do you think an hour passes without my remembering that?"

"No," she answered, adding silently, not in this house of death, not with every room holding a little shrine to him, and Aunt Martha still in mourning clothes after three years. They thought she should do that too, mourn Trevor every moment, sacrifice her life to remember his death.

Suddenly she knew she had to leave, before she said something unforgiveable to her uncle, before she broke her aunt's heart with some thoughtless act, before she gave up and accepted the life of a widow without having ever been a wife.

So she rose and faced her uncle. "Ada Rush has invited me to accompany her to Dorset with her. I am going to accept. Her brother will be escorting us, and I will take Mimi along."

"You mean to miss the Waterloo anniversary after all then."

"There is a church in Bincombe. I will observe it there."

He turned away, dismissing her. But as she went through the door, she heard him mutter, "Godspeed then, child."

The door to the library was cracked open, too powerful a lure to be resisted. Jessica inched open the door and slid through the opening into the reading room, breathing in the unique combination of dust and leather that meant old books. There was more dust than leather, unfortunately; she had spoken only the truth when she said that Wiley was no librarian. Oh, here in the reading room, he made a good show of it, with the glass cases displaying the more picturesque of the manuscripts, and comfortable leather chairs with lamps positioned nearby for illumination.

But though the room was dim, the lamps were unlit—there were no patrons to need light for reading. Alfred Wiley had continued his benefactor's policy of keeping the library closed even to scholars. Her father had been a shy man, reclusive by nature; Wiley, she thought, just wanted to keep all the Bacon artifacts to himself.

She moved quietly through the reading room and paused at the door that opened to the main collections area. Either the librarian had gone to lunch, or he was in the storeroom along the back of the second level. Otherwise, as he always did, he would have emerged from his office to ask her in that courteous voice whether she needed his assistance.

But the library remained silent, welcoming. Alone, if only for the moment, with her collection! She slipped into the main collection room, reaching into her reticule for a handkerchief as her passage stirred up a cloud of dust. A sunbeam from the distant window filtered through the motes, and her nose began to tickle. Sternly she ordered the sneeze away and walked purposefully if surreptitiously along the narrow corridor.

Here, where the books were kept, Wiley's deficiencies were most apparent. Disorder marked the vast room and its crisscrosses of mahogany bookcases, with boxes of documents heaped in the aisles. She bent to pick up a book on the top of a stack blocking her way. The title was spelled out in gilt on the leather cover: *Moll Flanders, Volume One.* She leaned against the end of a bookcase and leafed through the old book, smiling when she found the faint remains of a stain on the tenth page. How angry her parents had been when they found her at the breakfast table, reading this book out loud to Trevor! Her mother had warned her that the story was too advanced for a young girl, and too stimulating for a young boy; her father was more concerned about the jelly that had dripped from Jessica's toast on to the page. He had made her clean it herself—her first restoration job, and not a very good one at that. She had learned a good deal since then.

She glanced around for Wiley, and when she reassured herself that she was quite alone, dusted the book and stuffed it into her reticule. Later, in the little laboratory that used to be her dressing room, she would daub at the spot with a special solution, and, while she was at it, oil the cover and check the binding. When it was pristine enough to have passed her father's stringent standards, she would replace it where it belonged on the Defoe shelf. While she was at it, she would reorganize the Defoe items and make a list of those needing repairs.

And with those few acts, she would be doing more curating in one day than Alfred Wiley did in a year.

It always broke her heart to come here and see the chaos and deterioration. Wiley might tell her ingenuous

uncle that so many books were boxed because they were
scheduled to be restored, and that the long-promised
catalogue was only a few months away. Jessica knew
better. As long as her father lived, Wiley had performed
his duties well. But he had taken advantage of the laxer
supervision of her uncle to focus his attention on one
part of the collection. Now, if a book had nothing to do
with Sir Francis Bacon, it had nothing to do with Alfred
Wiley.

When I inherit, she thought fiercely, the first thing I
will do is discharge Wiley. *Without* a reference! And
then I will open it to scholars, especially other Bacon
scholars. When I inherit . . .

If I inherit.

And she wouldn't, if her uncle remained unreason-
able about her marriage.

And Alfred Wiley had to know that.

Absently she straightened out a shelf of sermon volumes, reorganizing her thoughts as she reorganized the
titles. Alfred Wiley only stood to gain if she didn't marry
before the deadline of her twenty-third birthday. He appeared to be a mild-mannered scholarly sort, but tenacious as he was about the Bacon holdings he considered
his own, she couldn't imagine he would let them go
without a struggle.

She located a white spot on her now-dusty handkerchief and applied it to the green leather cover of Dr.
Donne's sermons. Staring unseeing at the gilt letters of
the title, she recalled her uncle brandishing the poison-
pen letter, only the latest of several he had received
about her suitors. Uncle Emory hadn't let her read any
of them; he persisted in thinking she was too innocent
for such knowledge, and insisted on burning them. But
she had caught glimpses of three of the notes, and knew
enough from studying autograph manuscripts to make

some suppositions. No two of the letters appeared to be written in the same hand. This last one about Damien, indeed, bore the spidery hand of a man of the previous century, while an earlier one had been a bold modern scrawl.

It was unlikely that four separate people would have reason to scotch her marriage chances, and just happen on the same way to do it. No, it would have to be someone who not only had a motive, but also knew enough about her uncle to manipulate his protective instincts. And it would have to be someone with access to different scribes—or the ability to write in different hands.

Suddenly she replaced the book on the shelf and used the last clean corner of the handkerchief to dust off her hands. Quietly she moved through the stacks of shelves to the staircase that led up to the second level. She stopped to pull off her shoes, hiding them behind a box of unbound papers. Then she crept up the steps, her hand braced lightly on the bannister. At the top she ducked down and peered through the iron railing, over the tops of bookshelves, methodically scanning the aisles. Mr. Wiley was nowhere to be seen in the sea of books.

Still hunched over, Jessica tiptoed along the landing to the storage room. She flattened herself against the wall and peeked in through the open door. The room was unoccupied. The vault along the back wall that held the most valuable items was, as always, locked up tight. Only the solicitors had the keys to that door, a fact, she imagined, of constant annoyance to Mr. Wiley.

Retrieving her shoes, she went through the main room to the workroom along the side of the library. The door to Mr. Wiley's office was closed. Bolder now, she knocked, and when she received no response, she pushed open the door. A wave of hot air rushed out.

Resisting the urge to open the window, Jessica closed her mouth tight against the dusty air and steered a path through the piles of monographs that led to to the desk. She couldn't touch the papers on the desk, for it wouldn't do to leave any trace of her presence here. Fortunately, Mr. Wiley had left them scattered about in such a random fashion that she was able to get a variety of views of his handwriting.

Nowhere did she see a hand to match any on the poison pen letters.

She knew only a moment's disappointment, however. One sheet half-covered by the blotter bore the distinctively cramped signature. "William Shakespeare."

For an instant she imagined it was really the hand of the great bard. Then she called her pounding heart back into order. It was only a copy, surely, like those currently adorning the covers of some editions of his plays. Her fingers itched to touch it nonetheless, especially the odd little "h" with its short shaft and long furbelowed tail.

Instead she edged around the desk so she could bend down and view it straight on. As she stared at it, she fumbled in her reticule for her magnifying lens. With that aid, she could tell that it was not a printed copy, but written in ink on the same writing paper that littered Mr. Wiley's desk.

Curiosity kills the cat, Aunt Martha was fond of saying. Fortunately, Jessica told herself as she eased the page from the under the blotter, cats have nine lives.

She read rapidly, unbelievingly as the lines emerged. "Sir Francis Shakespeare" was the heading, in Mr. Wiley's clear flowing script. "The Signature above is that of an Illiterate man, a man who could not spell his own Name, who never attended School, nor owned a book. This cannot, therefore, be the Signature of the man who so Eloquently crafted the plays and sonnets attributed to William Shakespeare."

A distant door opened. She paused only long enough to read the next impossible line—"There is but one solution to this Puzzle. The works of 'Shakspere' are actually the Works of Bacon"—before shoving the page back under the blotter. Then she shoved her magnifier back in to her reticule, picked up her skirt, and dashed out of the office into the relative safety of the shelves.

When Mr. Wiley found her, she was kneeling on the floor between two stacks, assiduously reading a volume in the faint light. She assembled an expression of dismay and scrambled to her feet. "Mr. Wiley! I was—I was just looking for you. I wondered f I could borrow this book of Herbert's religious poems. Reading them might bring a bit of comfort to my aunt."

Mr. Wiley had never been one for open displays of dislike, even for the young woman he must regard as a rival. But Jessica had noticed that, as her father's deadline approached, the librarian was taking fewer pains to disguise his triumph. "I thought you understood, Miss Seton, that I do not allow books to leave the collection." He paused slightly, so that Jessica could feel the weight of his authority, then added, "As you know, that was your father's policy."

Jessica cared naught for the Herbert volume, but knew that Mr. Wiley would expect her to argue. She let her lip droop in a debutante's pout. "But sir, it is for my aunt. My father would certainly understand my borrowing it."

Mr. Wiley reached out an imperative hand and gripped the disputed book. Jessica put up a token resistance, then surrendered. With a sniff and a flounce, she pushed past him and out the door, secretly gleeful each time her reticule, with the stolen *Moll Flanders,* banged against her leg.

It was only later, in the privacy of her laboratory, that she allowed herself to consider the implications of what she had learned in Wiley's office. As she painstakingly applied the cleaning solution to the old stain, those few lines chased each other across her mind. Shakespeare the illiterate. Sir Francis Shakespeare.

And to feed this insanity, Alfred Wiley was using her beloved collection.

Chapter Three

Knowing I loved my books, he furnished me
from my own library with volumes that
I prize above my dukedom.

The Tempest, I, ii

Against the opulence of the blue-gray reception room,
the Prince Regent's attire was unusually sober, a plain
dark coat with a black mourning band around his arm.
Recalling the death of Princess Charlotte, half a year
earlier, John made his belated condolences. The prince
shook his head, raised his hand, murmured some dismissal. His somber eyes brightened only as they fixed on
the parcel John carried.

Still the prince was ever a gentleman, and never put
business before courtesy. "How good to see you, Captain. And how is my Cousin Tatiana? Well, I hope."

It was the Princess Tatiana who first introduced them,
this art smuggler and the royal collector, and the
prince's first question was always of her health and happiness. John was able to answer this, as her characteristically newsy seven-page letter had been awaiting him
on his arrival in London. "She is well. Planning a great
ball for one of her charities this summer."

"Ah, yes, the princess's charities. She will no doubt extort contributions from us both! But such a charming girl. I recall when she first came here to England, she told me that her cousin the tsar had no real claim to the throne—sometimes I wish I might remind him of that, when he is at his most imperial. But I forget! You brought her here, didn't you?"

"On the *Coronale*, as a matter of fact." He glanced down at the leather portfolio he held, hiding a smile. "Devlyn, you'll recollect, was her escort."

"Yes, yes. Fine man, that Devlyn." He paused, frowned, shook his head. "She was supposed to marry one of my brothers, you know. Clarence? Cumberland? I can't recall. Wanted Devlyn instead."

"Each to her own taste, sir."

John's diplomacy wasn't necessary. The prince gave a bark of laughter. "Who can blame her, after all? Still, now it seems that it might have been better for us if she had taken one of them after all. Now that—"

He broke off. Princess Charlotte had been the king's only grandchild—the only legitimate one, at least. The other princes were in a frenzy of nuptials now, determined to get another heir birthed before the king and Prinny died. But the prince had ever been a romantic, fortunately for Devlyn, and now only smiled ruefully at what might have been. "You tell her, my cousin Tatiana, to come see me next she is in London. She can bring that reprobate husband of hers too."

John matched the prince's effort to restore the lightness of their converse. "Devlyn will be delighted to hear himself called a reprobate, sir. I used to call him the Archangel Michael, when we were boys."

"That's right, you were boys together, down there in Dorset, weren't you?"

The prince peered at him, waiting for some response.

But John only nodded and started to untie the split-end knot that secured the treasure.

After an awkward moment, Prinny added, "Was this voyage on that *Coronale* also? A pretty little vessel, I hear. You had a pleasant passage, I hope." The regent was unfailing in his courtesy, making the necessary pleasantries, calling to the footman to bring brandy, though he never took his eyes off the package John was opening. He even left unspoken the accusation that John's arrival was three weeks later than he had promised.

"Yes, sir. I stopped off in France, to pursue another manuscript, but it came to naught." With an effort, he forced the regret from his voice. "So I have only this to show you."

"This" was the Jerusalem. John opened the leather portfolio and withdrew the manuscript, the gold gilt pattern of the cover cool and smooth under his fingers. He placed it into the prince's hands, then crossed to a table to bring a lamp closer. During the long voyage he'd had time to start its restoration, and as the regent reverently turned the leaves, the illuminations on the first six pages glowed bright as a Giacomo painting.

"It's very lovely. Very lovely." The prince lightly traced the ancient letters on one page, reading the text under his breath. Most of his subjects credited this man with small intelligence, but John knew better. The archaic Greek posed the prince no great difficulty. "It is a prize. Tell me, did you have very much trouble securing it?"

This, in the prince's polite parlance, was a request for a purchase price. He would pay it, whatever it was; John knew from long experience that the regent could refuse no beautiful thing once he had held it in his hands. It was no great sport to take advantage of him, and John never had, and wasn't likely to start now.

"No. The Vatican was straight on my heels— Alavieri'd gotten wind of my search somehow—but too late. I had no competition in the bidding, so I am able to offer it to you for £600." This was sixfold the actual price, but he had to pay for the voyage and leave a bit of room for profit.

Even so, the prince laughed with delight. "What a rogue you are. £600. You must have stolen it."

"I did my best not to," John replied dryly. "The sellers were not the worldly sort."

"Well, their naivete is my gain, I suppose. And you beat Alavieri, did you? Oh, this is a great find, Captain Dryden. And a great day! You have brightened my spirits." Then his mouth tightened, and he set the book on the marble table, keeping one hand gently on the gilt-laced cover. "I recall that there is something of—of a balance owing."

Ten thousand pounds, or thereabouts. There was the bust of Homer, and an opulent Renoir nude, and a sheaf of letters from Henry V to his bride Katherine, rescued from Napoleon's library after the first abdication. And a dozen other acquisitions, large and small, John had done on credit, without even his expenses covered.

The prince had never spoke of his troubles with Parliament, except an occasional muttering about the Commons' philistinism. "They know nothing of art," he might say, "of the nation's interest in preserving it." John was an art dealer, not a politician, so he naturally agreed that acquiring a twelfth-century Bible was more important than outfitting some regiment for battle or purchasing new coaches for the Royal Mail. Anyway, Parliament usually paid Prinny's shot eventually, after making the largest possible fuss in the newspapers and stirring up radical sentiments among the populace. But lately it had all been getting ugly, with rumors that the Regent had gone as mad as his father and was bent on bankrupting the treasury on frivolous furbelows like paintings and old books.

John crossed to the window. One wasn't supposed to turn a back on the sovereign, so he stood sideways, looking out at the carriages maneuvering through the crowded Mall. The prince had always been a good customer, generous in his gratitude, profligate with his recommendations. His ministers had doubtlessly informed him of John's background, and counseled against doing business with such a one. The foreign secretary, until recently John's occasional if secret employer, would have been vigorous in his warnings against converse, though he needn't have worried; John was nothing if not careful to keep his several professions separate.

Despite these warnings, the prince, however, always greeted him with that easy charm that took no note of class or position or past. He had the regal manner, certainly, but not the regal disdain so common in John's royal customers. The Bourbons, for example, were as haughty as if a revolution, executions, exile, and twenty years of war had only proved their divine right to treat the rest of the world as serfs. But not the prince.

John liked him. That was the trouble. He liked him despite his extravagant absurdities and his quite glaring lack of common sense. Prinny had been kind to the princess and Devlyn when he had the power to ruin them. He had almost single-handedly made John a major player in the close-knit London art world, forcing through his election to the Royal Society of Antiquaries by the simple expedient of threatening to revoke the royal charter. He had given, if anything, too much publicity to the more impressive discoveries, so that now every other dealer knew to track John Dryden's movements and purchases. And he had a love of beauty, and the far-from-flawless but essentially good taste that made him the nation's premier collector, whether the nation welcomed it or no.

He looked back to see the prince caressing the tattered ribbon that marked the reader's place. John sighed inwardly and crossed a figure off his mental invoice sheet. "A balance owing? I think not, sir. Or, perhaps a trifle, but anything more than that I would remember."

The prince blinked, hesitated, then gracefully surrendered. "If you say so, it must be true. I've never known you to mistake the slightest detail—it is what has made you so valuable to the nation, in your different ways. Do you know," he added, as if struck by the thought, "the King's birthday is very soon."

"Next week." The King had been hopelessly mad for years, but there were still ceremonies to mark his anniversary, the traditional end to the London season.

"You wait until then, and I will prove my gratitude. For the Jerusalem, I mean, of course."

Only a week till he received payment? John thanked him, but decided not to spend the £600 yet. He would probably end up whistling that down the wind, right after the £10,000 he had just forgiven.

He bowed, about to take his leave, then stopped. Perhaps there was some profit to be made out of this visit after all. The prince had a magpie's mind, full of trivial facts and irrelevant memories, especially of the halcyon days of his youth. "Do you know aught of a Frenchman, a collector of antiquities, named St. Germaine? He was of Chantonnay, in the Vendée."

"St. Germaine?" The prince leaned back in his chair, his eyes closing as he considered this. "There was a pretty girl named St. Germaine, years ago. Golden hair. But not in France."

John shook his head and resigned himself to a tale of one of the prince's many flirtations. It wouldn't even be salacious, most likely, for the prince's amorous emotions, it was rumored, had always been reserved for older women.

"No, not in France. It was during that bloody Terror. She came here with the other emigrées." The prince opened his eyes and frowned. "I don't know any collector by that name. But you know," he added ruminatively, "she married a collector, this Mlle. St. Germaine, I think."

John had been busy assembling a politely attentive expression, but this arrested him. "She married a collector? Here in England?"

"Yes, I'm almost certain. Not a well-known one, or I'd have the name right to hand."

"But he was a collector, her husband?"

"Must have been. I recall I sent them a Bacon letter for a nuptials present, and I should never have done so if he weren't a collector." The prince chuckled, his stomach rising and falling under the pristine satin waistcoat. "Usually I send spoons."

"You don't mean Parham, do you? He's supposed to have quite a Bacon selection."

"That's the one!" The prince beamed at him. "Sir Francis Bacon—that was the center of the collection. Not that anyone's ever seen it to judge its merits. Those Parhams have always been devilish close with that collection of theirs. Criminal, I often thought."

"Criminal indeed," John murmured. The Parham Collection was reputed to be a fine little library, but no one knew for sure, for the barons had always been chary of visitors. The collection had been closed entirely for a dozen years now, its contents the subject of speculation in the hallowed halls of the Royal Society. "So Mademoiselle St. Germaine became Lady Parham, did she?"

"Not the current Lady Parham. That's the brother's wife, I believe. Saw her at—at m'daughter's funeral. Not French at all. The French one must have died. He too, or his brother wouldn't be baron."

John thanked him and took his leave, stopping at the door for a last glance at the Jerusalem. But as he left Carlton House, his mind shifted to assimilate this last information. Rumor was all he knew of the Parham Collection, since the library had neither been acquiring or selling as long as he had been in the business. But if the daughter of the French collector had truly survived the Terror, perhaps—

It was too soon to hope. On a hunch, he rode to the Hall of Records in the ecclesiastical courts near St. Paul's. He was no stranger to the dusty stacks of ledger books here, having conducted occasional searches for famous names, hoping to unearth a prize like the Shakespeare will. Today his search was an expeditious one; he had a name and could narrow the death date down to the last couple decades. Within an hour, he was sitting crosslegged on the floor, taking notes on the terms of the last will and testament of Godfrey, Fifth Baron Parham of Linwood, filed in May 1812.

Entailed property to brother Emory. The brother inherited—there was no son then. John went carefully through the list of estates and houses and Chelsea lots, looking for anything that might be a collection of rare books. Minor bequests to servants and relatives. No bequest to a wife; she must have predeceased him. The residual—the residual to his daughter Jessica, under conditions outlined in trust agreement.

No trust agreement was attached. It would be in some solicitor's office, no doubt, signed and administered separate from the will. What the conditions were, what the residual was, the will did not disclose.

Forcing his disappointment away, he turned back a page. The brother was also named guardian to the minor child Jessica Seton, and trustee of her legacy, whatever that was.

He rose and replaced the document in its box, and trailing his hand along the dusty shelves, he moved back a year or so. Women might file wills too, if they had property separate from the marital estate. Lady Parham, it turned out, indeed had a will. She left everything to her husband, everything being a very short list—her interest in any property in France eventually restored to her family, and "the St. G trunk".

Absently, John brushed the dust off his breeches as he left the Hall of Records. Parham House, he had learned from the list of entailed property, was off Berkeley Square. He checked his watch. Three o'clock. A bit late for a morning call, but perhaps the Parhams were late risers.

The Parham Collection did indeed prove closed to the public, inaccessible even by appointment. And the Parhams were not at home to hear his appeal. A sovereign, disappearing into the butler's white glove, elicited the information that the baron and baroness were in Surrey for the fortnight. "And Miss Seton?" John asked, holding his hand out, palm up, as if in inquiry.

Quick as a bee, the second sovereign vanished from between his fingers. "Visiting friends, sir. Mr. and Mrs. Rush. In Bincombe. Dorset, I believe that is."

"It is indeed." John gazed longingly at the west face of the mansion, an angled wing where he thought the collection might be housed. But there would be time for that later. He might find his Dorset home a more fruitful field right now.

* * *

As John emerged from the dimness of the Devlyn Keep library, the glare of the sun off the water was blinding. Until his vision cleared, he paused in the doorway to the balcony that hung improbably over the bay. Devlyn didn't notice him; he was reading the *Times* with the silent concentration necessary in a house full of children and servants and princesses. The wind was up from the east, but he had tamed the newspaper by folding it into neat eighths and turning his back to the breeze.

All their lives John had seen his four-month-senior friend as a preview of his own future, and since they turned thirty he lived in dread that one day he'd visit the Keep and find that Devlyn had gone gray or bald or fat. But he looked as he always did, calm and cool, frowning slightly as he contemplated the events of the world. It was a testament to Devlyn's inner serenity, John supposed, that even life with Princess Tatiana had not worn him to a thread or driven him to dissipation.

John had sent a note round earlier warning of his visit, and now he could see he was expected. On the table next to Devlyn's chair were two glasses and an untouched bottle of brandy. John smiled at the excise stamp on the seal. "I see you've run out of the good stuff. I've probably still got a case or two you can have. Unmarked by English hands."

Unstartled, Devlyn looked up, as if he had known all along that he was not alone. He rose and held out his hand, ignoring the reference to one of John's more nefarious former professions. But he didn't refuse the offer either. It was a good thing for the princess, John thought, that the Archangel Michael always proved so corruptible. He'd be unbearable otherwise.

The legal brandy wasn't as bad as John had expected, and he sat down on the stone wall, letting the tension of the last few weeks fade in the warmth of the sun. The breeze was cool and the air sweet and salty. Far below him the sea was chopped into little white waves; across the cove near the village, he could see his pretty *Coronale* bobbing. This was a perfect Dorset afternoon, and were they still boys, they'd likely be out on the bay risking their lives in a homemade sailboat.

But they were both grown, and their converse was more formal now. With his glass, Devlyn gestured at the newspaper. "I see congratulations are in order."

John wished for once the Regent would have shown a bit of restraint and left Parliament in ignorance of his latest acquisition. At the very least, he hoped, the Regent had been discreet about how little he had paid for the Jerusalem, or John's other clients would start expecting the same kind of deal. "Prinny made a public announcement again?"

"Well, he always does, doesn't he? Every year, on the King's birthday. It's a law." When John only shrugged his incomprehension, Devlyn picked up the paper to study it again. "Perhaps I'm wrong to extend congratulations? I presumed it wouldn't have happened if you didn't want the honor."

"Devlyn, give me the paper." John made a grab across the table and got a hold of it. "What on earth are you talking about?"

Devlyn laughed and released his grip on the *Times*. "You mean you don't know?"

"I brought the *Coronale* round from Chatham. I haven't been on land for four days." There was nothing on the front page about the Jerusalem Manuscript or anything else to do with John. He let the wind tug it open and scanned the notices.

"Next page." In afterthought, Devlyn added, "Sir John."

"Gemini." John drew a deep breath as he turned the page. "He didn't really knight me."

"Worse than that."

"Worse? What could be worse?" He located the column with the twice-annual announcement of royal honors and orders and ran his finger down the list. His own name—the one he had taken two decades ago, anyway—leapt out at him. "Baronet. Baronet? What in God's name is he thinking?"

"I don't imagine God had much to do with it. This can't possibly be a case of divine revelation."

It was too much to take in. John started laughing, remembering the Regent's promise to reward him. Presumably creating a baronet was easier than paying bills on time. "It would never have occurred to me to pray for this, I assure you. And I don't know how he came up with such an idea. Parliament will declare him mad as the King!"

"I'd love to see Wellesley's face when he reads this. He's going to think it's because you've told Prinny about all those illicit operations you conducted for him when he was foreign secretary."

"Such as conveying your princess to these unsuspecting and unprepared shores? Yes, I deserve a medal for that little bit of smuggling. But a baronetcy?"

"Really, John, how did you accomplish this? Blackmail?"

Devlyn cherished few illusions, but that was one of them—that John was capable of nearly any mildly wicked act. John might resent that, except that Devlyn, once upon a time, would have been right. Enough of the outlaw still lurked within the art dealer to make John doubt himself at times. But not in this instance. "I beg your pardon. This honor was earned the traditional way, I'll have you know. I forgave a debt. £10,000."

Devlyn whistled through his teeth. "£10,000? I'd've expected a peership at least for that."

"There's been a great deal of inflation since your ancestor was named viscount, Devlyn. Even a barony would go for £20,000 these days." He gazed back at his name, unmindful of the wind whipping at the pages. "With any luck, everyone will think he's honoring my namesake poet posthumously."

Devlyn gave him a curious look. "You're not pleased with this honor, are you?"

For a moment, John couldn't answer. He smoothed the newspaper he'd crumpled and handed it back to Devlyn. "Oh, it's a generous act, you know. He didn't have to do this, and it might cause him all sorts of havoc. He knows Wellesley and Castlereagh and the rest will suspect the worst—I worked for the Foreign Office too long, you know. Learned too many secrets. But I'm out of it. They can't do anything to me now."

"Certainly it will be good for your business."

John shrugged. "Perhaps. Most collectors don't care about my position, you know, as long as I deliver the goods. But there might be one or two who will commission me first now. I don't know that I want that sort of client, of course."

Devlyn considered this while he filled John's empty glass with more brandy. "Is it an inverse form of snobbery you are exhibiting? You were never so proud before you became a baronet."

Baronet. The word sounded nonsensical, when applied to John Dryden. Sir John Dryden, Bart. He rubbed his temple with knuckles, wishing the Regent had just paid for the Jerusalem and had done with it. "It is rather amusing, isn't it? I have always fancied myself something of a democrat, and scorned such trappings. A man should rise by his own merits, not by his birth."

"Well, you've risen, that's for certain. Was it truly only a forgiven debt that motivated Prinny?"

"That and his gratitude for bringing the fair princess to our shores so long ago," John said ironically.

Devlyn smiled. "No, had he thought of Tatiana, he would have made you an earl."

John saw no profit in quibbling with this sentiment. He was fond of the princess, as a rule, but had never quite understood how his sensible friend chose to entangle himself with one of the world's more troublesome women. Diplomatically he changed the subject. "And I've just brought him a manuscript he'd been hoping for. The Jerusalem."

"Is that where you've been all spring? Jerusalem?"

"No. The manuscript is called the Jerusalem. But it's never been there, as far as I know. It was scribed in Alexandria more than eight hundred years ago. I found it in Greece, in a convent."

"Eight hundred years ago? And the nuns still had it?"

John said wryly, "They hadn't any sense of what it was. Used it for a doorstop. And they were all too eager to let it go for a pittance. Had to argue them into accepting the equivalent of a hundred pounds."

"Well, a hundred pounds is quite a price for an old book," Devlyn commented.

Annoyed by this dismissal of his great prize, John retorted, "Not at all. As I was leaving the convent, Franco Alavieri from the Vatican arrived. He told me he would have paid fifteen thousand pounds for it."

Devlyn drew in his breath at this new figure. Then, thoughtfully, he folded up the newspaper and secured it on the table with the brandy bottle. "You might have given him the manuscript, pocketed the fifteen thousand, and told the Regent you got there too late."

John regarded his old friend with dawning approval. "There's hope for you yet, Michael." But he could tell Devlyn was already regretting the suggestion. "Oh, I see. You meant that *I* might have done it, not that you would ever do such a thing. You know, you should appreciate me better. You might have to commit your own sins, were you not able to participate vicariously in mine."

"You have plenty to spare, I think," Devlyn replied. "So why didn't you sell it to the Vatican? Surely if the thought occurred to me, it occurred to you."

John almost said something foolish and sentimental, that the money didn't matter, that he wanted the Jerusalem to himself at least for the length of his voyage. But no one would believe that of the hard-headed businessman John Dryden. "Oh, I've my reputation to consider. And it is such a fine book. The Vatican would have buried it, you see. Not destroyed it—Alavieri would never have allowed that—but hidden it away in some corner of the library. They couldn't acknowledge its existence, you see, or they'd be acknowledging its authors. And the Coptics have been considered heretics since the fifth century. They practice monophysitism, you know."

Devlyn nodded gravely, then had to ask, "Some shocking ritual, I suppose?"

John laughed. "No. Oh, it's shocking enough to the pope, I suppose, but the rest of us wouldn't understand the fuss. Something about Christ having only one nature, not two, human and divine."

Devlyn agreed that this must be condemned in the strongest terms, perhaps forgetting that his own Anglicanism had long been considered heretical by the pope.

"Prinny apparently hasn't any difficulty with the heresy?"

"Oh, no. He's looking to build a rare-book library, and, if I know him, he will probably have a special display for heretics. It's a beautiful book, hardly aged at all. The binding is camel skin—most Copts were Egyptian, you know." Absently, he trailed his fingers on the stone wall, feeling instead the velvety texture of the book. "And gold leaf as fine as a hummingbird feather, vines all over the front, worth every bit of trouble—"

He broke off, embarrassed, knowing Devlyn could only wonder at his enthusiasm. But he tried to explain in a way Devlyn, a former soldier, might understand. "It's always an adventure, you see, because manuscripts are an odd trade. The buyers are few but intense, and intensely jealous. Alavieri was generous enough in defeat, or so I thought. But he had a trio of banditti waiting for me at the dock."

"What happened?"

"Oh, I was half-expecting it. My mare got away, and alerted my crew, and we made short work of them."

Devlyn was laughing, forgetting their adult reserve enough to lapse into a long-abandoned nickname. "Jack, you never fail to get into scrapes. Only you could turn some dusty old book into an occasion for pillage and derring-do."

Some dusty old book. John let that go by. Devlyn was an intelligent man, well-read, with a sure if conventional taste in art. He was also John's oldest friend, and probably knew him best—they had begun running together at five or so, as soon as John was old enough to escape the confines of the village and make his way up the hill to the Keep. But Devlyn, no doubt, understood this passion for old books less than John's earlier passions for adventure and art. A book is for reading, Devlyn said once, trying to puzzle this out, for conveying information. When it gets old and starts to fall apart, I'd buy a new edition so I'd have all the pages. But that's when *you* start wanting the book—when it's no longer usable.

So John took a certain pleasure in retelling a few of his Alavieri adventures. No one who had encountered the Vatican curator could ever think of the rare books trade as anything but the height of intrigue.

He didn't mention that moment, however, when Alavieri confessed his great misfortune of seeing and losing what he claimed was a work of Shakespeare. John was discreet by nature, and close by business habit. All he needed was Alavieri to hear that the Shakespeare play might have survived the Terror. He'd send an army of Jesuit warriors, not just a pack of thieves, after John.

He looked up to find Devlyn studying him. He was an observer, was Devlyn, and knew something was up. "Exciting, no doubt, these acquisition trips of yours. But now—now you've this new title, and it's sure to bring you more business. You've got a fleet of—what? Seven ships?"

"And the *Coronale*," John murmured, so as not to slight the lady.

"You could send them all out with their cargo, and spend all your time in London as a consultant and dealer. You don't have to make these trips, risking your life with the lunatics you keep meeting along the way."

"Alavieri's no lunatic," John replied defensively. "He's the best in the world. I'd give my right arm for half his ability and knowledge."

Devlyn raised his hand as if calling a halt to this. Still he gave it an ironic consideration. "Let me see if I have understood you correctly. You admire the man—a priest, by God—who tried to kill you over some old book?"

"It was nothing *personal.* I daresay, had he his druthers, he would let me live, and perhaps even take me on as a junior partner of sorts. But the Jerusalem is—it's more than an old book. And the book business is—"

"More than cutthroat."

"Well, yes. But I assure you, I am fit to the task. It is no more dangerous than free-trading, and I did that for years. It is surely less trying than smuggling guns to the Calabrian resistance. And Alavieri is only slightly more ruthless than Bonaparte."

"Somehow that doesn't reassure me. Whenever you leave on a voyage, I go out and look at that old raft we built, and think probably it is the last time I will see you."

Devlyn, John realized yet again, had a deep streak of pessimism down the middle of his practical mind. And it was disconcerting to find bits of maudlinity in a man of sense. But then, Devlyn had always cherished mementoes of his past—in one of the barns, next to the old raft, he kept the aeroballoon the princess had stolen from France. And he had kept John busy over the years, tracking down and retrieving the mediocre family portraits the late Lord Devlyn had sold to pay his gambling debts.

Restlessly John twisted the sapphire signet ring on his left hand. It had left a pale circle against the tan leather of his skin, mute evidence of the amount of sun he had gotten since he started wearing it seven years earlier. He shoved it back into place, and flexed his hands. He felt confined suddenly, both by his old friend's concern and the new change in his circumstances. Baronets, he gathered, weren't supposed to take risks.

"You're a fine one to talk, Devlyn. You were how long at war?"

"Nine years in the army. Seven at war, I suppose."

"And nary a scratch."

Devlyn shrugged. "But I am lucky."

"And I am smart. I earn my luck."

"Well, perhaps you are right. I must say, I never thought you'd earn a title, never in all my days." And so, with less than grace, Devlyn gave up. The role of the older advisor had never suited him anyway; he was no model for the staid and secure life, since he was married to a princess. "Just be cautious, won't you?"

A tiger kitten wandered through the door, wended its way around Devlyn's chair, and finally came to nuzzle at John's boot. He wriggled his toes to scratch the cat's throat. "I'll be here in cautious old England all summer, as it happens. Nothing very interesting will occur, you may be sure."

"Then you'll be able to come to Tatiana's charity ball next week."

Though he was here for that very purpose, John knew Devlyn would expect him to demur. He bent to pick the kitten up, and to hide any eagerness his expression might betray. "I hadn't considered it, actually."

"Do me this one favor, lad, and come. It will be nigh unbearable otherwise. All our charitable neighbors will be there."

The kitten was digging her claws into John's breeches, and he distracted her by stroking the stripe between her golden eyes. This set off a low chorus of purring. "You have charitable neighbors? Intriguing. And I thought I knew the neighborhood well."

"Social-climbing neighbors, then. They'll make a contribution to Tatiana's school, just to have a chance to say they have visited with the princess in her home. But Tatiana's Russian, remember, and her idea of neighborhood is rather commodious. She's got some coming from as far as Exeter." He tore off a piece of the newspaper and balled it up, tossing it up and catching it. The kitten stopped purring and started watching. Then, with a growl, she leaped off John's leg and seized the ball of paper, tumbling to the floor with it. Devlyn took the loss of his toy dispassionately, then observed, "Now that you are a respectable baronet, you have no excuse."

The Devlyns had always invited John to their parties, and sometimes, if he was in a defiant mood, he accepted. But Dorset wasn't as accepting of unconventionality as London—or perhaps they just knew him better. The mysterious past that fascinated a few London hostesses was no mystery here where John grew up. He might be a hero of sorts to the wilder youth on the South Coast, but to the gentry he was just the criminal upstart son of an apothecary. It would be entertaining, at least, to see how they would treat him now that he was titled.

Titled. Good Christ, what was the Regent thinking?

Devlyn must have sensed an opening, because he added, "Tatiana wants your consultation on decorating the ballroom."

"That, I suppose, is the clincher? In order to receive such a commission, you think I will jump at your invitation? I know nothing about decorating ballrooms."

"You need only endorse the plans she has. She thinks you have buckets of good taste—I expect it's the company you keep. Come, she will want to greet you anyway."

Devlyn led him back through the dark library, into the sunfilled great hall, past the bust of Napoleon John had gotten after Marshal Ney's execution. He remembered, back when they were boys, that the Keep was almost empty, stark even beyond the usual spare precision of a Palladian home, the only evidence of life the figures writhing on the Michelangelo-inspired dome. Now that

Devlyn had hired a staff, bought back most of the lost furnishings, and installed a new generation of Danes, the great dome no longer echoed with loneliness.

The primary reason for this change was approaching them even now, running down the stairs with a hand skimming over the oak bannister, her red hair loose about her shoulders like a girl's. The Princess Tatiana called out gaily, "John! Just in time for my party. Come see what I mean to do to the ballroom."

Devlyn smiled sympathetically and murmuring, "Better you than I," headed back to his refuge on the balcony.

But this was, after all, what John had been waiting for, a chance to get the princess alone.

Between them was none of the complexity that characterized his relationship with Devlyn. From the first, when the Russian princess had boarded his sloop for her secret voyage to England, they had been something akin to friends. She had the same ease that made her cousin the Regent an unexpectedly good companion: She noticed no one's class but her own, treating everyone with equal, imperial charm. He liked that, and liked her, and in this, as in most things, he would do her bidding.

"I'm no expert on decorating ballrooms, God forbid. But I will walk with you there."

So he let her bear him away to the empty space at the back of the Keep where he and Devlyn used to skate in their stockinged feet. Unlike the rest of the house, this austere room had resisted Tatiana's efforts to make it comfortable. It was so cavernous that their footsteps echoed like gunshots against the panelled walls, and they had to speak softly to keep their conversation from resonating. The sun through the tall windows glanced off the marble floor, but the light brought with it no heat. Even in his coat, John was shivering from the chill that rose from the stone.

But Tatiana was of a hardier race, and though her muslin gown was insubstantial, she never noticed that she had left her shawl behind. She stood bare-armed in the middle of the room and gestured around, proposing to make the cavern a romantic wonderworld via a crimson silk ceiling drape and a fountain of champagne.

She spoke with that gallant optimism that never failed to charm John. But he was a realist, and could calculate to a pound or so how much a ceiling of silk would cost. "At this rate, your highness, there will be little profit left for your school."

"I was hoping," she said, giving him a sidelong glance, "to meet that friend of yours, and persuade him to give me a good price on French champagne."

"No!" John shut his eyes, hoping to blot out the picture of Tatiana bargaining with a bloodthirsty South Coast smuggler. That she would probably win the negotiations did not make the vision more appealing. "Princess, please. Let me take care of getting you the champagne. Consider it my contribution."

Tatiana looked ready to argue the point, so he added, "*Part* of my contribution."

"But I did so hope to meet Shem the—what do you call him?"

"Shem the Shark. No. No. Devlyn would have my head if he knew I'd even mentioned knowing that one."

"Oh, if you insist."

She shrugged, conceding him the point. And for a moment he almost believed she was the one doing him a favor. Then he reminded himself how much champagne for three hundred—and a fountain—would likely cost him, and forced himself to interrupt her description of the planned school building. "Just a moment, if you please. In return for the champagne, I hope you will grant me a small concession."

"Anything!"

Her promise was rash but sincere, and so he said, "I would appreciate it if you would invite a Mrs. Ada Rush to your ball. Of Bincombe. And her husband, of course. And—any guest she might have staying with her this summer."

"Mrs. Rush." She scuffed her slipper on the marble dance floor and considered this. Then she looked back up at him, a wicked light in her eyes. "When did you start pursuing married women?"

Annoyed, he said, "I'm not pursuing anyone. It's merely a business proposition I mean to make."

"Certainly not with the Rushes. They don't collect art. She collects earbobs, as I recall, and he has quite a variety of cows. But they are not known for their art acumen."

John had never been deceived by the princess's frivolous manner. He had stopped underestimating her the day she got him a royal commission with a single offhand remark. In an earlier century, this woman might have made herself a tyrant like her ancestor Catherine the Great. So, though he generally guarded the truth jealously, he revealed a bit of it to her. "It's the guest."

"I thought as much." From the curve of her mouth, he could tell what else she was thinking, and she didn't disappoint him. "A lady guest?"

"As a matter of fact, yes."

She smiled sweetly. "I really ought to have her name to put on the invitation, John."

Reluctantly he said, "A Miss Seton."

"Miss Seton. Jessica Seton? Oh, good. I met her in London. Very pretty. Blonde, you know. They call her the Golden Girl—though she's not such a girl anymore. An heiress too, I hear."

John didn't travel in the same circles as heiresses, but he knew enough about society to take note of this. A pretty heiress and still a Miss? The two were usually mutually exclusive. "It's only a bit of her inheritance I'm interested in—the artistic part."

Tatiana made a disappointed face. "Do you think of nothing but your art?"

"Very seldom. Will you invite them or no?"

"Well, of course I will. I shall even mention your name—"

He cut off her sentence with an upraised hand. "I'd prefer the invitation came from you."

"You don't want it known that this graciousness is at your behest?"

"Just so. I want *no one* to know."

"No one? Not even Michael? But I tell Michael *everything*," she said, with that limpid innocence that occasionally fooled even Dryden.

But not today. He responded just as innocently. "You do? I'm glad. I was sure you wouldn't tell him about the Lieven brooch."

"It wasn't the Lieven brooch!" Mere words couldn't express her outrage; she had to stalk up to him and glare, so effectively that he fell back a step laughing. "The *Denisov* brooch. Peter the Great gave it to my great-grandmother. That—that Lieven witch took it from our rooms when my parents were exiled; I remember her rummaging around, pretending that she was there to help me, and all the while she was stealing my mother's jewels!"

"Appalling. And then when you saw it on the countess's bosom, you could hardly be blamed for expecting her to return it."

"And she offered me only insult in recompense! If I were a man, I would have—I would have gutted her like a fish!" Her hand sliced the air in an tight curve, and John, who had seen many fish gutted—though no countesses, as yet—could not help but appreciate her artistry.

The princess's violent Romanov ancestry would out, though fortunately usually only in rhetoric. At the time, however, he hadn't been so sure she wouldn't carry out her threats. He had been working for the Foreign Office then, positioning spies and laundering funds, and was steeped in the philosophy that the end justified the means. It was no great jump to decide that preventing the gutting of the Russian ambassador's wife justified a discreet little jewel theft. "I'm pleased that Devlyn understood. He's not usually so flexible."

"Understood?" She glanced at him exasperated. "Of course he didn't understand. I never told him."

"So I thought," John murmured. "Then we've established, haven't we, that there is at least *one* thing you haven't told your husband." He let the spot of blackmail work its way in, then added, "What's one more?"

"You're a rogue, John Dryden."

"Takes one to know one, your highness." And with a bow, he left her in the empty ballroom, sure that she would do as he bid.

Chapter Four

Dead shepherd, now I find thy saw of might:
"Who ever lov'd that lov'd not at first sight?"
As You Like It, III, v

Jessica pulled Ada behind an elaborate Oriental screen that served to hide the entrance to the kitchens. Though they had to keep moving aside for footmen carrying trays of food, from here they could see the whole ballroom and talk without being overheard or being drowned out by the orchestra. "Tell me who is here tonight."

Ada was taller, and could see easily over the top of the screen. She swivelled her head to survey the ballroom from one end to the other, and then waved her hand in dismissal. "Oh just the usual Dorset crowd, this early. No one very interesting yet —or eligible." She cast a sidelong glance at Jessica. "Still on the hunt, are you?"

"Don't call it that. You make me sound like a bird of prey. I'm just curious, and I thought that since you know everyone, you would tell me if anyone intriguing is here. I haven't even met the princess yet."

"Well, there she is." Ada gestured to the right with her fan. "She doesn't look like a princess, does she?"

Jessica stood on her tiptoes to peek over the top of the screen. Ada's fan was pointing at a small, slender woman with dark red hair, directing the footmen from the ballroom stairs. Her apricot silk gown was defying gravity, the little lacy sleeves hardly clinging to her shoulders. "Well, I don't know what a princess is supposed to look like—not like our own royal ladies, I expect. At least, she is marvellously pretty. And she has a dazzling dressmaker. I *love* that dress. I wonder how she keeps it up."

"Glue, do you think? It's just that when I think of a princess, I always expect a crown. She might have got one, had she married one of the royal dukes instead of Devlyn. I can't blame her," Ada said thoughtfully. "He's over there." The fan jammed towards the cardrooms, at a tall man in formal dress. "I'd choose him over a prince any day."

Devlyn, though admirably well-shouldered, was taken, and thus of no use to Jessica. She gave into her accustomed candor, for Ada already knew everything about Uncle Emory and his obstinacy. "What about the gentlemen here? Surely some of them are worth considering." A stir at the entrance caught her attention, for as the butler introduced the Earl of Tressilian, all conversation ceased. He was a dark, brooding man in full Navy splendor, and as he walked to the princess and lifted her hand to his lips with seductive grace, Devlyn started purposefully across the ballroom.

"Him, for example."

Ada was made of stronger stuff, though. "Your uncle wouldn't even need to get poison pen letters to disapprove of the earl! A grieving widower with difficult children and a drinking problem?"

"He's out of mourning, isn't he?" Jessica said a bit sullenly. "And he doesn't look foxed."

"Of course not. They say he only drinks alone, late at night." Ada laughed out loud as Devlyn reached his wife and without much ado led her away from the Navy man onto the dance floor. "Ooh, do you think they will duel? That would certainly cap the princess's party—her husband and her most illustrious guest meeting at dawn!"

"I don't think so, Ada. Lord Devlyn hardly seems the sort to shoot a man who merely smiles, however heart-breakingly." On second thought, Jessica decided, Tressilian wasn't the sort of man to make a comfortable husband. "Damien," she added with a chuckle, "goes mad with envy, whenever he sees that one. A real Byronic hero, right down to the brooding mouth. But you are right, Tressilian is not the sort to please Uncle Emory. What about that one there?"

"But what about Damien?" Ada asked with a significant look. "You're supposed to be madly in love with him."

Irritated, Jessica kept her gaze roaming over the brightly lit ballroom. "I never said I was madly in love with him. I said I thought, since he's run free in our house since we were children, that Uncle Emory might approve of him. I was wrong." Bitterness edged her voice. "Damien didn't even attempt to change his mind. Arguing, you see, is beneath him."

Ada sighed gustily in sympathy. "Not such a devoted swain after all. You would think, from his poetry, that he would slay dragons for you."

"He won't even put down his pen for me. I, of course, am expected to give up my collection for him." Jessica almost let the oppression overtake her again. Then she grabbed a glass of champagne from a passing footman and sternly reminded herself that she was at a wonderful party, surrounded by acres of silk and the light from a thousand candles, and that even if she couldn't marry any of these men, she might at least dance with them. "Lovely champagne, this. Ada, have a glass with me."

Absently, Ada shook her head. "Champagne makes me giggle. And since I'm already married, giggling does me no good!" She craned her neck to see past a knot of debutantes. "Perhaps that nice Lord Mumblethorpe will do. Your uncle can't call him a rake like Tressilian, for he isn't the least in the petticoat line. I think he'd make a most comfortable husband."

"I am certain he would—for the sort of girl who wouldn't mind being known as Lady Mumblethorpe." The champagne was having an effect; she could hardly get the name out. "As for me, I think I would give that prospect a pass, even did he look like Tressilian."

"You're so cruel, Jessie! Lady Anything-at-all would suit most girls. Hmmm. Is that a bishop coming out of the cardroom? He's young, isn't he, for a bishop. And not so badlooking, rather genial, in fact."

"I expect he won a good deal at picquet." Jessica let the bishop stroll past before she pulled Ada closer and whispered, "Do you think Uncle would want a bishop in the family? He'd have to watch his language!"

Ada laughed and added significantly, "And what's more, Jessie, you'd have to watch *yours!* And you wouldn't—I know you, you'd forget yourself and speak frankly while you were entertaining the Archbishop of Canterbury!"

"I would not! I've gotten much better than I was at school, I assure you. Living with my aunt and uncle has truly taught me the value of discretion in speech— blast!" A footman's tray collided with her arm, and after the exchange of apologies, she tugged at Ada. "We are in the way. Let's walk."

They strolled down the side of the ballroom, Jessica glancing sidelong at the other partygoers. It looked to be a glorious crush, all in all, for a rural entertainment. And Jessica was weary of the conundrum of her collection and its curator. It was easier to slip back into the irreverent camaraderie she and Ada had known at Miss Falesham's Institute for Young Ladies, when they were called "The Terrible Two."

Now she felt someone watching her intently, and raised her fan to hide her face. She stole a quick glance, though, and for just an instant met the gaze of the man standing a few yards away on the staircase leading up to the main part of the house. "What about that one?" she whispered. "I think he's staring at me."

She had to repeat it more loudly because the orchestra had struck up a mazurka, but finally Ada turned obediently and raised her lorgnette in the indicated direction.

Jessica groaned and tried discreetly to pull down her friend's arm. "You needn't let him know you're interested, Ada."

"*I* am not the interested one, *you* are! I'm merely doing reconnaissance work for you." But the lorgnette dropped, and Ada started away at a brisk pace, almost dragging Jessica along. "But that one is *not* a likely candidate, dear. Uncle would *not* approve, not in a thousand years, even with the spanking new title he's got."

Jessica risked a quick look back over her shoulder. He was still watching her. She kept walking, eyes forward, but his gaze felt like the brush of his fingers across the back of her neck. There was something indefinably alien about him, in his casual but wary stance, in the exotic lines of his face, in the opaque intensity of his gaze. "He's not English, is he?"

"Well, of course he is. He was born just down the road in Devlyn village. To the apothecary's wife."

Jessica felt a deep rush of disappointment. How very mundane, after all. But then, she reminded herself, that was rather mysterious. "A shopkeeper? At a ball like this?"

"He's not a shopkeeper," Ada replied. "He's the son of a shopkeeper. Or so the shopkeeper thought, anyway." Before Jessica could ask for elaboration of this cryptic statement, Ada had gone on with a hint of pride, "No, this one used to practice the South Coast's oldest profession."

Prostitution seemed unlikely, so Jessica ventured, "Fishing?"

"Nothing so dull! He does have a fleet of ships, I think, but he's after more impressive cargo. He was a pirate, you see."

Jessica couldn't help it. A deep thrill rippled through her, just as it might have years ago, when she and Ada were dreaming up outrageous Gothic plots for the edification of their schoolmates. But she sneaked another look and regretfully shook her head. "A pirate? Surely not. He looks the perfect gentleman."

"Oh, I agree, he does appear to advantage in evening dress. No one who didn't know him would ever imagine the truth, until they caught sight of him on the deck of a ship. The veriest corsair!"

Jessica stopped by the refreshment table and pretended to busy herself with a plate and fork. From this vantage point, she could see him out of the corner of her eye, without even turning her head. "He's not a pirate—I know that much. There aren't any left. And if he were a pirate, I hardly think Tressilian the naval hero would be stopping to address him."

It was true; the earl in his Navy uniform and the supposed pirate were deep into conversation now. Jessica felt a moment's regret that his apparent fascination with her had ended so soon. Wasn't that just like a man? But she supposed she was no more romantic than he, since she had already decided that this acquaintance wasn't worth pursuing if he couldn't help her win the collection.

Still, he was intriguing, from all the hints Ada had let drop so far. A new title, a dark past . . . "Perhaps he does look a bit piratical," she allowed, aiming her fork randomly at the display of food, her sideways gaze fixed on him. "So tanned, and those devilish winged brows. I can imagine him with a patch over his eye and a ring in his ear. Oh, Ada, tell me more. What's his name?"

Ada added another lobster patty to her plate, and frowned. "Oh, I can't remember. Manning, that's it. John Manning. Of course, he hasn't called himself that since he took up his illicit profession."

"Piracy? Come, now, Ada. I agree, he would make an impressive pirate. But he's here, at the princess's ball, and look, she's coming to greet him. I just don't think she'd welcome a pirate."

Reluctantly Ada gave in. "Oh, all right, he's not a pirate. That's just so much more romantic than a free-trader, for there are dozens of those around here. Not around *here*," she amended, as Jessica looked around the ballroom with renewed interest. "I daresay he's the only free-trader at this ball. But the South Coast just crawls with them. It is a sign of moral decay, my papa always said, how the villagers make heroes of outlaws like that John Dryden. And now he's *Sir* John Dryden. Papa must be spinning in his grave."

Jessica took another quick look at the elegant outlaw talking to the princess, and remembered where she had heard that name. "You don't mean that's really John Dryden?"

"*Not* the poet, dear. He's a century dead. I told you it was an assumed name."

"I know precisely when the poet died," Jessica said impatiently. "The collection has three copies of his last volume of poetry—'None but the brave, none but the brave, none but the brave deserve the fair.'" Jessica took Ada's plate from her hand before she could heap it even higher with lobster patties, and led her to a little table in a silk-draped alcove. There they could nibble and watch without observation. "But this is the *new* John Dryden, isn't it—the art dealer?"

"Well, that's what they say he used to smuggle. Isn't that unique—a smuggler who deals in art. But," Ada added reluctantly, "I gather he's gone respectable, and does everything legally now."

"I should say so. He's the Prince Regent's consultant on books, also, I think. They say he has the most extraordinary contacts on the Continent! And I know he's in the Royal Society of Antiquaries—and you must believe me, Ada, they are the stuffiest group. My father never applied to join, because he knew they would object to his handling of the collection. So that is John Dryden," she mused, pulling back the silk drape for a better look. "I wonder what he's doing here at the princess's party."

"I should think it would be obvious. He's—he's very close to the family."

Jessica watched as Sir John Dryden smiled down at the princess, and realized with a sinking heart what Ada's implication must be. "He loves her, doesn't he?"

Ada made an exasperated sound. "Jessica, you were

always one to suspect the worst! Of course he's fond of the princess! But it's not at all what you think." She leaned over and peered out around Jessica. Oblivious to propriety, she pointed her fork at Lord Devlyn, who had come up beside his wife. With the dark earl, Jessica recalled, he had seemed every inch the jealous husband. But he greeted Sir John with a smile and an outstretched hand. And then, while they clasped hands, Jessica blinked and the images of the two men seemed to merge. They were of a height, similarly slim, with the same dark brown curls, the same square-cut jaw—
"They are brothers."

"Half-brothers. It was Devlyn's father, not his wife, who was indiscreet, you see."

Now that Jessica understood their connection, she could also see the distinctions too. They weren't identical, by any means. Devlyn was plainly English; Dryden still looked exotic, foreign, with those winged brows and the cool challenging eyes. His dark hair was gilded with gold—a sailor was ever in the sun, she supposed. "It was acknowledged, then, their fraternity?"

"Oh, no. The apothecary raised him as his own. Never noticed, as far as anyone knew. My mother used to marvel at that. She said the two boys were always together, and everyone else could see the resemblance. Not Mr. Manning. But they must know, the two of them."

Now that she thought of it, Jessica realized it made perfect sense. Of course he was the bastard son of a lord. Where else would he have gotten that elegant manner, the interest in finer things, the impeccable taste an art consultant needed?

But the circumstances of this man's birth were not important, except that, perhaps, they had made him something of a maverick. And, for the plan that was half-born in her mind, a maverick might come in quite handy.

She rose and shook out her skirts, smoothed her hair back, straightened the pearls around her neck. "Ada, do hurry. I want to be presented to the princess. And soon, before he walks away!"

Sir John Dryden's eyes glinted ironically as the introductions were performed, as if he knew that she had come to meet him. Jessica put up her chin proudly; he had been the one who had challenged her to do this, watching her in that intent way. The orchestra struck up a waltz, and, as she knew he would, he asked her to dance. They left Ada and the princess smiling, as if they had engineered this themselves.

The waltz was no longer a scandalous dance, and Jessica, in three London seasons, had learned not to blush at being held so closely by a man. But this felt more intimate than she remembered. That was absurd, of course. She had often waltzed with Damien, and that should have been more intimate, for she had known him most of her life. She knew John Dryden not at all.

But somehow, even before he took her in his arms, she knew that his hand under the white glove would be hard and capable, that his arm around her waist would be taut, that she could look up and see her own image in his oddly reflective gray eyes. Instead she looked straight ahead, at the sapphire pin in his cravat, and told herself that this eerie familiarity resulted from her secret knowledge of his birth, his past, his connection to the world of rare books. It was a bit unnerving, to know so much about him, and he still a stranger. More unnerving still was the sense that he knew more about her than he had any right.

No matter. What counted was his unusual expertise, and his knowledge of the rare books trade. Casting about for an opening, she recalled the little notice that appeared in the *Times* last week, of an addition to the royal library. "I understand you recently procured the Jerusalem Manuscript for the Regent. I thought that had been destroyed during the Inquisition."

This was not, perhaps, the usual waltz patter, and it certainly captured his attention. "You have an interest in rare books, Miss Seton?"

She took pains to persuade him that she hadn't merely studied up in hopes of impressing him. "I hope to inherit a library soon. Perhaps you've heard of it— the Parham Collection."

He gave it a moment's thought, then replied, "Yes, I think I have heard of it. Quite a selection of Bacon memorabilia, I believe? But I understand that the library is permanently closed, and so of little moment to a dealer such as I, or to scholars either."

She heard the implied rebuke, and knew with some despair that she would have a hard job to restore the Parham's stature in the antiquary community. Perhaps, though, she could use his disapproval of the current policy to entice him into an alliance. She looked up at him, watching for a change in his carefully neutral expression. "Yes, Bacon is the center of the collection—a particular passion of my grandfather's, you see. But there is much, much more, mostly English, but also a few Continental items." There it was: a flicker of interest, just a slight narrowing of his eyes, a moment's cessation of breath. "If—when I inherit, I mean to do a full catalogue, and make it available to scholars. I hope then I shall have the wherewithal to begin acquiring more books. There have been no additions, you see, since my father died."

"The collection is concentrated on English books, you say? Have you any Elizabethan artifacts?"

"Oh, not very much. The collection was begun in 1611, but I think my ancestor hadn't any love for his contemporaries, and left them quite alone. That's a great gap, in fact, that I hope to remedy. We do have a few of Jonson's books, but they are a bit later, I think, the first from 1616," Jessica said, closing her eyes and envisioning the shelves for the sixteenth and seventeenth centuries. Her list perforce was a random one, for Mr. Wiley wasn't one for shelf maintenance. "A Coverdale Bible. Hakluyt's *Voyages*. Cawdray's little dictionary. A delightful little book of herbal medicines, illustrated, very primitive. An unattributed translation of Petrarch's sonnets—I think the Earl of Oxford is responsible, for my grandfather bought it from his estate. You know about the Bacon selections. And two First Folios, of course, but those are kept separate in the vault."

"That's all you have of Shakespeare—two Folios?"

The music ended as she opened her eyes to the sharp disappointment on his face. Defensively, she said, "The two Folios are quite good specimens, actually. And we have some Globe Theatre memorabilia, and an early playbook of *Twelfth Night*. But you know, much was lost when the theatre burned—there remains little to be had."

Sir John noticed that they were standing on the dance floor while everyone else headed for the supper tables and started to lead her back to Ada. Suddenly she thought she might lose him forever, this man who seemed to possess just the right combination of intellect, skill, and amorality to suit her purpose. "Wait! It is—so hot in here." It was a deeply stupid remark—for all the three hundred people were dancing here, and for all the hot red silk draped everywhere, this was the chilliest ballroom she'd ever known. Most of the ladies were clutching their shawls around them, and the men were slipping off into the cozier cardrooms.

But there was no sense in calling attention to the mistake by correcting it. She just forged onward, all too aware of what sort of invitation Sir John must imagine this to be. "Perhaps we could—walk out onto the terrace? I hear there's a lovely view."

Sir John kept a creditably courteous expression, neither lustful nor displeased. "As you wish."

Just in case he had misinterpreted her intent, she said, "I would like your advice on some obscure items in the collection that I might sell if—when—I inherit."

"Obscure?" There it was, the gleam of interest. Now she knew—curiosity must be his great weakness. "Obscurity" was all she needed to draw him out the French doors.

Even with the salt-tinged breeze off the channel, the night air was warmer than the ballroom. Sir John stopped for a moment on the garden steps and raised his hand to test the wind. It was almost an automatic gesture, and Jessica was reminded that he was, before aught else, a sailor.

Once out in the fragrant night, he took charge, guiding her down a dark pathway towards a broad flagstone terrace overlooking the sea. Here they were sheltered from a view by narrow tall yew trees, and the noise and music of the ballroom were far away.

She glanced back at the house, wondering whether their absence would be noticed. It would be a novelty, at least, Jessica decided, to be gossiped about for doing something improper like taking to the gardens with an outlaw. Her name was already a May game in the London clubs, for a crime no worse than getting and having to refuse a clutch of marriage proposals.

At the least this man was a most unusual outlaw. As

they passed a bank of rose bushes, he stopped to touch a petal with a gentle finger, then tested the thorn on the stem beneath. She waited for him to break the bloom off and hand it to her, as a gallant beau might, but he only let it go and continued down the path to the terrace.

The tide was out, and the surf was just a whisper against the rocks below. Jessica took a seat on the bench, tucking her blue silk skirt beneath her legs to ward off the chill of the stone. "You know the gardens well," she observed, as he took his own position leaning against the granite wall.

The moon was behind him, but whenever he tilted his head, as he did now, the light outlined the straight lines of his face. He gave her that look again, both quizzical and mocking. "I grew up in the village down the road. Devlyn—"

When his pause grew meaningful, she prompted. "Devlyn?"

Now the look was entirely mocking. "That's the name of the village. Devlyn. As well as the Keep here."

And your brother, she thought. But of course, he wouldn't admit that, not to a chance-met acquaintance. He was not, however, hiding his humble origins; in fact, it was almost a challenge, the cool way he alluded to his village birth. She wondered how to tell him she cared naught for his beginnings, that only his knowledge mattered to her. "Have they a fine library, here at the Keep?"

He shrugged. "None to speak of—merely current books. The old volumes were all sold to pay the gambling debts. Not," he added, as if she might get the wrong impression, "of the current owner. His father and grandfather were the gamblers."

They were Sir John's father and grandfather too, if

Ada's account was true. Of course, Jessica did not remark on that, though she said with special sincerity, "What an outrage, really! To break up fine libraries for that! I am fortunate—my father and grandfather cared for nothing *but* books."

"Well, if no private libraries were ever sold, I shouldn't have much in the way of merchandise, would I?" Another challenge—he was reminding her that he was in a trade, if the most rarefied of all. And he made his own purpose for accompanying her out here very clear. "You were speaking of some obscure items you might be interested in selling. Might I inquire what they are?"

At random she mentioned a few books she would not mind parting with, and saw him shake his head slightly, as if none of them suited him. Annoyed, she asked, "Was there a book you particularly wanted?"

After a moment's pause, he said, "I am interested in the Elizabethan era, especially Shakespeare and his set. Any scripts by playwrights of the time—"

"I don't think we have any of those. And the First Folios will not be available."

He turned and looked out to sea, his straight implacable back a dismissal. She wanted aid; he wanted Elizabethan. They were at cross-purposes, disappointed in each other already. Instinctively, Jessica rose from her bench and approached him, speaking clearly over the gentle rush of the surf. "But you must understand, I don't know the full extent of our holdings. My father added extensively to the collection, but hadn't time to do a complete inventory. Who knows? Perhaps stuck away in some box is exactly what you are looking for."

Only a few feet of stone separated them now. She leaned against the wall as he had done, mimicking his casual ease, then made the mistake of glancing down.

There was a sheer drop of fifty feet down to the rock-strewn water. Quickly she stepped back, trying not to appear unnerved.

But he was grinning as he turned to her. "A long way to the water, isn't it? I hung a rope from that tree when I was a boy—" he nodded back to a dark sturdy oak at the edge of the flagstones, "and anchored my boat down there, and would climb up and down for a lark." He looked down at the waves crashing below. "It's hard to believe I was so reckless."

"No, not hard to believe at all," she replied.

It was only what she was thinking, that he still must be at his best taking risks. But he withdrew slightly, into that civil reserve that reminded her how very different he was than the other men she knew. "You have uncataloged material in boxes, do you?"

"Yes, I know that's not the best way to treat books. But I haven't any choice yet. That is the first thing I mean to do, when I have the authority—a complete inventory." It would take a year or more, of course, but she couldn't keep the eagerness out of her voice.

"Perhaps you'll find that copy of the *Aeneid* that went missing during the Civil War."

"I don't know what you mean."

That ironic demon flashed again in his eyes. "I have heard that Charles I entrusted to the first baron a copy of Caxton's translation of the *Aeneid,* so that it wouldn't fall into the hands of Cromwell. In the muddle that followed—the war, and the King's beheading, and the Restoration—somehow the book never found its way home."

Jessica knew that book, one of the first printed in English, complete with the printer Caxton's spelling experiments. In fact, it was not boxed, but locked away in a display cabinet. She almost told him this, before she recalled that he worked for Charles I's successor. "Caxton's *Aeneid?* Oh, I doubt it's in any of the boxes. It would be too valuable to stash away!"

"And the Caxton guide to chessplaying—you don't expect to find that in a box either, do you?"

Jessica could only laugh, for it was true, the chess book was also supposed to have been a "gift" from Charles I. "Do you know everything?"

"No," he replied evenly. "I don't know what you want of me."

From the coolness of his tone, she realized it was time to tell the truth, or a bit of it anyway. "I only wanted a little advice. The library's curator—I wonder if you might know him."

"Alfred Wiley? He belongs to the Royal Society. I believe I have encountered him."

"What do you think of him?"

"I don't know him well enough to have formed an opinion."

Now, with the moon hidden by a cloud, it was too dark to see Sir John's expression, but she heard the restraint in his voice. He was not, she had already figured out, one to express himself indiscreetly. She should probably cultivate the same reticence, if she was to win his support.

But reticence was never one of her virtues, and now that an alternate scheme was taking shape in her mind, she could not keep still. "I'm not impressed with him. I think he does not do a very good job." She took a deep breath, and when she let it out she was able to speak without trembling. "The library is a shambles. You'd be dismayed, I know it. My grandfather Parham would—oh, he would take his riding crop to Mr. Wiley, I think. He has supposedly been updating the catalogue of the collection for years, and I dareswear he's got no more than a few pages completed, and meanwhile the condition of the books just keeps deteriorating." After a moment, she added in a low voice, "I can hardly bear to go in there now."

Sir John's hand had curled into a fist, but his voice was perfectly even. "So why hasn't he been fired?"

"Oh, my father liked him. They shared the enthusiasm for Bacon—I never understood it; I think Bacon is tedious in the extreme. So he appointed Mr. Wiley curator in the will. And my uncle and the solicitors know nothing of the field. They think libraries are supposed to be dusty and overstuffed with volumes and impossible to navigate. And they believe him to be a great scholar."

"He is, according to reputation."

Jessica shrugged. "Reputation? A dozen years ago, perhaps, he deserved it. But he has become narrow, I think. Nothing interests him but Bacon. And that is all he values in the collection. I'd give him the Bacon just to make him go away—well," she added in afterthought, "perhaps not all of it."

"Can't you prevail upon your uncle to discharge him?"

"I'm not sure that it is possible, given my father's will. And my uncle—as I said, he is duly impressed with the great scholar Alfred Wiley. And I am not, oh, not in my uncle's best books at the moment. But it is possible that, if I learned enough, I could persuade Mr. Wiley to resign."

She saw the ironic glint in his eyes, the half-smile that seemed so characteristic of him. "And how would you accomplish that?"

"Blackmail."

Now the half-smile became full, and she realized with a certain relief that she had impressed him.

"It is a ruthless one indeed, you are, Miss Seton." He

leaned back against the stone wall, his elbow braced behind him. "I don't know how I can help you, however."

"You are in a position to hear things about him, as a member of the Royal Society."

"Such as . . . what? Do you think the Antiquaries sit about and talk about each other's opium habits? Dishonorable behavior during duels? I fear I must disappoint you with the truth—most book-collectors have but one vice, and that one is not conducive to blackmail."

Impatiently she brushed aside an inquisitive ant, which had spent the last minutes climbing up her lace sleeve to her neck. "'I don't mean anything like opium habits. The man's a monk, I know that already. But perhaps he's been selling off bits of the collection—I wouldn't put it past him, as he cares for naught but Francis Bacon."

"I think I should have heard if he had been doing so. And I am not likely, you must know, to second-guess a colleague, especially if it might mean his dismissal."

She sighed, wishing he would just agree to help her as any proper gallant would. It was dispiriting how bereft of gallants nineteenth-century Britain was. "What about—what about some intellectual crime?"

"Intellectual crime? What do you mean?"

"Forgery."

"Of documents?"

He was wary again, leaning against the wall to put distance between himself and her charge. Forgery was a dangerous accusation these days, when William Ireland's Shakespeare forgeries were still turning up in important collections. Jessica thought to reassure him that she meant only poison pen letters, but knew how paltry, how personal that sounded, how unworthy of the title "intellectual crime." So, reluctantly, she played her trump card. "I don't know. I saw a signature of Shakespeare on his desk, the one from the will."

Sir John stilled his restless drumming on the wall. But she was learning something about this man: the very evenness of his voice was a clue to his discomposure. "A signature?"

"A copy. Mr. Wiley's copy."

She sensed him relaxing—it was relief, or regret, she couldn't tell. "That is not a crime, to copy out a signature. Have you an indication he meant it to defraud?"

"No. But—but he is using it wrongly."

"How could he use it wrongly, if not to defraud?"

His quiet interrogation unnerved her. He didn't trust her, and she supposed she couldn't blame him. She shouldn't trust him either; she knew him only by reputation, and that slightly. And what she knew of Wiley's crime suddenly seemed too nonsensical to be believed by this cool, remote man of business. So she prevaricated. "I think he means to publish some false suppositions about Shakespeare based on the signature."

It was not enough. He shook his head, to dismiss her suspicions as so much female fantasizing. "Shakespeare can withstand it, I imagine. He's held up pretty well through worse, I assure you. But if you are worried, why don't you tell your uncle?"

"It's not the sort of crime my uncle would consider a crime. I mean, it has only to do with—" She saw his quick glance toward the house, and knew there was no help for it. If she was to keep him here, she would have to slice off another bit of her precious information. "It has only to do with attribution. Of the plays." Ah, there it was. She knew how to capture Sir John. It only took a mysterious phrase, and he was all attention. "Mr. Wiley thinks that Shakespeare isn't Shakespeare."

"I beg your pardon?"

"He has adjudged from the signature that Shakespeare is illiterate."

He started to speak, then arrested whatever comment he had meant to make. She had surprised him finally, astonished him, in fact. And despite all her troubles, she smiled. It was such fun to be with a man who could appreciate the full horror of what she just revealed.

And so she stoked the fire with her speculations of the librarian's intent. "Mr. Wiley is writing a monograph about it. He will say that the man called Shakespeare was illiterate and uneducated, that he never went to school or owned any books."

"But that's absurd! He owned books, and he read them—he must have. The history plays draw extensively from Holinshed's *Chronicles*, just for one example. And he was surely well-read in the classics." He shook his head, relegating this to nonsense. "And if he were illiterate, how could he have written the plays?"

"That's precisely what Mr. Wiley asks. And his conclusion is—well, that he didn't. That he wasn't educated enough or intelligent enough to construct such masterpieces."

This last revelation struck Sir John silent. So she continued playing the devil's advocate, anticipating Mr. Wiley's argument. "You recall, of course, that in his eulogy Ben Jonson remarked that Shakespeare had 'small Latin and less Greek.' And he would know. He as Shakespeare's best friend."

"A rivalrous friend. That eulogy is one long covert lament that the world preferred Shakespeare. Jonson exaggerated his friend's weaknesses for effect; he must have. And anyway, small Latin and less Greek hardly translates to—to illiterate! Anyone reading the plays would know that their author knew Ovid well, and not only in translation."

"But Mr. Wiley would say that only proves that the writer couldn't have been Shakespeare, you see." She glanced up at him surreptitiously, watching his response. "Shakespeare didn't go to school, or take the Grand Tour. So of course he could know naught of—oh, of Ovid, or of Italy, or of elevated ideas and emotions, being naught but a glovemaker's son."

That last reference would do it, she thought. This apothecary's son, so elegant, so accomplished, would have no use for such elitism. But he surprised her. He shrugged, and looked away across the Channel to France. "It's a notion. I've never found the Italian settings particularly convincing—they rather sound like mere guidebook material. But I expect it can be argued Shakespeare must have visited there to admire it so. He seldom set a play in France, it's true.

"Perhaps he hadn't a French guidebook."

He looked back at her, his smile only a flash in the darkness. He was more composed now, but she saw his hand flexed into a fist at his side. "Perhaps." Elaborately casual, he asked, "So who was the real author of those plays, does Wiley say?"

"Who but Sir Francis Bacon?"

"Bacon?" He raised his hand in dismissal, found it still in a fist, and slowly opened it. "Nonsense. Bacon was a philosopher, not a poet."

Jessica abruptly consigned the devil's advocate position to the devil. "Exactly my thought. Bacon cared for evidence, for reasoning. For facts. A poet—"

"Cares for truth. Shakespeare cared naught for facts. He has Richard III as a hunchback—which is a truth, a higher truth, but has no basis in fact." He added, in a low voice, "It's an outrageous proposition."

Jessica smiled to herself. She had won herself, and poor abused Shakespeare, an ally. "Now you see why I am so mistrustful of Mr. Wiley. To think that he might use my collection to such a purpose!"

But even now Sir John seemed only half-convinced. "How? Oh, I will agree, his hypothesis is outrageous. But how can your collection help him prove something that isn't provable?"

In her haste to enlist his aid, Jessica hadn't considered that question, and for once she hadn't a response handy. "He could—I don't know." Slowly she spoke her thoughts. "There can't be any evidence in the Bacon section that Bacon wrote the plays, certainly, if Bacon *didn't* write them. But—but Mr. Wiley might find something that he could manipulate to indicate that. Of course, such a misinterpretation would be easy to prove false. . . ."

Sir John asked, "You said he was adept at forgery?"

"I think so." She decided not to tell him about the poison pen letters. "He copied out Shakespeare's signature very precisely."

"Could he forge something in Bacon's hand, do you think?"

"Such as a diary entry? 'Finished Hamlet today, will start Macbeth tomorrow'?" She was rewarded by his laugh, but his serious gaze never faltered from her face. And so she considered her own suggestion, testing it against logic, even if it proved illogical. Sir John would expect that sort of intellectual courage, she thought. "But if he has to forge proof, then he will have to accept he *has* no proof. He would be ruining his own case. So he wouldn't use the collection that way."

Unexpectedly, Sir John demurred. "I don't know about that. Collectors are an odd breed. Obsessive. When they are set on believing in something, they are sometimes blind to the truth. Someday I must tell you about the pope and the Aquinas portfolio."

"I know all about obsessive collectors," she said. "My grandfather traded his wife's wedding ring for an illuminated manuscript. He pulled it off her finger as she slept. She was furious." Jessica added fairly, "But it was a Book of Hours, from a Benedictine monastery no one had ever heard of, so who could blame him? Still, this is much more reprehensible an act than mere theft. You are suggesting that Mr. Wiley is not just blind to the truth, but might actually invent falsity. How could he believe in it, if he knows he invented it?"

"If he believes in the 'higher truth' of his theory, perhaps he won't cavil at a single falsehood, if it means he can persuade others. Think of it—he already believes in this mad idea, and without any evidence at all. It would be no great leap for him to invent proof—or destroy it."

She looked sharply at his shadowed face. "What do you mean, destroy?"

Sir John didn't answer immediately. He pushed away from the wall and started back across the terrace. "Come, we'd best get back." He waited for her to catch up to him, and when they were within sight of the house, he said softly. "Are the Folios all the Shakespeare articles you have?"

The path was so narrow that his arm brushed her shoulder as they walked, and her answer came distractedly. "I think so. They are kept in the vault, and only the solicitors have the key. Do you think—you don't think he would try to damage the Folios?"

He didn't seem to hear her inquiry. "What else is in the vault?"

The particular urgency of his question, the light in his odd silver eyes, made her hesitate. "Nothing Shakespearian. Unless it might be—" She swallowed back the words *in Maman's trunk*, and substituted, "something my father didn't tell me about."

"When will the vault be opened next?"

"When I inherit." *If,* came the mocking echo. "On my twenty-third birthday. July 23."

They were approaching the steps back up to the ballroom, and in the glowing light from the windows she saw his quick skeptical glance. "Earlier you said you *hoped* to inherit. I take it there are conditions on the bequest?"

"Just one. But it is of little moment." Jessica ruthlessly shoved the thought of her uncle's recalcitrance to the back of her brain. She had enough to worry about, with this last suggestion that the Folios might be in danger from their keeper. "I will discharge Mr. Wiley at the first opportunity, I assure you."

Sir John stopped with his hand on the knob of the French door. "When do you mean to return to London?"

Yesterday Jessica had decided she would not feel right if she didn't accompany her aunt and uncle on their Waterloo Day visit to Trevor's grave. That was a week from Thursday. Virtue such as this indeed brought its own reward—she would be in London to meet Sir John. "I am leaving Friday."

"Can you get me into your library without alerting Mr. Wiley to my real purpose?"

"I think so. If you call and leave your card, I will tell my uncle you are the Regent's consultant." She headed off his instinctive protest with the quick comment, "He is a bit of a royalist, you see. I can't count on winning his permission otherwise, and only he can order Mr. Wiley to accept a visitor."

"'That is, I hope you know, a very odd way to run a library." And with that observation, he bowed and opened the door into the ballroom.

Ada was waiting by the fire with an admiring look on her face. "You are so clever, Jessie."

"What do you mean?"

"Using Sir John Dryden to trick your uncle this way."

For a moment Jessica worried that Ada had eavesdropped on their conversation. But she reminded herself, if anyone had been listening, the uncanny Sir John would have noticed. "Really, Ada, what are you talking about?"

"You can't fool me. You mean for Sir John to court you. So when your uncle sees you mooning after an illegitimate upstart outlaw, he will suddenly decide Damien isn't so unworthy after all!"

Glancing quickly around, Jessica located Sir John over by the cardrooms and well out of earshot. "I'm not mooning over him—and you shouldn't call him names like that. He's every bit a gentleman, more so than most of the men here. And I wouldn't use him or anyone else like that."

But Ada only smiled. "Oh, no? Well, I know you better than that. I think you would use any weapon at your disposal to get that precious collection of yours."

For a dangerous moment Jessica wondered if her best friend was right. Then she shook her head. Her first concern was ensuring that Alfred Wiley didn't succeed at whatever he might be planning to prove his outrageous claim. And Sir John was the only man who could help her with that.

Chapter Five

Assist me some extemporal god of rime;
    for I am sure I shall turn sonneteer.
Devise, wit; write, pen;
    for I am whole volumes in folio.

Love's Labor Lost, I, ii

Monday morning, John presented himself at Parham House and was shown into the drawing room where the ladies of the house were seated in silence. Lady Parham was sitting rigid on the couch, working away at an embroidery hoop, shaking her head at a missed stitch. Miss Seton was more casual, with her sandaled feet drawn up beside her and her light gold hair drawn into a long braid down her back. A book lay open on her lap, but her abstracted expression indicated she wasn't reading a word.

Instead, she must have been waiting for him, to judge by the way she put aside the book and jumped up to greet him. She was nervous, he could feel it; as she introduced him to her aunt, her slender body was tense, her gestures quick and restless, her smile a shade too bright. Even after she took her seat, she kept getting up, rising to take the tea tray from the maid, crossing to the

window to open the drapes, going to the sideboard for
a spoon.

He knew better than to imagine that the mere presence of a morning caller could discompose her. She was
no green girl, but a woman of some sophistication, at
ease in the Devlyn ballroom and even outside in the
dark with a man she hardly knew. No, it was fear of
what this particular visitor signified, he thought, that
made her so restless—that and some innate intensity,
which her slight form seemed hardly able to confine.

His gaze was drawn back to her, no matter how often
he turned courteously to her aunt. Miss Seton was
pretty, but more than that she was bright, in all the ways
of the word. Her dark blue eyes sparkled whenever she
was curious—and she was always that. And her face, so
smooth and fair, was slightly flushed now. He imagined
that if he touched her cheek, his fingers would gather a
bit of that excited glow.

This young lady affected no fashionable nonchalance.
She found life an adventure, and didn't care who knew it.

He had long since learned that enthusiasm was dangerous. But deep inside, he supposed, he still thought life
was an adventure. Or he wouldn't be so quick to join
hers.

He watched her as she poured the tea, her slender capable hands never still as they moved from pot to cup to
sugarbowl. She made plausible small talk, but he had
enough secrets of his own to know when one was being
concealed. And he knew she was concealing something
now, had in fact been holding it back that evening on
the terrace, however candid that expressive face made
her appear.

But was the play part of her secret?

That the play Alavieri had lost was in the St. Germaine trunk, John had come to believe with the force of

divine revelation. He realized that such a belief took him a long way from his accustomed position as a skeptic, and dangerously close to Alfred Wiley's brand of idolatry. But John, at least, had some basis for his supposition. The young emigrée Annette St. Germaine must have risked death to save this trunk from the fires of revolution. If it had merely contained her favorite gowns, she would never have bothered, and never have made a special bequest of it in her will.

Alavieri had said proudly that only he recognized the hand of Shakespeare on the manuscript, that its purchaser was oblivious to its real value. That made some sense; most collectors, had they known of such a prize, would have announced it with great ballyhoo. But the Parhams—well, they weren't like most collectors. For near three generations now, this library had been closed to the public, withdrawn into obscurity by its reclusive owners and curators. For all anyone on the outside knew, the original scrolls of the Socratic Dialogues were stashed away in some flimsy wooden box, the victim of the Parham privacy.

Of course, he remembered something else that Alavieri said, that he should never let his hope overrule his sense. But John didn't think he was doing that. He wanted the play to exist, of course, but more than that, his certainty was the logical response to a chain of events started two centuries earlier.

But how much did this young heiress know? More than she revealed to John. She had not told him, for example, what he had just learned from a colleague at the Royal Society: that her inheritance was contingent upon her marriage. There was just one condition on the bequest, she had said airily, of little moment. But she had to have been dissembling—if marriage was of little moment to her, she would have married long since.

She must have felt his scrutiny, for she faltered in explaining to her aunt his role as the Regent's art consultant. She glanced over to him, guilt lurking in those dark blue eyes, and hastily rose and went to the desk to get her aunt's spectacles, in case Lady Parham should want to inspect his card more closely.

But the aunt waved the spectacles away, remarking crossly, "Do sit down, Jessica. You know your dashing about gives me palpitations. The Regent's art consultant, are you? Such a kind man. He sent the most affecting note of condolence when our sainted Trevor was taken at Waterloo."

That explained Lady Parham's mourning dress, which posed a contrast to her niece's bright peach and cream gown. John wondered how the girl managed to stay so lively in such company, for Lady Parham's mood rather matched her lugubrious costume. Maybe that accounted for the restlessness—Miss Seton wanted to escape from all the reminders of death. So did John, after five more references to "our sainted Trevor" in the next quarter hour.

The sainted Trevor must be the soldier with the sensitive mouth whose black-ribboned portrait hung above the mantel. John finished his tea and went over to give the painting a cursory glance. It wasn't painted from life, he surmised, but copied from a smaller portrait, for the minor details on the uniform were lacking, and the soulful expression was too obviously a post-sainthood embellishment.

"From Sir Thomas Lawrence's studio?" he asked, earning, as he knew he would, the approval of Lady Parham.

"Yes, it is, how clever of you to recognize his supervising hand. It was done from a miniature in my husband's study—that was all we had of Trevor. We had three of these done—one for Jessica, one for here, and one for our bedroom."

That would make for cheerful bedtime viewing. As a work of art, John vastly preferred the mantel itself. He ran his hand along the sleek curve of an oak-carved scroll, and Jessica, coming up beside him, said, "There's another Adam mantel in the library reading room. Perhaps Uncle Emory will give me permission to show it to you."

She said this loudly enough for her aunt to hear, and Lady Parham waved them distractedly away. "You go ask him, dear. He's in his study. I'll stay here with my sewing."

Uncle Emory turned out to be a wiry man with sidewhiskers and not the slightest suggestion of the Seton intellect. He showed no particular knowledge about the library in his home, nodding his head when Jessica explained their request. "My father and brother—that was their passion. I'm a hunting man myself. You say there's an Adam mantel in the lobby there? Fancy that."

An acquaintance with royalty was of more interest to him, and only after John promised several times to pass on his regards to the Regent, did Parham lead them downstairs and into the wing that held the collection.

He opened the heavy oak door but paused there, calling out, "Mr. Wiley! Mr. Wiley!" adding in aside to John, "Alfred Wiley is the librarian here. Fine scholar. Expert on Bacon, he tells me. Sir Francis Bacon, that is. Oh, here he is."

John noticed that Miss Seton edged back a bit, as if to make herself unobtrusive as Mr. Wiley emerged into the reading room. They were natural enemies, the librarian and his prospective employer, and she, at least, recognized it. Mr. Wiley, however, greeted them all with a slightly dotty geniality, as if he were a rustic king welcoming visitors to his domain.

The Regent's name worked its magic here too. While Parham fled back to his study (claiming that bookdust made him sneeze), and Jessica hung back polishing the display cases with her handkerchief, Mr. Wiley peppered him with questions about the prince's own library. "Has he any works of Bacon?"

"A few letters, and the usual volumes. He might be looking to acquire more, as a matter of fact. I understand the Parham has quite a handsome selection of his personal papers. Would any be available for him to survey?"

Mr. Wiley shot a glance at Jessica, who was standing straightbacked in front of the mantel, dusting it with the lace scrap of handkerchief, ostentatiously paying no mind to their conversation. Still, he lowered his voice. "The library is closed for now, in accordance with the late baron's will. In four weeks, however, I might be able to invite the Regent here to see what I have. In fact, perhaps we could arrange a bit of an opening celebration. Not, you understand, that I expect to sell my Bacon items."

My Bacon items. Mr. Wiley seemed less than certain that young Jessica Seton would be inheriting the library come July 23. Arrogant shag, this Wiley was anyway, expecting the nation's monarch to come to him, trailing a royal celebration behind. But John played along. "I must warn you that the prince is unlikely to come here at all, without some indication that it will be worth his while. If all you can have is a couple official letters signed by Bacon's secretary, I don't think I should be able to persuade him to make a visit."

The challenge worked. John had a glimpse of Miss Seton's startled face as Mr. Wiley, rigid with offense, led him back into the library's main room. "Just a couple official letters! Signed by a secretary!" Wiley muttered. "You'll see!"

John saw at a glance that the library was designed in a U with the reading room surrounded on three sides by the functional areas. This main room had an open area near the door, and an upper level, a narrow mezzanine lined with bookcases and accessible by some hidden staircase. The lower level was scored with rows of shelves perpendicular to the back wall.

And the shelves, he was glad to see, were filled with books. John set to calculating how many volumes there were: fourteen rows, say twenty feet long, three shelves along each row, subtract perhaps thirty percent for many of the volumes were, scandalously, tipped over to warp slowly into odd shapes: eight thousand volumes though, easily. And more were stacked on the floor between the rows, waiting to be reshelved—waiting patiently, to judge by the depth of dust on the covers.

The only light came from six tall windows, distributed symmetrically along the back wall. It was so dim that John could not make out the titles on the back of even the closest books. But he saw several he thought might be incunabula—books from the earliest days of printing, in the last half of the fifteenth century. He wished he hadn't left his spyglass on the *Coronale,* for he was hopeful that gold-tooled volume in the corner had been bound by Samuel Mearne, Charles II's bookbinder, and the Regent had a standing order for any Mearne books that turned up.

So much treasure in such disarray—it might have made John dizzy earlier in his career. But he'd seen monastic libraries in worse condition, including the Greek convent that hid the *Jerusalem* among piles of burlap sacks. Most of those libraries, however, were owned by impoverished and ignorant nuns and monks, who didn't realize what is was they possessed. This library was being neglected by a man who ought very well to know better.

John let his anger flare up and go out. He needed no further motivation, and so it would prove only distracting to curse Mr. Wiley's slovenliness and Parham's criminal laxity. But he felt a resolve build in the back of his mind: Now he intended to do what before he had only pretended to consider—he would help Miss Seton get control of this library. Young and inexperienced and feminine as she was, she could not help but do a better job than the men who had it now.

Besides, an inner voice said, she will have me as an advisor.

He looked back to see Jessica slipping away into the stacks of shelves. Clever girl, to take advantage of the diversion this way. He was tempted to follow her, for she was probably off to check on the St. Germaine trunk. But he had to play through his role of the Regent's consultant, erudite and enterprising, and always on the lookout for books. He even managed to keep from flinching at the state of the adjacent restoration room— the basin full of rags soaked in old mineral oil and paint, the broken books stacked haphazardly on the floor, a cup of tea abandoned on a shelf of vellum scrolls, a window open to London's sooty air. But he couldn't resist closing the Caxton edition of *Canterbury Tales* on the windowsill and spiriting it away to a shelf while Wiley's back was turned.

But the librarian showed no shame at the disorder around him, instead pointing to the set of cabinets that held his favorite pieces. Even hermits, John supposed, liked to show off their caves, and Wiley chattered like a debutante as he cleared a work table by pushing aside a dissembled copy of John Milton's pamphlet *Areopagitica*. Then, reverently, he opened a cupboard, pulled out a page with a pair of tongs, and laid it on the table. His hands were unexpectedly graceful, delicate and quick as he blocked the sheet with a leather-covered steel frame. "Forgers have magician hands," Monsignor Alavieri once instructed John. "It's all sleight of hand."

Finally, his elaborate preparations concluded, Mr. Wiley stepped back to let John examine the braced page. It was a ledger sheet, lined and cross-lined— Bacon's annual household accounts for 1612.

Wiley's voice was hushed. "You can see that he was not a profligate man. Expenditure for candles, only £2 for an entire year. Yet that same year, he records spending £50 on books."

This seemed little enough to marvel over, but at least it provided John with an opening. "He had quite a library, I expect. It is evident from the breadth of his writing that he was a well-read man."

"Well-read?" Wiley's eyes were hazy behind his spectacles, but this brought out the fire in them. "Well-read? The man was the greatest thinker of his time! The soul of the age!"

That ringing phrase rippled across John's nerves, and with its echo faded any lingering notion that Jessica had imagined Wiley's hypothesis. Soul of the age! John didn't react immediately, first taking a cotton glove from his pocket and pulling it over his right hand. "May I?"

When Wiley nodded, John picked up the accounts page and tested the texture. It was the cheapest of paper—another example of Baconian thrift. Shakespeare, John thought with some defiance, would be as profligate with paper as he was with poetry. "Soul of the age, was he? No, no, I can't agree with that. That is how Ben Jonson eulogized Shakespeare."

Wiley chuckled. It was an unnerving sound, like the squeak of an old metal gate in the wind. "Precisely so. Precisely so. That man Shakespeare—have you ever come across a volume from his library?"

John shrugged and replaced the page on the table. "Books he owned? No. I've always been more interested in finding his manuscripts. I never have. Perhaps none exist."

Wiley showed no reaction to this last leading comment. Probably he didn't know about the lost play; then again, perhaps he knew enough to hide such knowledge. "You haven't found any of his library, because he had no library!"

"How do you know that?" So that he wouldn't appear more interested than he ought, John started to assemble the abused Milton pamphlet. He noticed the anomalous type on the third page, and with a bit of his mind realized that such an egregious mistake must indicate a pirated version—perhaps one using some stolen plates from the official printing in 1644. He made a mental note to check this sometime, and brought his awareness full back to Wiley's response.

"I went through Warwickshire years ago, looking for books with his name on it. It's scarce two centuries since his death, but there wasn't any trace, not in any library in the county!" As if he had just proved the world flat after all, Mr. Wiley slapped his hand on the table, making the Bacon list jump in alarm.

Carefully, John matched up the edges of the Milton pages, and resisted groaning at the inadequacy of Wiley's evidence. Instead, in a temperate tone, he said, "Well, perhaps he left his books to his daughter and son-in-law. It stands to reason. His son-in-law was an educated man, and they inherited most of the personal items, as I recall."

"But there *are* no books! Even had he given them away, we would find them still, volumes with his name on it."

John was so taken aback by the meagerness of this that he could hardly frame the obvious response. "Perhaps he didn't write his name in his books. I don't, when I buy a book—I only put my card in it, in case it might be mislaid."

"It was the custom of the day to sign the frontispiece of a book," Wiley replied austerely. He stooped and opened a cupboard, pulling out a red-bound volume. Carefully he lay it on the table. "Go ahead. Open it."

John set the Milton pamphlet down and with his gloved hand opened the cover of the book. It was an obscure scientific text, written in Latin.

"See?" Wiley pointed at the flowing signature on the frontispiece. "Francis Bacon. A fine hand, he had. And—" He closed the book and replaced it in the cupboard. "A large library. Books were possessions of considerable value, and when one lent them out, one wanted to ensure they were returned."

John focused his attention on the Milton pamphlet and reserved his comment that perhaps Shakespeare valued his books so highly that he didn't lend them out. And he balled up all the rest of his objections and hid them away in the back of his mind. He would get nowhere arguing with a man with an *idée fixe.* "That is true," he remarked when he'd gotten control of his voice. "So you found no volumes owned by the Bard? I suppose it made you wonder whether he kept a library at all."

"It did. It did make me question just how well-read this man from Stratford really was." Wiley lovingly replaced the household accounts list in its oilcloth cover and replaced it in the cupboard. "As I said," he added,

"Bacon had one of the great libraries of the day. I wrote a monograph on it for the Royal Society's journal. Perhaps you read it?"

"I did indeed." John closed his eyes for a second and mentally sifted through several years' worth of tedious Society monographs. "You mentioned that he had a copy of Copernicus's *De revolutionibus.*"

"Yes, I have it here in the library." He made a sweeping gesture at a nearby shelf. "It was rather a comprehensive piece that I wrote, if I must say so myself. I am writing another, you know, but this is not nearly so tame."

John took a deep breath and moved back from the table until he felt a shelf against his back. He felt confined, suddenly, in this room with a madman. No, not a madman, just another obsessive collector. "Not so tame, is it? Well, anything likely to shake up the Royal Society of Antiquaries will gain my interest. What is its subject?"

Wiley laid a finger wisely along the side of his nose and nodded portentously. "Bacon, of course. And his heretofore unknown accomplishments. I daresay it will revolutionize Elizabethan-era scholarship forever! But," he added with a raspy chuckle, "you will have to wait to read about it. In a month or so, I expect to find just the evidence I need to complete my argument. For now, I think I must leave it at that."

"Indeed." It was all that John could trust himself to say until he had walked back into the reading room. Only then could he turn back to Wiley with some measure of equanimity. "I would like to tell my client that soon he might have a chance to view what you have here. Have you a catalogue of the Parham's holdings?"

"A catalogue?" Wiley asked, as if John had requested to be provided with an elephant. "Oh, I've started on one. Just the Bacon items so far. Let me find a copy for you." And he plunged back into the library, muttering to himself.

A list of Bacon papers would be of little help in furthering the quest. But when Wiley emerged with the little book, John accepted it with thanks, reminding himself that a few months ago he would have regarded this as a great boon. No other dealer had any idea what the mysterious Parham Collection contained, and here, on the first six pages, were copied out what Wiley, at least, considered the most valuable holdings. It was just that the little book felt too light in his hands, as he knew that it would not mention a play attributed to Dekker or Munday or any of the actor-playwrights who collaborated with Shakespeare.

Wiley, meanwhile, was poking his head back into the main room. "Miss Seton! Miss Seton! Where is that girl?" He turned and said confidentially to John. "She is quite bold, you know. She comes in here without invitation and thinks she has free run. She picks up books and wants to take them, quite as if she owns the library!"

"But she does, doesn't she? Or will soon? She is her father's heir, is she not?"

Wiley smiled. It was a pleasant smile, a gentle, sympathetic smile. "The collection is separate from the entailed property, and separate from her personal legacy. She hasn't yet fulfilled the conditions set forth in her father's will, and there is little chance that she will. So the collection cannot be said to be hers, in any way at all."

His mouth snapped shut just as Jessica entered through the door to the main part of the house. She came up beside John, every inch the debutante suddenly, smiling up at him as if they were social acquaintances. "Oh, you are finally done, Sir John? My aunt was wondering if you would stay for lunch."

It was clever of her, to sneak back out of the library

and pretend that she had been elsewhere all along. Wiley appeared mollified, but then, he probably hadn't yet seen the telltale cobweb, silver against her golden hair. Unobtrusively, John brushed at the back of her head, and the cobweb disintegrated under his fingers, melting away into the silk of her hair. As his hand dropped, she looked up startled at him, then made a funny face as she raised her hand to where his had been and felt the stickiness.

To distract Mr. Wiley from this quick grooming, John thanked him and assured him that the Regent would hear of Bacon's household accounts. "And watch the Society journal for my monograph," Wiley reminded him in an urgent undertone as they passed through the door. "In a month or so, no more. Revolutionary, I promise you!"

Once back in the main hall, Jessica broke her uncharacteristic silence. "I didn't actually talk to my aunt, but I'm certain she would like to have you stay for lunch."

"We haven't time for lunch. We must talk, and privately. Can you go for a drive—just to the park?"

Her eyes widened, and too late he remembered that he wasn't the sort of driving companion a young lady should be seen with. But before he could withdraw his suggestion, she said only, "Let me get my bonnet—and comb the spiders out of my hair!"

Chapter Six

> The very instant that I saw you did
> My heart fly to your service, there resides
> To make me slave of it, and for your sake
> Am I this patient logman.
>
> *The Tempest*, III, i

Rendering herself spider-free took only a moment, but explaining to Aunt Martha that she was missing lunch to go driving in the park threatened to take much longer. Ruthlessly she pretended not to hear the questions about exactly who this Sir John was, beyond the Regent's art consultant. "I shan't be gone above an hour or two, Aunt!"

She waved gaily and escaped down the stairs before her aunt could protest. She tied her bonnet on with quick jerks, thinking how absurd it was that she was still answering to her aunt and uncle when she was almost twenty-three. If she had been allowed to marry, she would have her own household, and she might drive with anyone she pleased.

Sir John was waiting in the hall, reading the meager excuse for a catalogue as if it were Holy Writ. The sun through the stained glass window splayed colored light on the pages and across his tan hands, striking off his sapphire signet ring. When he saw her, he marked his place with a card and closed the book, putting it away into his pocket. As he smiled, his gray eyes became mirror-like, reflecting the sunlight. "Sometime you must go through this list with me, telling me which items your father acquired, and which your grandfather acquired. Each, I'm sure, added his own stamp to the Bacon holdings, but I haven't much of a sense of their preferences yet."

For just a moment, she had imagined that his smile was for her, for the new bonnet that tilted so rakishly over her eyes. She knew an instant's disappointment, then shook her head at her own foolishness. She'd known men's admiration before, often enough, and once or twice something far deeper than that. And it had not been enough. Now she was with a man who treated her not as an heiress to be captured, nor even an object to be adored, but as—as a colleague. She had best enjoy this unaccustomed equality while it lasted, for without a doubt she would not experience it with many other men.

And if it was her collection that most attracted him, well, that's why she had sought him out, after all. So, lightly, she told him, "I shall tell you all I know about my ancestors' acquisitions—under one condition."

He stepped back to let her go through the front door, and as she brushed past him she sensed the guardedness of his stance. "What is the condition?"

She glanced up in exasperation. "Well, you needn't think I will expect your firstborn! I merely hope you will let me copy that list before you return the book to the library. Mr. Wiley has never let me have one." She bit back a bitter comment and continued with determined brightness, "I have a list I've done from memory, but

I've only come up with about six hundred book titles.
And nowhere near that many manuscript titles."

"You have a very good memory, I think."

"Not good enough, I fear."

"He's only listed the Bacon works, and not all of
that."

"Well, I can add those to my list, then. I'm certain I
didn't recall all those."

It was a bright June day, with only a few clouds float-
ing above the chimney tops and trees of Berkeley
Square. As his phaeton was brought round, Sir John
hesitated on the steps, turning his face to the light
breeze and his gaze towards the gray horizon. "Storm
brewing." He caught her startled look and added reassuringly, "Not till tonight. You needn't worry that the
picnic will be ruined."

"Picnic?" she said faintly, but she supposed if he could
conjure up a storm from a brilliant day, a picnic would
not strain his ingenuity. He tossed a gold coin to the stableboy bringing the fashionable phaeton and sent him
down the street with a low-voiced order, and once again
Jessica found herself revising her estimate of him. He
must have an unexpectedly romantic streak, she thought
as he helped her onto the high perch, planning a picnic
for her this way. While he was busy with his horses, she
surreptitiously bent to look on the floor for a basket of
delicacies, under the seat for champagne bottles, back to
the tiger perch for a serving groom. But the phaeton
was meticulously bare of picnic paraphernalia.

She had forgotten about his maverick streak. His idea
of a picnic apparently had nothing to do with a linen ta-
blecloth, crystal champagne glasses, and hovering servants. As they stopped at Piccadilly—he was headed for
Green Park, instead of the more populous Hyde Park—
the stableboy ran alongside and handed up a couple

green jars and a cloth parcel tied up with string. Sir John transferred these to Jessica and rewarded the stableboy with a grin and another coin, then urged his horses across the busy street.

Jessica was too surprised to comment, but only sat there with the parcel radiating heat in her lap, a cold jar clutched in each hand, her feet braced against the floor, praying that his driving skills weren't limited to steering ships into dock. Fortunately, they arrived at the park without mishap, and he pulled up in the middle of a little grove of trees.

"I didn't want you to miss lunch," he explained, taking the parcel from her lap and vaulting to the ground. He held up his hand for a jar, then deposited the goods on the grass under an old oak tree. And then, with that impeccable courtesy that accorded so well with the cool elegant accent, he lifted her to the ground.

There was a moment, before her feet found the earth, that her body brushed against his and she recalled that too-intimate waltz at Devlyn Keep. Then he dropped his hands from her waist and took the other jar from her, set it down against the exposed tree root, and went to see to the horses.

The sunlight filtering through the leaves spread like a canopy over the green, isolating them in a pastoral oasis in the middle of the city. It was inviting, the deep soft grass, the dappled shade, the ancient tree, but for just a moment she was unable to enter the pretty scene.

Why the prospect of sitting alone with Sir John seemed more improper than driving alone with Sir John, she couldn't say. And why she was so conscious of the impropriety, she didn't know. She was no green girl, living in terror of ruination. She had been alone with men before, for as long as a half-hour, and felt no more than a *frisson* of guilty pleasure. But here, in broad daylight, in the midst of a crowded city, she felt that same sense of danger she knew last week, when she had shared a bit of darkness with this man.

"You'll pardon my shirtsleeves, I hope," he said, tugging off his coat. And then, to her mingled horror and pleasure, he spread it on the grass and bade her sit. It was a Weston coat, she could tell from the precision of the cut, and he was sacrificing its pristine folds for her comfort. He had his gallant moments after all.

She could do no more than graciously accept, arranging herself so her sandals didn't touch the superfine fabric. As he sat across from her on the exposed root, stretching his long booted legs out before him, her thoughts skipped with alarming rapidity from coats to gallantry to queens and finally, inevitably, to the collection. "Did you see in the reading room that we have not only a copy of Hakluyt's account of the first expedition to Virginia, but a copy of Hariot's scientific notes about the second?"

"Oh, my coat won't get so muddy, and I can't think you will reward me by lopping off my head, as Elizabeth did to poor Raleigh."

And then as he tilted his head to the side and smiled at her, she realized why she felt in such danger to be alone with Sir John Dryden. It was that eerie intimacy—that certainty that he knew her very well, even without knowing her at all. For he had traced her thought-skips backwards, and arrived at their debarkation point—Hakluyt and Hariot's employer, Sir Walter Raleigh, who had once spread his cloak over a puddle so the queen's shoes wouldn't get muddy. "How did you know what I meant?"

He shrugged and with dexterous fingers made short work of the elaborate knot in the parcel. "You think quickly—but clearly. Don't you?"

"No one else thinks so." He only understood, she realized, because his mind worked in the same way. But there was danger there too, in imagining them kindred. They couldn't be, of course; they were as different as night and day.

She had to halt the inner debate to accept the napkin and the meat pie and the apple as he handed them to her in rapid order. The mechanics of juggling the food and the jar of lemonade were sufficient to divert her, but still she hesitated before beginning the feast.

He saw her frown at the jar, and smiled again. "Don't think of food poisoning, Miss Seton. Think of this as a culinary adventure."

Because he had read her mind again, because she did like to think of herself as adventurous, because he raised his own jar in salute, she laughed and took a sip and told herself that lemon probably killed all evil humors. And then, to distract herself further from speculation about their commonality, she returned to the subject that haunted them both. "What did you think of Mr. Wiley?"

He set the rest of his meat pie down on the napkin, as if Mr. Wiley had deprived him of his appetite. "You are right. The man's a menace."

Sir John, she knew already, wasn't one to exaggerate; if anything, he deliberately kept his responses muted. So "menace" must reflect a severe antipathy to the librarian. "What did he show you?"

"Bacon's candle expenditures. For some reason, he thinks the Regent will want to snap that up. Where did you slip off to, by the by?"

"Back to the vault. You made me worry about the Folios, so I thought I'd best check on them. As far as I can tell, they haven't been touched."

"I thought you said only the solicitors had a key to that vault."

"Oh, I didn't get into it. There's a tiny slit in the door, and I could see that the case holding the Folios was still on the shelf."

He turned his apple in his hand, studying it with remarkable concentration. "What else is in this vault?"

She was not deceived by his casualness. The little catalogue Mr. Wiley had given him wouldn't be enough to quench his curiosity. So she took her time, biting into the meat pie and chewing meditatively before replying. "Oh, all the illuminated manuscripts, and a few parchment scrolls, an early codex, one of the early printed editions of the Psalter—" she waved her hand vaguely. "Too much to enumerate, really. But it hasn't been opened since my father's death."

"Does Wiley know what the vault contains?"

This question came brisker. Aha, Jessica thought, the vault fascinates him, for some reason—a reason he hasn't shared with her. It was a necessary reminder that they might be allies now, but they were not comrades. She looked squarely into those reflective eyes and told the truth. Fortunately, the truth revealed nothing crucial. "My father surely told him. He has never been in it, as far as I know. No one has, since my father took me in there before he died."

"No unknown treasures, then?"

For once, she was glad that her father had been so close with his information. Very carefully, she said, "I know only the known treasures." She looked away, disillusion stinging at the back of her eyes. She should know better than to trust so quickly, especially a man with so many secrets. He wasn't the sort to be a white knight, sacrificing his own interests to help her.

Perhaps he sensed her withdrawal, because he told

her then of his interview with Wiley, reminding her that
whatever his real purpose, they had one goal in common. "Wiley didn't mention Shakespeare's signature. Instead, he told me that he has found no book bearing
Shakespeare's name, therefore he had no library,
therefore—he implied, but did not say—that Shakespeare must have been illiterate."

"An illiterate actor? I suppose the Globe hired someone to read him his lines?" Jessica scoffed, then frowned.
"But that is curious, isn't it? That Mr. Wiley never
found books with Shakespeare's name inside?"

"Curious. But meaningless. First, as I told him, not
everyone defaces a book by writing in it. Second, Shakespeare has no living descendants, so his possessions were
probably dispersed a century or more ago. And third,
Wiley is a curator, not a dealer. I doubt he knows how
to search for a book. I suspect he just sent letters round
to the Warwickshire landowners, asking if they had any
of Shakespeare's books. How would they know? Most
probably never set foot in their libraries, and only figured that someone would have noticed if they owned
such a prize. So they would never bother to search the
shelves, much less the cupboards and under the floorboards."

"The floorboards?"

"Certainly. That's where Royalists hid their valuables
during the Civil War. That's how I found that sheaf of
medieval caricatures—the Royalist owner had been executed by Cromwell, so I suspected he never had a
chance to dig the treasures back up." He added in afterthought, "Perhaps I might discover which Warwickshire
landowners were executed as Royalists, and—"

Then he shook his head briskly and rose. He walked
over to his horses, slipped their bits, and shared out the
remains of his apple between them. Over his shoulder,

he said, "Wiley also neglected a possibility that no librarian should ignore. Libraries are full of paper, and frequently they go up in flames. And everything is lost. It's possible that Shakespeare's library—and perhaps his manuscripts and notes and personal papers—has burned in the last two centuries." He added casually, "I was in France recently, looking for copies of the Stephanus Bible and a few other items. The Revolutionaries, you know, respected books no more than they respected churches. They sacked and burned many libraries. It's impossible to count what has been lost."

"My grandfather—my maternal grandfather—was killed in the Revolution. His chateau was burned." Jessica didn't know why she mentioned this, for her family seldom spoke of it. She'd had to piece the story together from details her parents let slip. But they were long dead, and their reticence reflected the same suspicion that had led to her father's strange will and the isolation of the collection. Not that her motive in revealing this was so noble—she just wanted to impress Sir John. She might not have rescued Bibles from their burial grounds, but she knew a few good book stories too.

And she had succeeded in capturing his interest. He left the horses and returned to sit under the tree, circling his knee with his clasped arms. "Where was the chateau?"

"Near Chantonnay, in the Vendée. He had a great library, you know. I gather he was something of an Anglophile—he often travelled to London to find volumes. That is how he met my father."

"And so he arranged your mother's marriage?"

"Oh, no, I don't think so. He wasn't so farsighted as that! But my mother knew no one else in England after the Terror. My father must have thought he owed it to his friend to take care of her. Mother always said he married her for her dowry."

"What was that?" Sir John asked quietly, leaning closer.

"She meant it ironically. She had no dowry. Everything was lost in the Terror. Except—"

She saw the silver flash of his eyes, the sudden tension of his body. "You know, don't you? You know about the trunk. Did Mr. Wiley tell you?"

He had the grace to look guilty, but that only lasted a moment. "No, he never mentioned it. The Prince Regent told me about your mother coming here as an emigrée. He said he sent them a Bacon letter as a wedding gift."

Automatically she murmured, "How good of him to remember." Conflicting emotions flooded her. As always, when she thought of her parents, she felt the wrench of loss, of incomprehension—they were unknown to her in so many ways. And she felt betrayed by this man, who withheld so much from her, even as he claimed to be an ally.

But, she thought, clasping her hands tightly around her drink, perhaps she was taking it too personally. She had been keeping much from him, too. It was only politic to test a potential ally before revealing secrets.

She studied him from under her lashes, wondering what else he knew about her family and her collection. "I did not realize that the Regent was aware of my mother's trunk."

Sir John shrugged and looked away. "Is it kept in the vault?"

"Yes. It's always been there."

"What's in it?"

The question came too quickly, betraying him, and he must have realized it. He picked up his drink and assumed a careless expression, but she had already learned what she needed to know. Whatever he wanted from the trunk he could only hope was really there. She shrugged, just as he had, insouciant, unconcerned. "I don't know. No one does, as far as I know. It's never been opened."

"Surely there is an index of the contents somewhere."

"I've never seen one. There wasn't one attached to the will, I know that. I don't think that even my father knew what is in it."

Sir John capped his jar of lemonade, shaking his head all the while. "I don't understand your family at all. No catalogue, no index of the contents of the trunk—what if there's a fire? How will you know what to save?" In a sardonic tone, he added, "But then, you shouldn't have time, as you would have to go to the solicitor's office first to get the key. And how do you know that solicitor hasn't been conspiring with Wiley to steal works from the vault?"

Since that was Jessica's worst nightmare, she could only say, "I don't know. I have worried about that myself."

"Without an index, you'll never know. If I had been advising your father—" He didn't finish the thought, but his tone made it clear that they would all have been better off now. "Closing off treasures this way—why did your mother save those works from a conflagration, bring the trunk here, then lock it up for a quarter century?"

Jessica couldn't answer for a moment, torn between her sense of betrayal and her need for an ally. Common sense provided the answer. She couldn't defeat Mr. Wiley on her own. Sir John might have his own aim in this, but as long as it didn't conflict with her own, she would let him pursue it.

And besides, it was her parents' reclusiveness that caused all these problems, when they decided to tie up the collection in legal knots to keep the world away. Sir John was, by comparison, a veritable model of openness.

So finally, haltingly, she said, "My family has never been welcoming of the outside world. I don't know why. I am not that way. But as for the St. Germaine trunk— that was a test for my father, I think. My mother was not one to trust fate or other people. I suppose that was common in those who survived the Terror. She always said that she knew Father had married her to possess the trunk. She meant it jokingly, I'm sure, but she must have thought there was some truth in it. And Father always retorted that the day they were married, the trunk was sealed, and so he had never even gotten a glimpse of the treasures inside. He did love her, I think."

"He must have been mad about her." Sir John didn't sound as if he approved. "For it's madness, sure enough, to lock up—whatever it is they locked up. Are you sure your father didn't know what he was forgoing?"

"Yes. He presumed that it was the best of the collection, but Mother used to tease him, reminding him what an eclectic collector my Grandfather St. Germaine was. Whatever St. Germaine might consider priceless, the world might not agree." Despite the tension that gripped her, she felt the memories course warm through her, and, almost unaware, she smiled. "Father would groan and swear that he would go to the vault and break open the trunk. But he never did. So I think he never knew."

"Your mother must have been bewitching."

Jessica noted his sardonic tone, and wondered if he meant that he would never let a woman bewitch him that way. It would be interesting to test his resolve—but she wouldn't, of course. It would serve neither of their interests. "Oh, she was. I wish she'd have lived long enough to teach me some of her tricks, for she got away with the most outrageous things. And my father—oh, I think he liked to speculate about what she was hiding from him. The lost plays of Sophocles! A fifth Gospel!"

"He thought, did he, that it was something lost? Something unknown?" When she was too puzzled to reply, he added, "He didn't speculate that it held another Guttenberg Bible, but an unknown gospel. Not just an early Latin translation of *Oedipus*, but one of the lost Sophocles plays. That's a signal, don't you think?"

"It's just that he knew more about the St. Germaine method of collecting than anyone else in England. He thought my grandfather was ripe for the plucking by any sharp, because of his predilection for oddities. And he disapproved, in principle. But he must have dreamt all kinds of dreams, imagining what that trunk could hold."

"Ah."

That was the last comment Sir John made for several minutes; he took to staring off into space as if he were silently calculating a string of variables. Jessica began gathering up the crumbs of the meat pie to throw out for birds, glad of the respite to consider what more she should tell.

For the time being, she had not choice but to trust him. But she would have to take care. Any more information about the trunk, he would just have to earn, by working for her purposes before his own.

Finally he broke his silence. "Does Wiley knows what is in the trunk?"

She took off her bonnet and smoothed the satin ribbons, considering this. "Why do you ask? Do you think he wants something from it? Something that might help his case against Shakespeare?" When he only shrugged in reply, she tied the ribbons into a bow, then pulled them loose. Then she looked up at Sir John. "I know that Mr. Wiley was the one who persuaded my father to have it opened when I inherited."

"What do you mean?"

"After my mother died, my father revised his will. That is when he decided to keep the library closed to new purchases and sales until I was grown. Yet he spoke of leaving the trunk sealed. He picked out 1843 as the date of its opening, fifty years after my grandfather's death. But Mr. Wiley suggested that he make it twenty-five years instead."

"1818."

"Yes. And since the library was to transfer on my birthday that year anyway, Father just appended the disposition of the trunk to the trust conditions." Reluctantly, she added, "I suppose I should be grateful to Mr. Wiley."

Sir John smiled. "Don't strain at that, Miss Seton. I think you are right to think he has his own dreams of what that trunk contains. There are, I understand, conditions on your inheritance?"

This abrupt change of subject silenced her. Finally, she said, "Just one."

"Your marriage."

Yet another indication that he knew more than he ought about her. He must have spent the last couple days studying up on her life. It would be flattering, if it wasn't so unsettling. "Yes. I must marry before my twenty-third birthday—next month."

Now he was the one to be puzzled. He regarded her with the concentration he must have applied to a disputed text. "Why not just marry? Are you morally opposed to the institution? A Wollstonecraft disciple?"

She laughed hollowly. "I have nothing against marriage. I would be married six, no, seven times over, had I my druthers." At his confused frown, she added, "Oh, not literally, for that would be illegal, to have seven husbands. I mean that I have received seven proposals that were acceptable to me. But not to my uncle."

"But you are of age——" He broke off, then nodded. "I see. He must approve the marriage. Rather feudal of your father. These seven suitors—none of them suited?"

"They aren't ghastly, if that's what you imagine. They are all gentlemen, and good decent men besides. Some are family friends, in fact. But my uncle——"

"His standards are more exacting than yours?"

His tone was neutral, almost silky, but for some reason she took offense. "I know what you're thinking. What everyone thinks. That no woman of any sensibility could truly find seven different men acceptable as husbands. Well, I have no sensibility to speak of. I want what other women want, of course, a husband and children. But I want something more—my collection. I am no romantic, but I would be grateful to the man who helped me secure all that." Fiercely she added, "I would make any one of them a good wife, had I the chance."

"But your uncle will have none of them. Why not?"

"Because——" She gazed down at the napkin twisted in her hands. But she could feel his intense regard on her face. "My Uncle Emory would approve no man but Trevor."

"The sainted Trevor."

His tone was so deeply ironic that despite herself she smiled. "Yes, the sainted Trevor. Father and Uncle both meant me to marry him. That way the collection would remain in the family."

"I'm surprised your uncle doesn't just marry you off to his current heir."

"Oh, I thought of that also. But our cousin Gerard has been married for decades; he's much older than I. Besides, my uncle's refusal has nothing to do with the collection. He doesn't care about it very much. But my father knew that Trevor did care, and that my uncle would do anything for him. That's why my father had no hesitation putting Uncle in charge of my marriage. But when Papa died, he had no idea that Trevor would take up soldiering." Bleakly she added, "Neither did Trevor, of course. That was Uncle Emory's idea."

"To make a man out of the boy, I suppose."

She glanced up startled. "Precisely. How did you know?"

"I had a father too. Only he thought manhood had something to do with taking over his business. It would have been safer than Waterloo, I suppose." Then, quickly, as if he regretted the personal admission, he said, "So now your uncle is consumed with guilt over his son's death, and determined to make you suffer for it."

It was something she'd thought, of course, but never before put into words. "Yes," she said slowly. "It's as if he thinks that he can have no other son, so I should have no other husband."

"You don't need his permission to marry now."

She shook her head blindly. "That's what Damien said. He was the last one. He said we could just marry without Uncle's permission. But then I would lose the collection."

"You must see that you are very likely to lose it anyway."

"I do see that. I do." She forced some resolve into her voice. "But while I have a chance to change my uncle's mind, I will do whatever I can. If I can discredit Mr. Wiley, perhaps my uncle will be more reluctant to turn the family legacy over to hired hands. Or," she added bravely, "at the very least, another man will be given charge of the library, and it will be made available to scholars. Will you help me? My uncle might listen to you. You are a man, and the Regent's consultant, and neutral in the matter."

He did not answer directly. "Are you prepared to ruin Wiley?"

"Yes."

He regarded her not with censure, precisely, but with interest, as if she posed a particularly intriguing problem. "Really?"

She thought of the poison pen letters, the neglect of the library, the insolent way he denied her the use of her father's collection. "Yes. He would ruin me, if he could. I think he has tried. We are at odds in every way."

Her pronouncement must have sounded vainglorious, because he smiled one of those annoying masculine smiles. "You would hate him too, if he were holding your life away from you and laughing."

The smile faded. "No. I am not one for hatred. If I feel that, it only lasts a moment."

"And what replaces it?"

"Intent." He added, "It is so much more effective."

"Well, then, Sir John," she said deliberately, "what do you *intend* to do?"

Again he didn't answer. She was learning that he was not one to commit himself. But as he took out his watch and glanced at it, she thought that he would not fail her. He had something at stake too—perhaps an altruistic love of Shakespeare, perhaps something more secretive than that.

"We'd best get back before your aunt calls out the watch."

Jessica shook out her skirts and adjusted her sandals.

He rose and held out his hand to help her to her feet. Then, absently, he touched an edge of the napkin to his tongue, and applied the wet cloth to the corner of her mouth. It was so intimate a gesture, but so automatic, that she could only accept it as causally as it must have been intended. "You must ordinarily picnic with children! Have you nephews and nieces?"

He looked down at the new gravy stain on the handkerchief and hesitated for just a fraction of an instant. "One of each."

She remembered that Lord Devlyn had a son and a daughter, but only said, "Is it a brother or a sister who gave you these messy relations?"

"A brother." He stuffed the handkerchief back into his pocket. "Dennis. He took over the apothecary shop when my father died, and the house too."

Perhaps this unusual loquacity was meant to divert her from realizing that he had, in a way, disowned another brother, another nephew and niece. But she couldn't say that; it wasn't surprising, she supposed, that he would be close with that scandalous secret.

And it wasn't surprising that he changed the subject. "You have no siblings, have you?"

"No. There was only Trevor—he was my cousin, of course, but we were reared together, like brother and sister."

"And your parents expected you to marry?" He sounded as disapproving as when she confessed that her parents did not make lists. He was not, she realized, very impressed with her family.

"*We* expected to marry also." She had to pause to strip the defensiveness from her voice. "It's not unknown, you know, in our set, for first cousins to marry. It keeps the family holdings together for generations."

He gathered the remains of their lunch into the cloth

and tied it up with quick jerky motions. "Other sets might see that as a strange reason for a marriage, almost incestuous, in fact. But then, I suppose, *your* set would regard that as a hopelessly middle-class perspective."

And before she could respond, he went off to untie the horses and lead them back to the cartpath. She gathered up the lemonade jars, feeling unjustly rebuked. She had not called him middle class. She was no snob, after all; she had proved that today, coming out with him without even a moment's qualms about his background. She might even admit to finding it exotic.

But he soon regained his composure. As he helped her into the phaeton, he said levelly, "I will help you. I will talk to your uncle, suggesting to him that the Regent or some of my other clients might be interested in my account of the library. If we can get a few hours in the library without Wiley hanging about, we can begin searching."

"For what?"

He didn't answer immediately. But when he had tugged at the reins to get the horses moving down the path, he admitted, "I don't know yet. I just know something must be in there that will help our case."

The anxiety that had plagued her since his cold dismissal of her class vanished. Our case, he had said. Jessica still had her ally, one she could trust to be ruthless enough to match Alfred Wiley.

Chapter Seven

As Jessica entered the dining room for supper, she heard thunder roll in from the east and a sudden spatter of rain on the windows. She should have known better than to doubt Sir John's prediction.

She took her seat as the windows rattled from the force of a thunderclap. In the next moment, the room glowed eerily from a lightning flash, then dimmed again. Jessica thought of lightning fires and library destruction, and resolved, as soon as she inherited, to modernize the house's defenses.

Grace was interrupted by another thunderbolt. Aunt Martha shuddered. "And after such a lovely day. You saw no sign of rain, did you, Jessica, when you went on a drive with that Sir John?"

"No, Aunt. But he said there was a storm coming—he's a sailor, you know."

Aunt Martha leaned back to let the footman ladle soup into her bowl. "What an unusual man that Sir John is. Where did you meet him, dear?"

In Aunt Martha's parlance, *unusual* could mean *unacceptable* or simply *uncommon*. Jessica decided that to be safe, she'd best bring in the heavy defensive weaponry.

"At a ball at Devlyn Keep. The princess herself introduced us."

"The Princess Tatiana?" Aunt Martha brightened. "Such a charming lady. And Sir John was at her ball?"

"Yes. He's a boyhood friend of Lord Devlyn, I believe."

Her aunt Martha accepted this identification without demur, but Uncle Emory hurrumphed, then went back to his soup. Jessica wondered if he had heard about that other connection between Lord Devlyn and Sir John, but knew better than to ask. Still, she had an inexplicable desire to discuss this enigma of a man, and so she turned back to her aunt, who loved harmless gossip. "He is very discerning, don't you think? He knew right away that portrait of Trevor was from Lawrence's studio."

"Quite the gentleman. It's hard to believe he's in trade. Of course," Aunt Martha said, ruminatively breaking her bread into small pieces, "I suppose a royal art consultant isn't quite in the same sort of trade as a haberdasher. He cuts a rather striking figure, I think."

"Looks like a foreigner to me." After making this pronouncement, Uncle Emory sank back into silence, gesturing to the footman to fill his wineglass.

Jessica knew a moment's unease. If Sir John was to aid in her quest, he needed to win the confidence of her uncle. But it sounded as if he had lost it already—and she had a good idea who might be to blame.

Aunt Martha, oblivious as usual to the tension at the table, confided, "Your uncle is hoping that Sir John will persuade the Regent to visit Parham House. Sir John sent a note by this afternoon, offering to survey the collection to find items that might lure him here."

Sir John had apparently wasted no time. But, to judge by her uncle's expression, neither had Mr. Wiley. Deliberately she introduced that name into the conversation. "Did you tell Mr. Wiley that Sir John might be coming again? It might prove a bit embarrassing, if Mr. Wiley would turn away the Regent's consultant, or discourage him from looking around."

Her uncle's head snapped up at the mention of the librarian. "I told him to give Dryden reasonable access to the collection. And Mr. Wiley—he told me a thing or two about this consultant."

"Oh?" As if unconcerned, Jessica buttered her bread with long, smooth strokes of the knife. "I didn't know Mr. Wiley got out enough to learn anything of those around Carlton House."

The mention of the royal residence mollified him a bit. "Well, he's encountered him in this antiquary society. Doesn't fault his ability, mind you, for Dryden's very well thought of there at the society. But—"

The arrival of the footman with the next course cut off his comment. But Jessica knew what was coming. Her uncle waited only for the footman to walk out with their empty soup bowls before picking up his fork and pointing it at her. "His antecedents are cloudy, my dear. Mr. Wiley suggested he is a mere tradesman's son, dressed up as a gentleman."

Dressed up as a gentleman. That annoyed Jessica enough to impel her to intemperance. "Sir John *behaves* as a gentleman, too, Uncle. And his antecedents aren't the least cloudy. He told me straight off that his father is an apothecary in Dorset. I can't see what that has to do with his consulting on the collection."

"It has nothing to do with his consulting, but it has everything to do with your going out driving with him."

Jessica's heart sank. It hadn't taken Mr. Wiley very long at all to start his poisoning. At least this time he had done it openly. "It was an open carriage, and in the middle of the afternoon. Even so wicked a creature as an apothecary's son can't get up to much under those conditions."

Her irony made no impression on her uncle, who only regarded her dourly. "He is utterly ineligible."

Aunt Martha, who had been so complimentary of Sir John only a few minutes earlier, chimed in. "Yes, dear, he's not of our sort. Even if he does associate with the Regent, and has a title, truly, you can't be seen with a tradesman's son."

"And," Uncle Emory declared, "don't you think of presenting him to me as a suitor."

"A suitor!" Jessica felt the heat rise in her face. "I—that's absurd. I haven't any intent of—of snaring him." Her voice shook as she continued, "I know you can't understand this. But more than anything I want to ensure that my family's collection is secured. And I've told you before, I don't trust Alfred Wiley, and I don't think he's doing an adequate job. Sir John is an objective observer, with great experience in the field. While he's doing the Regent's work, I hope he might—" For a moment she couldn't think of a plausible reason for them to associate, but she took a deep breath and found that the words came to her eventually. "That he might—unofficially, of course—make some recommendations on what volumes most need to be restored, and which might be best preserved under glass. The sort of duty," she added bitterly, "that Mr. Wiley hasn't seen fit to perform for years now."

Uncle Emory glowered but only remarked, "I don't know why Sir John should go to the effort to do so—unless he has some ulterior motive."

"His *motive* might just be the desire to keep the collection from deteriorating further! Perhaps he just cares about preserving the nation's heritage!"

Her ringing endorsement had an unintended effect. Uncle Emory couldn't accept an altruistic apothecary's son, but self-interest he could understand. "No. He's a tradesman. More than likely he knows what's what, and knows once your father's bequest is executed there will be items selected for sale. He thinks that, if he is in on it from the first, he will be chosen as the dealer."

Aunt Martha said helpfully, "Well, I don't know what's wrong with that, Emory. After all, he certainly knows his business. And only think if the Regent would ask to be shown some of the library. We could have a reception—music, perhaps, a Venetian breakfast?"

He nodded slowly. "Perhaps. Well, I know one thing. He's no fool. He'll want to stay on my good side as long as I let him into the library. So you can just cross him off your list of potential suitors, my girl. He won't be likely to jeopardize his future by courting you."

Jessica felt the panic rising in her—fear that this new association would be barred to her, anger that her own wishes counted for nothing, dread that Sir John would face insult because of her. "Uncle, please! Don't—please don't say anything to him! I'm sure he hasn't the slightest intention of that, and it could only embarrass all of us if you do."

Uncle Emory considered this grudgingly. "That's so. I should be charitable, I suppose. His birth is no fault of his own, after all, and he's making himself useful, and hasn't once mentioned sending us a bill. And, as I said, he's no fool. I'm sure he learned long ago to keep his distance from his betters, or he wouldn't be tolerated as he is. But you—you, miss, you just keep your distance too, and don't be thinking you might make him lose his head and pay you court. I assure you, I will never, never approve such an unequal marriage."

Jessica had won her goal: Sir John would be allowed

access to the library. But she knew a gnawing dissatisfaction. She pushed away her roast beef, unable to eat it for the sour taste in her mouth. "I don't know why you think that will intimidate me, sir. After all, you haven't approved any of the *equal* marriages that have been proposed for me."

"Don't you be impertinent, young lady! I am your guardian, and—"

"And I am of age," Jessica cried, to remind herself if not him, "and if I want to—if I want to learn to stand up on a horse and join Astley's Circus, I can! You can do nothing but deny me my collection, and you're intent on doing that anyway!"

Uncle Emory rose slowly, and his voice trembled with fury. "Go to your room, Jessica. I won't have such insubordination at my own dinner table."

Jessica was glad to escape, knowing that she had suffered too much provocation and gone too far in retaliation. But she didn't go directly to her room. She stole through the front hall into the west wing, and found her way by lightning flash to the door of the library.

It was locked, as she knew it would be. She leaned her forehead against the cool wood, drawing deep breaths, calming herself with the thought of the wisdom of the ages that lay just beyond this door. She had to take the long view of her situation.

As bleak as her prospects seemed at the moment, she had made some progress. If nothing else, she had enlisted Sir John in her quest to secure, if not inherit, the collection. And she had gotten her uncle to consider that Alfred Wiley might not be the world's greatest authority on rare books. If she could just keep chipping away, perhaps Uncle Emory would relent and let her marry. And even if he didn't . . .

She raised her head from the door, listening to the relentless rain and the erratic rumble of thunder. There was a message there, she thought, if she could only translate it. Perhaps it was that July 23 would not be the day of her death. She would live on, even if she didn't inherit. And the library would live on too. She might still have some influence on its fate, if Uncle Emory allowed it—if Wiley didn't ruin it first.

She tried the door again. It was still locked tight. But that was no real obstacle. There were many ways to open locked doors—and she'd bet her life that Sir John knew every one.

The next morning Sir John sent his card up with the message, "Meet me in the library." Jessica pocketed the card, made some excuse to her aunt, grabbed her reticule from the couch, and escaped downstairs to the west wing. She found him with Mr. Wiley in the main collection room. The heavy air was more electric than usual, and she suspected she had interrupted a verbal fencing match. We will have to get rid of him, she thought, giving Mr. Wiley a bright and completely false smile.

But Mr. Wiley showed no inclination to be gone, sticking to them like a burr in the guise of showing Sir John more treasures. Jessica trailed along after them, scanning the shelves, looking for something—anything—that might prove helpful. But all she saw were books in need of reshelving, manuscripts in need of repair. She cast a longing look over her shoulder towards Mr. Wiley's cluttered office. If she could sneak in there, she could steal that monograph he was writing . . .

But he would surely find it missing, and blame her, and suspect their scheme. Then the advantage of sur-

prise would be lost. Jessica resigned herself to the direc-
tionless search Sir John apparently planned. It was so
unlike him, she thought, not to have a plan in mind—

Just then, when Mr. Wiley stooped to pull a book
from a lower shelf, Sir John caught her eye and winked.
She smiled back, immeasurably relieved. He had a
scheme, after all, but hadn't had time to share it with
her.

With the adroitness of a Machiavelli, he procured
them the time and the privacy they needed. He collected several books, spread them out on the table in the
workspace, and pulled a magnifying glass from his
pocket. Then he glanced around. "Where is that volume
of Hakluyt's memoirs? I have a client who claims Raleigh as an ancestor. He might be willing to trade some
Bacon for that."

That was enough to send Wiley out into the reading
room, where the Hakluyt was locked in a display case.
Once the librarian was out of earshot, Sir John took her
by the arm and drew her over into the shadows of the
shelves. For a moment, as she felt his calloused fingers
on her bare arm, she imagined what her uncle had
imagined might be true—that Sir John meant to court
her. But in the dimness his face was alight with something other than affection.

"We haven't much time to search. Tell me, does
Wiley ever leave the library in the day?"

"Not for long enough." She separated a stack of
books on the nearest shelf and peered through at the
corridor, worried that the librarian would find them
conspiring. "And, I've noticed, he's taken to locking the
door sometimes even when he's here. But you haven't
told me yet what it is you think we should be searching
for."

"An index of the contents of the St. Germaine trunk."

"But—but if there were one, wouldn't my father have known what the contents were then?"

"Not if the index is hidden."

Jessica frowned. He kept coming back to that trunk. Whatever he thought was in it, he must want it very badly. She determined to find out before they went much further. "You have utterly no evidence that an index exists. None. And there's plenty of evidence it doesn't."

The light in his eyes faded, and she was sorry she had been so brusque. Then he set his jaw stubbornly. "I know the way collectors operate. They wouldn't just stuff a trunk full of treasure and make no index. Your grandfather must have told your mother what to save— and if it's as extensive a selection as I think, one of them must have made a list, or items would have been forgotten in the heat of the moment."

"That's only a hunch. And a tenuous one, considering you knew neither my mother or my grandfather."

"I tell you, I know collectors."

"Why are you so obsessed with this index? It won't help us defeat Mr. Wiley. We need evidence against him, not against—not against my mother and my grandfather!"

Exasperated, he replied, "What kind of evidence do you want then?"

"A copy of this brilliant monograph about Shakespeare's illiteracy. Even my uncle would be able to see how wild a notion that is."

"So tell him. Why do you need a copy?"

She let her breath out in annoyance. "Because otherwise he will ask Mr. Wiley if it's true, and Mr. Wiley will profess ignorance, and make helpful little observations about how spinsters so often give into their imaginations

and believe their fantasies are real. And then—and then
Mr. Wiley will be warned that I know his secret."

"Precisely. Better that he remain entirely unaware as
long as we can manage it. Your uncle is an estimable
man, no doubt, but I don't think you should count on
his discretion."

"But—"

Sir John cocked his head, then laid a rough finger
across her mouth. "Hush," he whispered. "I hear him
coming. Now no more provocations, Miss Seton. Let me
take the lead here."

His finger was gentle enough on her lips, but this last
request—or was it a command?—made her twist away
and out from behind the shelf. Just as Mr. Wiley
rounded the corner she sped out the back of the workroom, into the corridor that led to his office. Sir John
could stay there and fence with the librarian if that's
what he wanted to do. She was going to conduct her
search while she still had access to the library.

What with her fear of discovery and the chaotic condition of the office, Jessica again had to confine herself
to the desktop. Edging around it, so as not to tip over
any of the precarious piles of books on the corners, she
scanned each sheet of notepaper, gingerly lifting the
blotter to peer underneath. The page she had seen pre-
viously was gone, and for just an instant she wondered
if she had been indeed imagining things.

Then she took firm hold of her emotions. She wasn't
the lunatic in Parham House—Wiley was. He had probably squirreled the monograph away somewhere, waiting for some final dubious "proof" to emerge from the
collection. She tiptoed around a decade's worth of unbound journals and pulled open the nearest cupboard. It
was jammed with papers. She knelt down and lifted out
a handful, using her thumb to fan through the pages.

She would need all afternoon to go through one cupboard.

Despairing of the task, she replaced the pages and rose, brushing off her skirt. The floor hadn't been swept for years, she thought; Mr. Wiley never let the maids in to clean here. Struck by a thought, she spun around, knocking a book from the desk.

She made a grab for it, but missed, and it landed with a crack on the floor. Immediately, to still the reverberations, she put her foot down on it and held her breath. When there was no response from the workroom, she exhaled and replaced the book on the desk, sending up a prayer of gratitude that Sir John was keeping Mr. Wiley preoccupied.

As she expected, the rubbish basket was overflowing under the desk. Deciding to sacrifice her dress for convenience, she sat down on the floor and sorted through the crumpled papers.

She didn't find what she was looking for, that incriminating statement about Bacon as Shakespeare. But she did discover another rendition of Shakespeare's signature on a coffee-ringed sheet of paper. She smoothed out the wrinkles and folded it carefully, then put it inside the cover of the novel in her reticule. After restoring the rubbish basket to something akin to its earlier disorder, she slipped back into the corridor.

When she came to the corner, she flattened herself against the wall and slowly edged over till she could see into the workspace. Mr. Wiley was just turning away from her. Suppressing a gasp, she pulled back, pressing her face to the wall, breathing in the dry scent of old paint and plaster, listening hard.

They were discussing bindings, Mr. Wiley holding forth on the possible identity of the bookbinder Bacon had used. She stole another glance; Mr. Wiley had his back to her, but Sir John saw her and with a quick jerk of his head sent her back into hiding. He raised his voice slightly to say, "Bring that volume over here to the window, will you? Perhaps I can identify the bookbinder's stamp." After a moment, he added, "See? If you hold it up to the light, you can see it. No, look closer."

She took this as a signal that Mr. Wiley was well-diverted and, still pressed close to the wall, she slipped around the corner and sped down past the shelves to the door. Her light leather slippers made a scuffing noise on the wood floor, but the adroit Sir John covered this up with another speculation about the binding. She glanced back through the shelves to see him looking over Wiley's shoulder, amused and annoyed. With a slight gesture of his hand, he urged her away. Laughing silently, she passed through the door and into safety.

She waited on an upholstered bench down the hall from the library door. Her heart stopped pounding after a few minutes, but she was still exhilarated by her adventure. She slipped her hand into her reticule, touching the edges of the folded sheet where it stuck out from the book, afraid yet to bring it out and look at it again for fear that Mr. Wiley would emerge.

But only Sir John came out of the library. She called out softly to him, and smiled as he turned and shook his head in admonishment. When he came up to her, she took his arm and drew him towards the backstairs. "Come," she whispered urgently when she felt his arm tense in resistance under her hand. He doesn't like being led, she thought with a tiny thrill. He would soon learn that neither did she. "I must show you what I found."

As always, curiosity proved the lure. Stealthily they went up to the gallery that ran the length of the next floor. Sir John closed the door firmly and then pulled a sidechair in front of it to serve as a warning of an interruptor.

The long narrow windows overlooked the garden, letting in a trace of flowery fragrance and the glare of west light. On the other wall, half in shadow, were the portraits of dead Setons. Tacitly they pretended to study the portrait of a fearsome baroness, done in oils on a dark background. "You didn't take a copy of Wiley's monograph, I hope," Sir John said in a low tone.

"No, I couldn't find it. What a mess that office is! But I found this." She pulled out the page and opened it for him to see, but didn't let go when he reached out for it.

He made a low, exasperated sound deep in his throat, something rather like a growl. "I shan't keep it, I promise."

Reluctantly she released it, and he spread it out against the uncomplaining baroness's bosom. Framed by his square, hard hands, the signature looked spindly, like an elderly man bowed down by his sins. "By me, William Shakespeare": The "W" in William began with a long wavering diagonal stroke, and the last letters in Shakespeare trailed off into illegibility.

"Not a bad forgery," Sir John pronounced at length. "He's got that bow on the 'h' dragging below the line, as Shakespeare always did, but the 'y' doesn't trail far enough. The ink and the paper are modern, of course, so there's no chance he'd be able to fool anyone. I don't think that's his aim, anyway. He's just testing it, I think. But he's got a good hand, does Wiley. Now," he concluded, folding the page back up and handing it back to her, "how do you intend to replace that in his office?"

"I got it out of the rubbish, I'll have you know. He'll never miss it."

He acknowledged her resourcefulness with a quick grin, and, encouraged, she added, "Perhaps I should go through all the rubbish thrown out from the library. If I can only get to it before it's merged with the rest of the house's trash, I can surely find an entire early draft of his monograph."

"You must be joking. Going through the rubbish? No, no," he said, "we have more important things to do. We must search the library for that index of the—"

"Of the contents of the St. Germaine trunk. Yes, I heard you the first time you said that, Sir John. And it makes no better sense now. Even if there is an index— and I don't concede there is—what good will it do us? It won't prove Mr. Wiley a scoundrel or a lunatic, or turn my uncle's head, or win me back my collection. What good will finding it do?"

"It might serve as protection. If we have the index, if we know what the trunk contains . . ."

When he didn't continue, she exclaimed, "What? Do you think Wiley means to do some harm? Tell me!"

"I don't know," he finally answered. "He told me that in a month or so he will have what he needs to prove his case. A month or so—what happens then?"

He knew of course, but she sighed and repeated the schedule that felt emblazoned on her brain. "My birthday is in a month. The collection will be turned over to—to the legatee." She wished she could say "to me" with a real conviction, but she thought it might be tempting fate. "And the vault will be opened. And the trunk unsealed."

"If the evidence he is anticipating were in the extant collection, he would have already claimed it. So he must know—or believe—that the evidence is still hidden away." He walked slowly to the next picture, a sweet-faced man in a gold-edged ruff and velvet doublet. "Perhaps, when he advised your father to seal the trunk for a mere quarter-century, he got some clue as to what might be in it."

"But my father didn't know! Oh, he had his speculations, but he didn't know."

"I suspect your father's speculations might be credible, based as they were on close evaluation of St. Germaine's collecting practices. And it could be, you know, that he took a look at that index, after your mother's death."

His insistence on speaking of the index as if it were an established fact almost persuaded her. Her mother was a list-making sort; she used to keep track of books she read and plays she attended. It would have been in character to keep a list of the books she had smuggled out of France. "It will take us weeks to search the whole library. And we haven't got weeks, at least not weeks without Wiley. He's surely going to get suspicious about our coming in together every afternoon."

"Oh, I think I scotched any suggestion that I appreciated your presence. I took advantage of your scarpering off that way to tell him we'd had an argument."

She couldn't help but admire his resourcefulness in using whatever opportunity presented itself. "What did we argue about?"

"That Milton pamphlet. I said you had insisted it was the official edition, and that I had shown you the anomalous type on one page and proved you wrong. You did not admit defeat—I take it you seldom do—but only flounced out in high dudgeon."

"I never flounce, in high dudgeon or otherwise," she said witheringly, then added, "What did he say?"

"Oh, he was torn between congratulations for putting you in your place and defense of the collection's inviolability to fraud. But he was clearly pleased to think that no accord exists between us."

"So we'd best not re-engage his suspicions by returning to the library together?" Jessica knew a moment's disappointment at the prospect. Sir John gave her hope, that was what it was. She didn't want to risk despair without her constant exposure to his cool objective optimism.

"Not during the day, certainly."

Without explaining this cryptic remark, he crossed to another painting—a Hoppner portrait of her father. It didn't look very like him, Jessica thought, coming over to touch the little brass plate that identified the subject. Her father had always been shy around strangers, but during the portrait sittings he had covered that up with a righteous glower more appropriate to his brother Emory.

"Is there a picture of your mother?"

"No. She would never sit for one. She didn't care for representational art; no one in the family really did."

"So I see," Sir John said ironically, and she laughed.

"Oh, I know, it's a most indifferent collection of paintings, don't you think? It's because we care only about books." She glanced up at him, knowing that he collected art as well as books, and wondering if she could explain her family's bias. "Books are beautiful, but not—not consciously so. They are books, first of all, you know. Something useful. The beauty is extra, added by the artisans who were supposed to just be recording words on paper, and not making art. Somehow that makes it more precious than paintings which are deliberately, and only, art." She stole another glance at him, but only saw herself reflected in his silver eyes. "Do you understand what I mean? Don't you think that, withal, the book is the most lovely thing invented by man?"

He smiled, and she saw the warmth even in those cool eyes. "Oh, you should see my sloop full-sail on a breezy afternoon. Then you will see the loveliest thing invented by man. But books—they come close. Their beauty is not a *raison d'etre*, but a result of our need for them."

There was a moment of that perfect amity that Jessica, with a bit of her consciousness, knew Mr. Wiley should not witness. Instinctively she glanced up and down the gallery, to make sure all the doors were still closed.

And John, too, must have thought it best to break the connection. "We will have to break into the library at night."

This, at least, had the effect of diverting her from whatever connection had flickered between them. "Break in? You mean—" For a moment, she was too taken aback to speak. Finally she whispered, "You mean, fiddle the lock on the door."

"I would prefer the window," he replied with commendable aplomb. "If we used the door, they would know it was an inside job. And I noticed a likely looking elm tree, just outside the window."

She breathed, "How perfect! How—how exciting! Oh, let's do! Tonight!"

When he grinned at her, she saw that the elegant art consultant had been replaced by that pirate Ada had dreamed up. Jessica felt her mouth curve in an answering smile, and wondered if the upperclass heiress had vanished into an—oh, an adventuress—something daring and wild and indiscreet.

So it was somewhat deflating to hear his dismissal, though his excuse was impeccable. "Not tonight. The Regent has returned from Brighton for the weekend, and I'm to dine with him. Tomorrow night."

Reluctantly she replied, "We're going to Surrey tomorrow."

For a moment he looked dismayed, then, evenly, he

asked, "Do you mean to spend the summer in the country then?"

"The summer? Oh, heavens, no!" She saw the relief flash in his eyes, and wished she knew how to interpret it. He didn't want to lose his accomplice, probably. "My aunt is probably the only person in the kingdom who finds London air salubrious in the summer. Hay gives her sneezing fits, you see. We're just going down for the Waterloo anniversary, and will be back Monday."

"I suppose I shall have to do it myself then." Dismay spread through her, but he continued, "You can help me narrow down the search considerably though. Tell me, where might your mother have hidden the index? Had she any favorite authors, volumes?"

Jessica brushed angrily at her skirt, having just noticed its deplorable dusty state, and recalled her resolve to keep this maverick in line. Craftily she said, "I suppose if I put my mind to it, I could remember something like that."

He was annoyed, she could tell from the set of his jaw. But he said very politely, "Will you put your mind to it, then?"

"I might . . . if you wait till I return to do the burglary."

"It's not a burglary," he said crossly. "It's only an—an unauthorized visit."

"You will wait for me, then?"

"I will be wasting my time otherwise, I suppose. If I wait, then, you will tell me where your mother is likely to have secreted the index?"

She didn't let her exultation show on her face. "Well, I do have another condition."

He turned away from her, towards the door. But he didn't walk away. "What is this preoccupation you have with making conditions?"

"I don't like anyone having the advantage of me. Especially," she added, "if he is hiding something of import to me."

"What do you think I'm hiding?"

She paused to put her thoughts into a coherent sentence. "You are hiding your interest in the St. Germaine trunk."

"Not very well, apparently." Resignedly, he faced her. "What do you want to know?"

"What you think is in there. Why you are afraid that Wiley will get it."

He moved restlessly to the narrow window and looked out at Berkeley Square. Indecision played across that exotic face, replaced at last by resignation. He had, she thought with relief, decided to trust her. "I have—a colleague, who many years ago, got his hands on a prize. Something we would all have searched for, were we ill-judged enough to believe in it. My colleague, once he saw it, believed. But he hadn't the funds to purchase it, and it went instead to a French collector. Recently, my colleague taunted me with a poor substitute for this prize, and told me the one he had held in his hands was destroyed in the French Revolution. That is what he presumed, anyway."

"But you don't. You believe the French collector was my grandfather."

"The collector of oddities."

"How—how odd was this prize?"

When he answered, his voice was hushed, almost a whisper, as if the words might echo off the high ceiling and alert the world to his suspicions. "It was an autograph copy. A handwritten playscript. Several actors would have been involved in its writing. The Lord Admiral's Men, I think."

Lord Admiral—"Shakespeare was in that company, wasn't he? But surely you're not thinking that—"

John said flatly, "I've never known this man to be wrong when he makes a judgment. And your grandfather must have seen it too."

"That's why you were so interested in the signature." She couldn't take it all in just yet, that her mother might have hidden a script of Shakespeare from the world— from her husband, from her daughter. "But what is this play?"

"I don't know. Not one of the ones we know. My colleague said only that it had something to do with a riot."

"A lost play. My father—he must have suspected it. And yet—"

"I know. It's astonishing that he didn't break open that trunk. I would have."

She caught a glimpse of the hard light in his eyes and knew it was so. She also knew, if she weren't very careful, this man might break into the vault as casually as he suggested breaking into the library. Could he be as dangerous as he looked just that moment? Yes, she answered silently. But, for the moment, at least, his dangerousness was in her service. To remind him of that, she asked, "Do you think Mr. Wiley knows about it also?"

"He must think something in that trunk will help his case."

"But—but it won't!" Jessica shook her head in confusion. "If it's in Shakespeare's hand, it will prove him wrong!"

"He must think it is in Bacon's hand."

"And when he finds out it isn't—"

Jessica couldn't go on, so John finished it for her. In

a hard voice, he said, "He will very likely destroy it. The only literary work in Shakespeare's hand."

Her head was too dizzy to ask the questions she had—how long he had known, how much of their acquaintance he had planned, whether he would have told her if she hadn't forced him. She could only lean back against the wall, her tumbled hair brushing her father's picture, and whisper, "Maman concealed a lost play."

Sir John waited quietly, leaning against the window frame, the sunlight outlining his slim form. She stared down until his shadow crept across several planks of the bleached oak floor. Then she took a deep breath and gathered tattered reserves. "What do you think we should do?"

He straightened and turned to study her. Quietly he said, "Tuesday night, we will do the job. You might make a list of possible hiding places. I will send you a note with the other details."

She nodded and bent to pick up the reticule she had let drop to the floor. Then she started towards the door. John stopped her with a hand on her arm. "Will you be well enough alone?"

His gentle tone almost undid her. Alone. She supposed that was true; she was more alone than she had realized. "I will be well enough. It's just—oh, it's just too much to contemplate. My mother, my father—always keeping things from me. And now they might keep the collection from me, and *he* might get it, and ruin it. . . ."

The steady pressure of his bare hand on her bare arm gave her the will to say what she had never let herself think. "It's all so unfair. Not just to me, to everyone who cares for books. And they were both so secretive, and my uncle—he could make it better, but instead he only makes it worse. Why didn't they just leave the collection to me, without all these complications?"

Fiercely she said, "It's mine by right. It is. But I know everyone thinks that because I want the collection, I must be greedy and grasping."

"I don't."

"You don't?" She looked up at his face; the afternoon sunlight cast shadows across his eyes, but she saw kindness there.

"I think you are the only Seton in several generations who really knows what the Parham Collection should be, and the only one capable of making it reach that standard. Your father should have known you better, and trusted you more."

Then he released her hand and opened the door. "Tuesday night. We will make it come right again."

Chapter Eight

Tell me where is fancy bred?
Or in the heart or in the head?
Merchant of Venice, III, ii

With time at a premium, it couldn't be helped. But John wished he hadn't picked one of the longest days of the year to resume his criminal career. At the very least, he thought, England might have moved to a more southerly latitude for the occasion. It was near ten o'clock, and even back here in the mews, far from the streetlamps, he could still see the numbers on his watch.

The stableyard was empty, and the lights in the carriage houses were winking off one by one as the stablemen went to bed. Still, John kept to the shadows as he approached the back wall of Parham House. He wore the loose black cotton trousers and black jersey of his free-trading days, when a moonless night and invisibility meant safe landings and high profits. The last time he had worn these had been another moonless night, in a fortress in Brittany, though his only profit had been the cautious joy of the Foreign Office agent when he realized he had been rescued.

The gate was locked. John pushed up his sleeves and

leapt for the top of the wall, hands open, as if into the shrouds of the rigging. He felt his fingers scrape the rough granite then catch, and thought, I am myself again. And at that thought, he knew a moment's despair. A felon's heart, he had, and always would, no matter what clothes he wore.

He pulled himself up and paused balanced on the wall. The darkness was deeper here in the shadows of the house, and he could not see the ground. But he launched himself into the twilight, landing lightly in a crouch. He stayed still, holding his breath, but there was no sound from the dark house.

He crossed to the elm tree to wait for Jessica, who had been strictly directed to wait until full dark. He found himself wishing Devlyn would come to town and sit him down and talk him out of this. All their lives Devlyn had tried to dissuade John from one folly or another, succeeding so seldom that it was a credit to his hard head that he persevered. But this time, John thought, I might be more open to persuasion. It was folly indeed, this felonious search, this absolute certainty about the lost play, this alliance with an heiress. He knew Devlyn well enough to anticipate his arguments: the risk an arrest would pose to his career, the hazard of Wiley—or worse, Alavieri—learning of his aim, the impropriety of involving a noblewoman in a felony, the danger of letting her too close. Unfortunately, John's memory couldn't reproduce the combined effect of Devlyn's reasoned tone, his eminently sensible approach, his half-concealed caring. And so, though he recited the points by rote, John remained unpersuaded. The felon's heart always won out over the rationalist's head.

And it always would after all, for now Jessica was stealing up to him, her bright hair stuffed into a cap, her eyes alight with laughter. They were allies, and he couldn't end that. If he did, she would be alone again, and that he couldn't allow.

Poor little rich girl, he thought, holding out his hand to take the bag she'd looped around her shoulder. Bright and brave, just like Tatiana—

It was an errant thought, but true enough. When he first met the princess, she had been alone in a world of privilege, her enemies wearing the masks of family and friends. Oh, hers was a more dangerous world, the Romanov court, where a small misstep could be punished by a quiet execution.

Jessica had less at risk—not her life, only her life's work. That was enough, though, to win her an out-of-practice knight errant, one far more errant than Tatiana's.

And it was worth it after all, for Jessica's laughter bubbled over as she whispered that surely it was dark enough, and she couldn't wait any longer, and did John like the burglary attire she had stolen from the laundry of the stableboys.

"The breeches are too big," she whispered, tugging at her thigh to demonstrate.

"Good," he replied with feeling, and she laughed. This was no green girl—she knew what he was thinking, and must have found it amusing that the sight of her slender form even in too-big breeches and a boy's shirt tight across the breasts might make him think that. To distract himself, he stared up into the branches of the elm tree and calculated their route to the window. "Let's go," he said, and compliantly she edged over to him, so he could put his hands on her waist and help her up to the first branch.

He'd done something like this before, guiding the climb of other bright-eyed ladies in the rigging on his ship, to show them the view that couldn't be had anywhere but the crow's nest. But his senses were especially heightened now, as if the light breeze scraped up every nerve ending. Her calf was slender but surprisingly firm under the rough breeches, her skin warm where his fingers accidentally caught in her wool stocking. The excitement she couldn't quite contain radiated like heat from her body as she scrambled for the next branch.

"Let me go," she murmured, but he didn't. He guided her foot to the fork in the tree, then slid his hand up her calf to the back of her thigh and gave her a gentle shove. Once she slipped, and he found himself with his arms around her waist and his face against her silky fragrant neck. If he hadn't spent his youth climbing masts in hurricanes, he might have fallen right out of the tree.

Once he'd managed to untangle himself, he got her settled on a sturdy limb and started on the window. He edged out on the branch, and when it swayed ominously he braced his knees against the window frame. It was dark enough now that he had to feel with his fingers to find the slight gap between the two casements. He slipped his knife into the gap and ran it up to the latch. With a twist of his wrist, he dug the knifepoint into the latch and flipped it up. Jessica exclaimed admiringly, but he shook his head as he pushed the casement open. "Easy as it was for me, Alavieri could do it too—if he could get up this tree. Then your prizes would be gone. Not that anyone would notice, since your family hasn't bothered to catalogue."

"Monsignor Alavieri?" she inquired, completely missing his point. "The consultant to the Vatican? But he wrote that lovely essay on the ethical values of book collecting."

"Precisely." He stood up on the branch, balancing for

an instant on the balls of his feet, and, grabbing the window frame, swung into the library. When he had his feet planted, he turned and held his hand out to her. She took it and stepped onto the window, as daintily as if she were descending from a carriage. But then, as if she'd put on a boy's nimbleness when she put on a boy's clothes, she let go of his hand and jumped lightly to the floor.

Then she peered around the dark room. "We're in the work area."

He pulled the drapes shut on the window and started for the next. "Yes. Careful, the table's right in front of you. Can you find the lamp there? I brought a flint."

So had she, and he let her win the argument of who got to light the lamp, just so he could see her face in the glow as she turned the flame up and set the lamp on the table. Her cap had come askew; he pulled it off and her hair tumbled down, pins falling to the floor. With a corner of his mind he counted the *clinks*, reminding himself that they must pick up every one, so as not to leave evidence of their entry.

But for the moment he just caught another pin when it loosed as she shook her hair free.

He had never seen her with her hair down. It fell around her face in tangles, golden as the lamplight. He reached out to pull off the last clinging pin, letting his fingers rest just for a moment on the lock of hair. It was a moment of synesthesia, of sensual confusion, when he *felt* a warmth that was but a reflection of flame on gold, when his desire was stirred by the aesthetics of sweet femininity in rough masculine attire.

I am losing my mind, he thought very clearly. And it's all I have just now. He dropped his hand, turned away from that aching vision, reached out blindly to one of the nearby shelves, and closed his fingers on a volume.

But he could see her still, on the edges of his vision, her hands tangling in her hair, capturing the radiance and taming it. "Wait," she said, as her fingers combed it through and began a plait down over her shoulder.

He set the volume back on the shelf and bent to feel through the dark for the discarded pins. The floor was reassuringly solid, cool to the touch. He traced the gaps between the floorboards, finding the last pin when it jabbed his finger. "Here." He handed her the pins, one by one, and quickly she bound up her hair, pinning the braid to the top of her head. It was a curiously intimate moment: Their quest was arrested so that he could watch her braid her hair.

When she finished, she jammed the cap into her pocket, a minor blessing, for it left the gold untarnished. She seemed not to have noticed that the world had changed for an instant there, but perhaps she was better at hiding her feelings than he knew. The glance she gave him was level and discerning. "Where do we start?"

"You promised to show me this famous vault."

The vault was in a storage room, down the corridor and up a staircase hidden by a wall of shelves. The lamp illuminated a cluttered room, a glue-spotted table, and a wooden panel instead of a wall along the narrow end. John knocked with his knuckles against the panel; it was constructed of the heart of oak, as thick as the hull of his ship. In the middle was a sturdy door of wrought-iron over oak. Each of the three bolt-latches was secured with a massive falling-pin iron lock. He hefted the middle lock in his hand and said with some relief, "I might be able to take this off with a four-pounder aimed close, but a pistol certainly wouldn't answer. Hold the lamp up, will you?"

With Jessica beside him, holding the lamp near his

shoulder, he could just see into the half-inch slit cut into the door. But the darkness within was so total he could distinguish nothing. Disappointed, he withdrew. "Are you sure the trunk is still in there?"

She lowered the lamp and took her own turn at the aperture, with no greater success. "During the day, more light gets in, and I can make out the trunk amidst the other items. I check it as frequently as I can."

And when he looked again, he could almost see it there, an aura in the darkness, glowing as if powered by the treasures within. Once again he felt with disconcerting clarity that his grip on his own thoughts was loosing, that he wanted something so much he was surrendering logic to desire. But then that unaccountable certainty returned. The script was there, and it was safe, at least for the moment.

John felt in his pocket and brought out a small square of beeswax wrapped in sailcloth. Molding a thin sheet between his hands, he pressed a bit of it against the back of each lock. This way, if anyone opened the lock and closed it later, the seal would be broken. It might be too late to remedy, but at least, as long as the seal remained intact, they might rest easy.

"Now what do we do?" she asked as he finished.

He freed the breath he had been holding. "That is for you to decide. You know where your mother's secrets are."

She liked that, this momentary surrender of command. She tried to hide a smile, he noticed, but a tiny dimple appeared in one cheek to betray her. With a slight ring of authority, she said, "Come this way, then, and don't forget the lamp, will you? We'll look in the French area, first. Corneille and Racine."

Unerringly she led him through the dark labyrinth of shelves to one at the other side of the library. She held up the lamp so he could see the volumes, all with elaborate bindings the French were known for. He ran his finger down the slender spine of Racine's *Andromache*, tracing the gilt of the title and the lacy engravings set across the bands. "Fine work, this binding. Padeloup, is it?" he asked. "Or one of the Deromes?"

"I don't know," she replied, amusement lilting her voice. "But we'll have time to catalogue later. Now we're looking for this index you're so certain my mother hid."

He was glad she had set the lamp down on the floor, so she couldn't see the unaccustomed flush her rebuke had brought to his face. "You know, I am used to being in charge. I haven't been ordered about like this since I was a boy."

"Just as well. It doesn't seem to have any effect on you. Here." She slipped in between him and the bookshelf and handed him several volumes. Then she took a handful herself and began to page through them.

"Careful," he warned, as she held one by the spine and shook it. She made a face at him, then held the book up and, closing one blue eye, peered through the gap between the spine and the binding.

"Check the casing too." He followed his own advice, opening the cover of a book and running his fingers over the inside, finding no telltale bulge. "If the pages are but glued onto the binding, she might have prised them up and put the index underneath."

"I hardly think my mother would have needed to tamper with a book's binding, Sir John. She would have merely hidden it in the pages, I believe."

John ran his hand along the back of each shelf, steeling himself not to wince at the brush of spider corpses and a decade's worth of dust. "When you take over this place," he muttered, "remind me to give you the direction of the cleaning concern that maintains the British Museum. An army of maids couldn't do this up without laying waste to the books."

"It is lamentable, isn't it?" Jessica gazed around her and sighed. They were still speaking in whispers. It was not so much that fear of being overheard, so far from the rest of the house, but rather the need to listen for opening doors and approaching footsteps that kept them hushed. "I have tried to sneak in and dust, at least, but Mr. Wiley has always caught me out. No doubt it is the worst-maintained library you've ever seen."

"Not at all. This is pristine compared to your usual monastic library, which has been neglected for centuries. I found one, in fact, that had been closed up a century ago after a bit of flooding, and never cleaned. Mildew everywhere. And the rodents. I never knew horror till I saw a rat sitting on an old refectory table, feasting on a codex of the Psalter."

She liked such stories, he could tell from the sparkle in her eyes. And it was pleasant to realize that her theatrical shudder had less to do with the thought of the rat than the nature of his meal. No one else he knew, except for the antiquated antiquaries at the Royal Society, would even recognize the rarity of a Psalter from the codex period, or mourn its fate so sincerely.

It was too dangerous, this appeal of hers—the curious mind and the lilting voice and the willowy body. "What next?" he said, as curtly as he could make himself sound.

She drew back a bit from this coldness, but after a moment she picked up the lamp and started towards the corridor. "The classical section. Aristotle was her favorite philosopher."

The subdued quality of her voice made him sorry, so

more gently he said, "I should have known. Aristotle the scientist, always making tests."

She looked back startled over her shoulder. "Tests? Oh, you mean making my father promise not to open the trunk. Yes, she was an Aristotelian! It drove Papa mad; he was a Platonist, of course."

"Insisting on absolutes? Absolute beauty, absolute truth? What did your mother think of that?"

"She said she would believe it when she saw it. All she had seen, she said, was absolute wickedness—the Terror, you know."

The classics shelf was not, as he foolishly hoped, filled with ancient papyri, but printed editions and modern translations of the earliest works. "With that kind of debate over the dinner table," he mused, fanning the pages of *Niomachean Ethics,* "I'm not surprised you turned out the way you did."

"What do you mean, the way I did?"

Surprised by her defensiveness, he closed the book and replaced it on the shelf. "Intellectually seeking. I didn't mean to offend you. It's an admirable way to be."

"Most people don't think so." She flashed an apologetic smile. "I shouldn't be so thin-skinned. But I have heard most of my life that intellectual curiosity isn't the ideal quality in a young lady."

"I know." He did know; intellectual curiosity was no virtue in a shopkeeper's son either. "But you do have all those dinner debates to recall fondly."

"What were the debates at your dinner table?"

He laughed and scanned a modern Greek translation of *The Republic.* "Well, you may be sure that Plato and Aristotle didn't figure into the conversation. Food. Was the beef too tough, were the berries ripe enough. My father liked to talk about his business, trying to interest me in it, but of course the reverse happened. And

Dennis—my brother—and I would argue about whose turn it was to help wash up."

As Jessica pushed aside a book and looked behind it, she was frowning, probably at his reference to washing up. An heiress would not have had to help her mother wash up the dishes. He took some perverse pleasure in that, so much that he couldn't go on to confess that his mother actually did little housework, as they had employed two servant girls who left at dinnertime. That would have spoiled the story.

But when she replied, it was only to ask, "What happened to your father's business, if you didn't take it over?"

"He left it to my brother, but only after I told him I planned to tear the building down if he were foolish enough to leave it to me."

She glanced back at him assessingly, and he sensed she was trying to fit him into some schema of the world as she knew it, into some confluence of class and birth and ability. Good luck to her, he thought, replacing a book on the shelf. He'd done his best all his life to make that impossible.

But she surprised him again. "It is ironic, don't you think, that you went so far to avoid inheriting the family business, and I will do anything I can to inherit mine. I can't help but think your father—"

She broke off there, and he wondered what it was she couldn't say. That his father must have been disappointed? That he had had the right idea? Perhaps it hadn't to do with his father at all, but with hers. "Fathers are usually incomprehensible, in my experience," he said with some intention of comforting her.

But that only emphasized what he didn't want to consider: how much alike they were, under the obvious differences. Both were incapable of filling the roles carved out for them—idle noblewoman, shopkeeper's son.

"How did you do it, then," she asked, "learn so much about art?"

He was surprised to find himself telling her the truth. "It was free-trading that did it. I was—oh, afraid to go home after my first voyage, and so I joined another crew on the way to the Ottoman Coast." It was so long ago that he couldn't remember what they were there to purchase, but he recalled very well the heavy scent of incense that floated out over the harbor to greet them. "I found some ceremonial torch-holders from the early Roman era in the marketplace in Ismir, and that got me started on dealing in ancient artifacts. The statuary came later, when I'd gotten my own ship and had more room for cargo. I was never much interested in paintings, though I procure them for clients. Mostly dimensional art. And books, of course."

"Why books?"

He shrugged. "I expect it's to make up for my illiterate childhood."

She gave him a wary look. "You weren't illiterate."

She was learning to ignore his more provocative statements—he would have to be more persuasive, he decided. "No, but I seldom read. As a boy, I wanted only to sail, and hadn't much use for school. But then there were those long voyages, and nothing to do when the work was done. The only books aboard were the Bible, and Robinson's *Elements of Navigation*, and Dr. Johnson's edition of Shakespeare. I'd near worn the covers off by the time we were back in the Atlantic—oh, not the Bible. But the plays, and the sonnets, and navigation, of course."

"What was the first book you bought?"

"The first rare book? Ben Jonson's *Works*. I wanted

one of the Shakespeare folios, but most of them are kept hidden away."

She ignored this ironic reference to her family's vaulted treasures. "Do you still have the Jonson?"

"No. I sold it. I'm a dealer, you recall."

She shook her head with the same consternation that he had witnessed with other collectors. "But if you loved it, how could you sell it?"

His answer must needs be inadequate, for no collector was likely to see a dealer's motivation as anything but mercenary heresy. But he tried to explain, because— because he wanted her to understand. "I sold it so I could buy something else I loved. I don't need to keep it, to have it. Just to hold it. And I wouldn't sell it just to anyone, only to someone who could appreciate and care for it. Then I find something else—it's the discovery, not the possession, that is my aim."

To his surprise, she did not take issue with this. Instead, she asked, "Is that what you're doing with me?"

"I don't know what you mean."

"Helping me with the collection. Are you doing that because you want to make sure it is appreciated and cared for?"

He couldn't answer immediately, because he couldn't easily untangle his motives. Initially, of course, he wanted to find the lost manuscript. But now . . . "Yes, I suppose so. You will be a better steward than Wiley, and better than your father too. And," he added honestly, "I want to be the first to know what the collection—the entire collection—contains."

She closed the book she was searching and brought it to her breast in an unconsciously supplicating gesture. "You said before 'When you take over this place.' Do you think that I might somehow—somehow—inherit it? I confess, I am losing hope."

Hopelessness was not a emotion he could let her experience, and so, uncharacteristically, he made a rash prediction. "I think that no matter what happens July 23, you will shortly be charged with the care of this collection. Wiley can't last long as trustee." Not, he added silently, when I'm done with him. "And you are the most likely replacement."

She bent her head, but not before he saw the glow in her eyes and cursed his unprecedentedly wayward tongue. She was taking that as a promise, not just a prediction. And even out-of-practice knights errant knew better than to break promises made to distressed damsels.

Gently he took the classical volume out of her hands. "That's the last of it in this section. Where do we look next?"

Recalled to the present, Jessica said, "Oh, have we time to search more? She liked Robert Herrick and the other Cavalier poets, but those volumes are scattered all over the library."

He checked his watch. It wasn't midnight yet. "Another half-hour, perhaps. The watch will come by at one, and we'd best be gone by then."

Their search through the Cavaliers was fruitless, and Jessica grew hesitant when he pressed her to come up with some new possibility. "Oh, I don't know! It's been so long since she died, and sometimes I hardly recall how her voice sounded. . . . Perhaps it's just that you—I mean we—are mistaken, and she made no index."

"She made an index," John said firmly. "Now think. Whom did she wish to hide it from?"

"My father, I suppose. If she meant it as part of the test . . ."

"Was there some favorite author or book that she

kept secret from your father? Where he wouldn't think to look?"

She gave it some thought, her brow furrowing prettily in the lamplight. "There was some playwright he disapproved of . . . let me think. A scandalous sort, I think, of the Restoration theatre."

"All the Restoration playwrights were scandalous."

"This one was a woman. That was why my mother liked her, and why my father disapproved. He didn't think women should be scandalous in public. Oh, what was her name? I recall that she was a friend of John Dryden—" She shot him a quick look. "The first John Dryden."

"Aphra Behn."

"That's it! How did you know?"

"Oh, I've come across her name before. She was a spy for the Foreign Office, did you know? They treated her badly." In fact, they had abandoned her in Holland, preferring not to believe her prediction that the Dutch would take Chatham and burn the fleet. They were wrong; she was right. And in his experience the Foreign Office hadn't changed much in a century and a half. "No one reads her any longer. Tell me, where would she be shelved?"

There were no Behn scripts in the shelf devoted to Restoration theatre, though there were several cookbooks and an angler's companion. John closed his eyes wearily, imagining searching through every one of eight thousand volumes in the next quarter hour. Wiley, he thought, not for the first time, should be excommunicated by the Royal Society.

But Jessica was staring off into the distance, her blue eyes dark with concentration. "I once came across Maman pasting a Behn novel into the casing of another book, so that Papa wouldn't know what it was she was reading in the evenings. She just laughed and told me it was our secret. I think he would have been more upset to know that she had torn out the inside of a book to do it, of course. It must not have been a valuable book. Now what was the title?"

He held his breath so that she could muse on this in utter stillness. It sounded right, a hidden book, a secret marital defiance, just the sort of action that Jessica's infuriating mother would take. And he knew he could count on Jessica to puzzle it out.

"A gray-blue cover, with a bit of floral gilting in the corners." Her eyes squeezed shut; even her fists clenched with the effort. "A slender volume, folio-size. Quite new. I can see it right before me . . . oh, what does the spine say?"

John could not answer this, nor do anything but keep his silence so she could concentrate. Hurry, hurry, he thought, stealing a look at his watch.

As if in answer, she said, "Hannah More."

Naturally. It was a clever trick, for More was another woman playwright, a century younger, but an evangelical religious writer, far more proselytizing than provocative. And in due course, they found her works in the middle of a grouping of sermon books. John saw the gray-blue leather volume first, grabbed it, and then paused gripping it, testing with his thumb for the slight empty rub that meant a loose binding. Then with enormous resolve, he handed it to Jessica.

She held it for a moment, studying the cover. *"Percy. By Hannah More."* Then she opened it. *"The Lucky Chance. Aphra Behn."* Tentatively she held the book open with her thumb and forefinger, and gave it a little shake. A thin white packet fell to the floor.

With one mind, they knelt to pick it up, their hands colliding on the folded, sealed paper. Then they sat down together on the floor, their backs against the shelves, their heads touching, to examine it in the circle of light cast by the lamp.

"My mother's hand." Jessica's hand trembled as she pointed to the first line scrawled on the front: "If you are truly honorable and truly love me, Godfrey, you will put this back unopened." And her father's: "Annette: If you ever again question my honor or my love, I will show you this."

It was an eerie moment, this dialogue between lovers long-dead, and John sensed that Jessica was close to tears. It seemed natural, imperative in fact, to take her face in his hand and bend to kiss her—a distraction from sorrow for her, from desperate curiosity for him.

And inevitably it became more than a distraction. Her lips parted under his—no, this was no green girl, he thought, closing his eyes and letting the paper drop so he could pull her closer. He slid his hand across her back, every nerve telling him that there was nothing between the rough linen and her skin. It was so very sweet, the taste, the feel of her, the radiant moment in the darkness.

And inevitably it was only a moment. He had been too long at sea, acute to every slight change in the rigging's song, to let even this block his hearing. He drew slightly away from her, and when she murmured some inarticulate protest he laid a finger across her lips. There it was, the creak of a door opening from the hall. He grabbed up the paper, stuffed it in his shirt, and in one fluid motion rose and tugged her to her feet. "Douse the lamp," he whispered. "Take the More book too. We'll go out the way we came in."

They were out the window and scrambling down the tree as the heavy steps echoed in the main bookroom. John left the casement open behind them, though the book dealer part of him argued the malignant effect of soot; already a plan was forming in that other part of his mind, the felon part.

As they landed on the ground, Jessica whispered that she had left the kitchen door off the latch. "Tomorrow," she said, and rose on her tiptoes to kiss him boldly if lightly on the mouth. Then she vanished into the dark house.

He waited by the door until the sound of her footsteps faded. But he left it too late. The French doors flew open and three footman erupted from the back of the house. One caught sight of him and shouted for the others to follow, and like brawny ghosts in their white nightshirts, they thundered towards him.

John took off through the kitchen garden, his boots digging into the soft dirt and uprooting plants as he set his sights on the back wall. Behind him a pursuer stumbled on a cabbage or a beet and went down with a curse and a thud. But the other two kept coming on. As he passed a tree, John reached out and grabbed at a branch. A soft fruit—a pear?—came off in his hand. Without breaking stride, he twisted and threw it backwards at the nearest footman. He got a glimpse of the pear squashing against the man's pristine nightshirt, then focused his attention ahead, where the wall stood high and inviolate.

Sucking in a lungful of air, John jumped at the wall. He hung there for a long instant, grasping for purchase on the rough granite. Someone grabbed at his boot; he kicked backwards, freeing his foot, and hauled himself up on the wall. A hand swiped at him, but he sprang to his feet, balanced there, and then, laughing, launched himself into the darkness.

Chapter Nine

Conscience is but a word that cowards use,
Devis'd at first to keep the strong in awe.
Richard III, V, iii

Jessica was nightgowned and hugging herself, thinking of John's hard eloquent mouth, when the pounding of feet in the hallway told her she could legitimately awaken. Rubbing her eyes, feigning drowsiness (though she had never felt more awake), she emerged from her room. Her aunt was in the bright-lit hall, clutching a wrapper around her and holding a brass candlestick high as a threat to anything that might come up the staircase.

"Jessica! There's been a burglary!" she cried.

"Oh, aunt, no! Where is he, the burglar?" Jessica cried back, enjoying herself enormously. "Surely not in the house still!"

"I think not," Aunt Martha said, with a bare hint of disappointment. "There's no trace of him, except in the library, your uncle says. The footmen chased him through the back garden, but couldn't catch him. The watch have been alerted."

Jessica knew a moment's unease, thinking of John

trapped in the street when the alarm was up. But then she remembered the flash of silver in his eyes when he heard the library door open. It might have been pleasure in that kiss they shared—certainly he'd responded in other ways—but it was more likely excitement at the thought of a chase. She reminded herself that he had eluded excise police and French privateers and Barbary pirates and Vatican priests—a few footmen and watchmen would pose him no great peril.

And so she was able to take pleasure in the chaos he had left in his wake, trailing along behind her uncle as Mr. Wiley, his voice quavering with outrage, said he had returned to the library for a forgotten volume and found the open window, the misplaced lamp. Jessica didn't let herself worry that the lamp's position by the shelf of religious works was any evidence—John surely knew what he was doing, and anyway, the telltale More volume was even now stowed safely away in a box under her evening wraps.

As they gathered again at breakfast, her uncle was still unsettled, made more so by Aunt Martha's oft-pronounced fear that they would all be murdered in their sleep. Jessica thought to soothe and provoke both. "It was the library the burglars entered, not the living quarters. And there was no evidence they got any further than the bookroom. I think they must have been after something in there—oh! Perhaps the Baconalia! Or—who knows what!" She added craftily, "Poor Mr. Wiley is so distrait, I know he can't think of what to do. He must be in terror that the burglars will return. And he won't have any way to prevent it."

Her uncle peremptorily waved away the footman who had come to pour more coffee. "That tears it. I'm going to call in that Dryden fellow for a consultation. If he ad-

TAKE ADVANTAGE OF THIS SPECIAL OFFER, AVAILABLE *ONLY* TO ZEBRA REGENCY ROMANCE READERS.

You are a reader who enjoys the very special kind of love story that can only be found in Zebra Regency Romances. You adore the fashionable English settings, the sparkling wit, the captivating intrigue, and the heart-stirring romance that are the hallmarks of each Zebra Regency Romance novel.

Now, you can have these delightful novels delivered right to your door each month and never have to worry about missing a new book. Zebra has made arrangements through its Home Subscription Service for you to preview the three latest Zebra Regency Romances as soon as they are published.

3 **FREE** REGENCIES TO GET STARTED!

To get your subscription started, we will send your first 3 books ABSOLUTELY FREE, as our introductory gift to you. NO OBLIGATION. We're sure that you will enjoy these books so much that you will want to read more of the very best romantic fiction published today.

SUBSCRIBERS SAVE EACH MONTH

Zebra Regency Home Subscribers will save money each month as they enjoy their latest Regencies. As a subscriber you will receive the 3 newest titles to preview FREE for ten days. Each shipment will be at least a $11.97 value (publisher's price). But home subscribers will be billed only $9.90 for all three books. You'll save over $2.00 each month. Of course, if you're not satisfied with any book, just return it for full credit.

FREE HOME DELIVERY

Zebra Home Subscribers get free home delivery. There are never any postage, shipping or handling charges. No hidden charges. What's more, there is no minimum number to buy and you can cancel your subscription at any time. No obligation and no questions asked.

TO GET YOUR 3 FREE BOOKS
FILL OUT AND MAIL THE COUPON BELOW

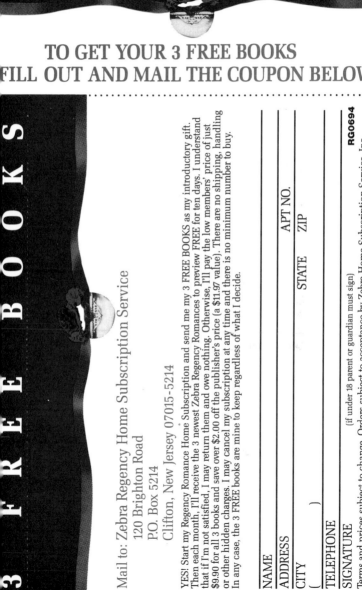

3 FREE BOOKS

Mail to: Zebra Regency Home Subscription Service
120 Brighton Road
P.O. Box 5214
Clifton, New Jersey 07015-5214

YES! Start my Regency Romance Home Subscription and send me my 3 FREE BOOKS as my introductory gift. Then each month, I'll receive the 3 newest Zebra Regency Romances to preview FREE for ten days. I understand that if I'm not satisfied, I may return them and owe nothing. Otherwise, I'll pay the low members' price of just $9.90 for all 3 books and save over $2.00 off the publisher's price (a $11.97 value). There are no shipping, handling or other hidden charges. I may cancel my subscription at any time and there is no minimum number to buy. In any case, the 3 FREE books are mine to keep regardless of what I decide.

NAME _____

ADDRESS _____ APT NO. _____

CITY _____ STATE _____ ZIP _____

(____) _____
TELEPHONE

SIGNATURE _____ **RG0694**
(if under 18 parent or guardian must sign)

Terms and prices subject to change. Orders subject to acceptance by Zebra Home Subscription Service, Inc.

GET

3 FREE

REGENCY

ROMANCE

NOVELS—

A $11.97

VALUE!

ZEBRA HOME SUBSCRIPTION SERVICE, INC.
120 BRIGHTON ROAD
P.O. BOX 5214
CLIFTON, NEW JERSEY 07015-5214

vised the Regent on setting up the royal library, he'll know what to do to secure this one."

And so it was that when Jessica entered the drawing room on some flimsy pretext, she found the cool Sir John bending over the table, drawing plans on a parchment sheet, with Uncle Emory watching and nodding sagely. Mr. Wiley was sitting apart on the settee, his face set, his arms crossed at his chest.

John rose as she approached. Gone was the dark dashing outlaw of the night before, though danger still emanated from his slim form. In his subdued impeccable clothes, he was cool again, remote, as if their crime and their kiss had never occurred. But just as she felt her spirits plummet, he took her hand—a formal, public gesture, but one he made intimate, by stroking her palm with his calloused thumb before releasing her.

It was like a secret kiss, like the kiss they had shared only hours earlier, daring and sweet and tantalizing and temporary. As Jessica bent her head to hide the color that rose in her cheeks, she told herself that this intimacy was only a bit of excitement, a flirtation with danger like their criminal activity. He wasn't for her; he was too alien, too apart. It couldn't last—but while it did, she meant to delight in it.

So she glanced sidelong at him, letting her eyes show her inquiry, knowing that only he would see it. His response was a slight shake of his head before he returned to his consultation with Uncle Emory. And she was left to puzzle that out. Did it mean the index didn't contain what he'd hoped? No. If his hopes were dashed, she would know it; she would see the loss in his eyes no matter how he tried to conceal it. She would have to wait for a more private moment to learn what he had found.

That moment came soon, when Uncle Emory rose to show the parchment to Mr. Wiley. Jessica poured a cup of tea, keeping her gaze focused on the liquid leaving the spout, and whispered, "So tell me!"

John took the cup from her and shook his head warningly. "Not today—Wiley's keeping watch on me. I will get a note to you tomorrow. And we are supposed to be at odds, recall."

To further that impression, Jessica did not have to invent any annoyance. It's my index, she wanted to remind him, but instead she poured another cup and carried it to Mr. Wiley. He took the tea with a distracted polite murmur, and went back to scowling at Sir John's drawing. In a show of fellow-feeling, Jessica peered down at the plans and then sank gracefully down beside the librarian, hand on her heart, as if overcome with dismay.

"Really, Sir John! Bars on the windows? An armed guard in each room? This is not the Tower of London, you know, but a library!"

Mr. Wiley stared at her, no doubt astonished to have so unlikely an ally. But he soon recovered, and pointedly addressed his own remarks to Lord Parham. "Miss Seton is right, my lord. Surely such contortions aren't necessary. I would find it impossible to work in such an atmosphere, with guards peering over my shoulder and rifling through the shelves."

John regarded him with that assessing gaze that seemed to take his measure to the inch. "You have an alternative plan, Mr. Wiley?"

"Yes, I do. It was merest luck that sent me back to the library last night for the document I had forgotten, but that is the right approach—to be there at all times. I mean to move my quarters into the backroom."

Jessica bit down hard on her protest. The flash in John's eyes told her he had the same thought—Mr. Wiley in the backroom, with the vault, with the trunk.

No, it was too dangerous. She swallowed hard and managed a smile. She even patted Mr. Wiley's hand—or fist, rather, for it was bunched on the settee between them. "How brave of you, Mr. Wiley! But—but someone broke in last night. He escaped, didn't he? And my aunt said he got clean away, without being identified. What if he didn't get all he wanted? He might be back!"

"What did he get, by the way?" John asked with a casualness that must have fooled everyone but her. "Have you done an inventory to determine what's missing?"

Lord Parham shot a sharp look at the librarian. "We can't tell if anything is gone. None of the Bacon, that's all we know."

"Oh, yes, I'd forgotten. There's no current catalogue. My word, that will make it difficult, won't it?" John came over to retrieve the parchment, carried it back to the desk, and as he added to the list there he murmured to himself, "Task number 13. Inventory of major pieces."

When he returned the plan to Lord Parham, he added, "Miss Seton's right. If the burglar means to return, Mr. Wiley won't be safe there. You need trained, trustworthy guards, especially at night."

"A guard will be little protection," Mr. Wiley observed, his eyes sharp behind their lenses, "if the threat is an internal one."

"Internal?" Lord Parham and Jessica echoed.

Mr. Wiley subsided into a remote silence until John said roughly, "Out with it, Wiley. What are you implying here?"

The librarian sat up straighter and smiled. "Implying? I mean to imply nothing. You are uncommon tetchy, Dryden. I wonder why."

"Well, *I* wonder why you looked at me when you

spoke of an internal threat. If you've an accusation to make, make it."

"If you insist. . . . It's just that, anticipating Lord Parham, I sent a messenger to your flat early this morning. And you were not there. The doorman told me you hadn't come home."

Sir John's smile went steely. "I shall have to thank the doorman for paying such close attention to my whereabouts, and keeping you apprised. Or perhaps you would prefer that the next time I decide to spend the night elsewhere, I consult with you first, Mr. Wiley?"

"It's just that I can't help but wonder why you would spend the night elsewhere. You show an uncommon interest in the collection, Dryden. And we know about dealers—Tell him, won't you, about how you procured the Mesa Royale manuscript? The story was the talk of the Royal Society. There was a rope ladder involved in that, wasn't there?"

"Why don't you tell the story, Mr. Wiley, since you know it so well?"

The librarian waved a dismissive hand. "The particulars are of no account. But your absence from home last night worries me. I can't help but wonder what would have drawn you from home."

"Wonder all you like. But keep it to yourself, if you please. There's a lady present."

But, as Jessica rather hoped, Mr. Wiley seemed to have forgotten that she was sitting next to him. "You mean to say, that you spent the night with your mistress? Her name might not be amiss then."

He could not, however, ignore Parham's outraged exclamation. And John, his voice tight with anger, said, "Lord Parham, if you have need of it, I will furnish the name of the friend in whose home I spent the night— but elsewhere. This conversation cannot be of any interest to Miss Seton, and we shall, if necessary, resume it in a more appropriate setting."

Jessica opened her mouth to protest, but her uncle overrode her. "I shouldn't ask anything of the sort from you, Dryden. A man's nights are his own. Wiley, what are you thinking of, making such a suggestion with my niece present? And to the Regent's own consultant here?"

With his patron glaring at him, Wiley could do nothing but murmur an apology—to Jessica, not to the man he had insulted. And Uncle Emory was mollified enough to try to compromise between the two divergent security plans. He agreed to Mr. Wiley's suggestion of a single guard, stationed in the garden at night, while a footman sat up in the hall outside the library door. "Bars too, I suppose. No doubt you have some recommendation on a firm to install that, Sir John?"

John shrugged, as if unconcerned that his sage advice had been mostly disregarded. "I will send a trustworthy man for you to interview. He worked on Carlton House. If he does not satisfy, I will give you other names. If there is nothing more, I'll take my leave of you."

He bowed to Jessica. That momentary acknowledgment of camaraderie was gone now, and, ignoring her silent signal to wait, he started for the door. But Uncle Emory, at his most imperious, accomplished what she with her eyes and expression could not. "Just a moment more, Dryden. Jessica, you may stay too, this concerns you. Thank you, Mr. Wiley, you may go back to the library now. You might start that inventory Sir John suggested."

Mr. Wiley left, muttering about inventories and upstarts. John's gaze followed him, and the chill hadn't left his eyes when he turned back. Jessica suppressed a shiver when he looked at her. She knew how kind, how gentle he could be; she doubted not his essential goodness. But when he looked like that, she remembered how little she knew of his life, his past, the experiences that had made him alternately so approachable and so aloof.

And when she saw her uncle's expression—awkward but resolute—she knew with dread that John was about to live through another of those experiences. "Don't, uncle," she hissed, but he silenced her with an impatient chop of his hand.

"Dryden, I hope you won't take offense at what Mr. Wiley says. He's a scholar, you know, not much for the social graces. Seldom sets foot outside that library."

John inclined his head without comment, but that was enough to encourage Uncle Emory. "I mean you to know that I appreciate your counsel on this matter. It is most conciliating of you."

John did not speak. Even his eyes were at their most unrevealing, opaque and reflective.

And Parham, seeing himself in the other man's eyes, cleared his throat and shifted nervously. "But—well, I think it's in your interest that you know right now. If you have designs on this collection—on my niece—"

"Uncle . . ." Jessica's agonized whisper wasn't enough to cut him off.

"—You'd do best to understand that won't serve. I'm sure you realize that I cannot approve of such an unequal match. You are a creditable man, I have no doubt, but you are ineligible."

Instinctively Jessica started towards John, to beg his pardon, to pull him out the door, to make it right somehow. But he raised his hand to stop her. The chill hadn't faded from his eyes, and his glance hardly brushed her. Then he never looked her way again.

Instead, he addressed her uncle in a voice as hard as

ice. "I give you no leave to declare me eligible or ineligible, or declare me anything at all."

"Give me leave? Give me leave? I am the girl's uncle!
I'll *take* leave to warn you off, I will, and be damned to
your arrogance!"

"It is not arrogance, Lord Parham, to resent such a
charge. I came here at your behest, to do you a service.
I have no designs on your niece or her collection."

Distractedly Jessica thought that the first part of
John's statement, that he was here at her uncle's behest,
was only half-true. The second part might be similarly
ambiguous. But where would that leave them?

"Well," Parham said, visibly relieved, "that's fine
then. We'll need speak no more of it."

But John was too angry to leave it at that; she saw the
resolve he had to bring to loosing his clenched fists. "I
don't think you understand. If I wanted a woman, and
she was of the same mind, nothing you could say would
gainsay me. I mean no insult, but I do not accept that
you have any right to dictate to me."

Uncle Emory took a step back, as if he finally felt the
force of John's chilly anger. "By God, you are a slippery
one, Dryden. I'd call you insolent, but you're too
damned polite, even when you insult me." He regarded
the younger man with something close to astonishment.
"I'd call you an upstart, but you don't ask for any favor.
You aren't anything I know, and I don't know what to
make of you."

"It isn't your place to make anything of me." John
gathered up his riding gloves, jamming them into his
pocket. His voice was level, though, as if he were giving
instructions to a crewmember. "You will not treat me as
a servant, or as a thief, or whatever it is you prefer me
to be. If you have no use for my aid, tell me so, and I

will leave. But I am an Englishman, and no man's lesser at that. I suggest you keep that fixed fast in your mind."

He bowed to Jessica and left without another word. As the door closed behind him, she turned on her uncle. "How dare you! He has been nothing but good to us, and you—and you insult him so!"

"Well, he insulted me, too, did you hear?"

"He told you that you had no right to order him about, and he's correct. As you have no right to tell me I can't see him if I wish."

"Your father left you in my charge! That gives me the right!"

"No. You have only the right to withhold my inheritance from me." Jessica covered her mouth with her fist, remembering what great power that right gave him. But it was not enough to control her, no matter what he thought. Her hand dropped to her side. "No more than that."

Parham must have sensed they were on the brink of some terrible confrontation, for his tone became more conciliatory. "Now Jessica, surely you are not interested in that man. Oh, he's handsome enough—least your aunt thinks so; he looks like a damned foreigner to me. But he isn't our sort, not in any way. He couldn't make you any kind of husband!"

It angered her, and hurt her too, to think that he could disdain a man like John Dryden. And that anger took shape in hot words. "He's a good man. Better than most! He would never have insulted a man as that—that supposed *gentleman* Alfred Wiley insulted him! And he would never have insulted me, either, by making unwanted advances—and yet that is what you accused him of doing!"

"I accused him of no such thing! I merely meant to

warn him that if he thought to improve his lot with marriage, he should look elsewhere!"

"But that is an insult! To him, and to me!" In despair, she turned away and started for the door. But she halted with her hand on the knob. She had to try to explain, at least, even if it would do no good. "Oh, Uncle, don't you see? You as much as called him a fortune hunter, and me a prize only desired for my fortune!"

"I said nothing of the sort. But he's no fool. He can see where the main chance is—and you're the likeliest target for him, if he's looking for a fortune."

Jessica drew in her breath to protest this, but then just raised her hands to rub her aching temples. She got nowhere arguing with her uncle; she never had persuaded him of anything. Sometimes she thought he didn't even hear her. Softly, as if to herself, she said, "I am real to him, at least. As I have never been real to you."

"That's nonsense, girl, and you know it! You are my own brother's daughter, my niece—"

"No. I can't say I feel that's true, that you look at me and see your niece. I feel that I was never more than Trevor's bride. The future mother of your grandchildren. And now, I don't know. Vestal virgin at his tomb—"

Parham drew back at this, his face whitening. "How can you speak this way, Jessica? After all I've done, given you a home, to give me such offense!"

"It's because I don't care any longer, do you see? I realize you might offer me a home, but you haven't really any room for me after all. I wish—oh, I wish Father had just appointed a solicitor for me. Then I shouldn't have fooled myself that my guardian cared what became of me. I would have known I was just a case to him, a file in his cupboard. And though he might not have stirred himself to make me happy, he wouldn't have actively worked against it."

Parham raised his hands to his ears, as if he wouldn't even let himself hear this. "Well, if you think your happiness lies with such a one as John Dryden, you are beyond foolish. Beyond foolish! Any of those others would have been better than this one. At least they are all of gentle birth and good families!"

Jessica released the breath she had been holding and forced back the furious comment she had been about to make. "Well," she said, opening the door, "they weren't good enough for you either. So I expect it doesn't matter what I do. I've given up trying to please you."

She let the door close behind her, then sagged back against it, too weak to go up to her room. She could hear her uncle pacing about in the room behind her, back and forth, back and forth, as he used to in those days after Waterloo. For a moment, guilt weighed her down. Her uncle never meant to hurt her, or anyone else. It was just that he had his own narrow view of how the world was supposed to be.

Then she pushed away from the door. No. She wouldn't make excuses for him anymore. He was her uncle, and she loved him despite it all, but she wouldn't, couldn't let him dictate her future any longer.

She thought of John's face when he realized that he was facing another insult, the latest in a lifetime of them. That's what he resisted most of all, being trapped in an identity he hadn't made. His need for freedom was so strong, to do as he wished, to be as he wished, that he must hate to be labeled *tradesman* or *ineligible* or, worst of all, *bastard*. So he surrounded himself with that deliberate distance, pushing her and everyone else away.

She had crossed that distance, once or twice. He might deny it—in fact he did deny it, when he denied he had any designs on her. But she knew the truth. She might be a maiden, but she was experienced enough to know when a man desired her, no matter where he spent the night later. But desire wouldn't be enough to cross that distance again.

She was sorry that an insult had made him retreat, sorrier still to discover within herself a fierce protectiveness. He would not welcome that, she thought, and neither did she. This was a man who could fight his own battles, and didn't need her help at all.

Chapter Ten

And keep you in the rear of your affection,
Out of the shot and danger of desire.
The chariest maid is prodigal enough
If she unmask her beauty to the moon.

Hamlet, I, iii

Jessica met her friends as planned at Ranelagh, but as soon as she could she pleaded a headache and called for her carriage. She could wait no longer.

When the carriage clattered to a halt in a quiet street near Manchester Square, she told the groom that she wouldn't be long. She didn't need his disapproving look to remind her that she was committing social suicide, or would be, at least, if anyone recognized her entering this residence for gentlemen. So she gathered her taffeta cloak around her, put up her hood even though the heat smothered her, and in a muffled voice asked the doorman to direct her to "Capitaine Dryden's rooms, s'il vous plait."

John's set of rooms were on the first floor, above the monastic-like courtyard. Her knock was answered promptly by a bantam-sized man with a bandanna about his neck and a patch over one eye. A real pirate,

Jessica marvelled, down to the hoop in his ear! But when she asked for Sir John, the pirate's scarred face knotted with the same disapproval her groom had shown. "Follow me, please," he said, as glacial as a prince's butler.

Jessica couldn't help glancing about her curiously as they passed through a wide corridor. The walls were covered in dark blue, the paintings illuminated by gold sconces. She thought she saw a Giotti landscape over the staircase, and surely that watercolor of a ship in harbor was by the young Turner. The pirate strode onward, but she hung back to peer at the brass plate under a bust of Achilles. Fifth century BC, sculptor unknown, it said, and she gave the marble nose a gentle rub before running to catch up with her guide.

He threw open the door to a library. "Miss Seton to see you," he announced, then as soon as she was in the room, he held out a hand for her cloak, and soon as he had it, withdrew, pulling the door shut firmly behind him.

The library was dimly lit, except for a pool of light over the desk. John had been frowning at some papers, but when he saw her he put down his quill and rose. He was coatless, his cuffs folded back over his forearms. He rolled down his sleeves, but not before she saw the tattoo of a trident on the inside of his wrist. It made her shiver, to glimpse that secret emblem—a free-trader's symbol no doubt—and she found herself weak with longing to study it, to touch it, to kiss it.

She battled back the impulse—lord, wasn't his mouth enough to draw her?—and began talking before he could protest her appearance. "I couldn't wait till tomorrow to find out about the index. Tell me, do, before I expire. Did it say what we hoped it would say?"

"I don't know," he replied, shrugging his coat on and

coming around the desk. He wasn't precisely welcoming, but she hadn't expected that, not after her uncle's performance. "It is from your mother and grandfather; I thought you should open it."

She was silenced by this gallantry. She knew exactly how desperately he wanted to know what was in that index, and how difficult his restraint must have been. Finally she said, "Well, I'm here now. Let's open it."

"We can't. It's not here." He added with a grin, "Do you think I could have withstood the temptation, were it here in my rooms? No. I left it at my friend's house. It is safer there anyway.

"But—but when will we open it?"

"When we get there. I hope you don't mind a bit of a walk."

Jessica looked down at her insubstantial sandals. "I've got my carriage—"

"No. We must walk. Come see."

When she joined him at the window, he tugged the velvet drape back an inch or so. "Look down there, in the street. Do you see anyone?"

She turned her head sideways so she could apply both eyes to the task. After a moment her vision adjusted to the darkness, and she could see a dark figure on the walk opposite. "You mean that man near the lamppost?"

'There's another at the corner. They or a couple colleagues have been there for the last two days."

"Mr. Wiley hired them."

John inclined his head. "Perhaps. They perk up whenever Arnie or I appear, so I'm taking no chances."

"Do you think they saw me enter?"

"No doubt. But don't worry. Arnie is a master at diversion."

He let the drape drop back into place and crossed to

the door to call his manservant. "Arnie, tell the door-man to call for Miss Seton's carriage. And bring her evening cloak with you when you return."

A diversion! Jessica could hardly catch her breath. This was nearly as exciting as breaking into the library—stealing away to a man's rooms, finding a pi-rate, being watched by suspicious men. "They are why you didn't come home last night, aren't they?"

"Considering what I was carrying, I thought it the sensible course. I left the index there."

"Oh." A flush crept up her face as she remembered the implication of this. "Is that where we're going—your friend's house?"

"Yes. It's only a half-mile or so, in Cavendish Square."

Cavendish Square was rather an elegant area for the courtesan crowd, but, Jessica told herself, his friend could be a wealthy noblewoman. Bending her head to hide her fierce blush, she asked, "But what if it is incon-venient for your friend? I can't think she would be pleased to see me."

The startlement in his eyes relieved her, though his laughter was unexpected. "Not *that* friend. I am not so lost to propriety as all that! No, this is a perfectly re-spectable friend, who is, moreover, not in town. So you will not be exposed to the curious stares of servants. Ex-cept for Arnie, of course, and he doesn't gossip."

She felt an immeasurable but ignoble relief that his night had been passed innocently. But disquiet followed immediately. *Not that friend* meant that there was such a friend, and as she stole a glance at John's face, Jessica knew nights with that one wouldn't be so innocent.

She was on the brink of demanding some clarification when Arnie reappeared with her evening cloak. "Put it on," John told him.

Arnie started to spread it around her shoulders, but

John shook his head. "No, Arnie, I mean for *you* to put it on. You're going to draw off our friends in the street by taking a ride in Miss Seton's carriage—as Miss Seton."

The horror on Arnie's face was almost comical, but Jessica knew better than to laugh at a pirate. "But—but Captain! I won't fool no one!"

"You're about the same size. Just pull up the hood and keep your head down." John took the cloak from his numbed hands and held it up. "And don't say anything."

Arnie had turned to shrug on the cloak, but he still muttered, "And what do I do when we reach her house, I ask you?"

"You'll think of something. Jessica, do you have a handkerchief?"

Fascinated by the transformation of pirate into heiress, she only nodded, and burrowed in her bag without taking her gaze off Arnie. "Here," she said, handing the scrap of lace to John.

He transferred it to Arnie. "Hold this in front of your face and sniff every now and again. The groom will think you've suffered a romantic disappointment, and leave you quite alone."

Arnie, still protesting, trudged out of the room.

Jessica waited till the door was closed to give into laughter. "You are going to disgrace me! I'll have you know, I do not dissolve into tears on such occasions, especially in front of servants."

"Well, your servants will accept your tears sooner than they will accept Arnie's eye patch. Let's watch."

This time he opened the drape at least two inches. He was a head taller, and could look out over her, as long as he stayed so close behind her that she could feel the brush of his sleeve on her shoulder. Was he remem-

bering that kiss when they were even closer than this?
Now, he couldn't be, for he was laughing and pointing
at Arnie, huddled in her cloak, stepping daintily up into
the carriage.

"You needn't worry. He will do well enough, as long
as he doesn't encounter your aunt or uncle."

"They are abed, I'm sure."

"Then he will just wait until the carriage is being
taken back around to the stables to sneak out of your
house. He's had a great deal of experience—used to
play all the ladies when my crew performed Shakespeare at sea."

Jessica was only slightly reassured, but firmly she
pushed her worries aside. There was nothing more she
could do about it, and at least she had achieved her
aim. She was here with John, and they would soon be
in possession of the precious index.

One of the watchers departed at a fast walk after the
carriage. "We'll go out the back," John said, letting the
curtain drop back into place. He looked her up and
down, at her fine lilac gown, her hair up, pearls at her
neck, and though she saw the gleam in her eye, she
knew he was not about to compliment her beauty.
"You're rather formal for this sort of outing. You would
have done better to wear boots," he added, gesturing at
her Grecian sandals. "But I reckon it can't be helped."

"You could send for the index, and we could open it
here."

But she was relieved when he shook his head and returned to his desk to retrieve a ring of keys. "No, I don't
want it in this house. It's safer where it is."

The night was cool and dry, but Jessica felt flushed as
she followed John down the mews lane, hugging, as he
did, close to the wall. It was near midnight, and dark as
pitch back here where there were no streetlamps. She

kept her eyes focused on John's tan coat, trusting him to find a way through the night to their unknown destination. She wasn't experiencing fear, precisely, more that pleasurable trepidation thunderstorms sometimes brought; she knew she was safe with John, but she could imagine being in danger here without him.

Without her protective cloak, Jessica felt blessedly unencumbered. There was some kind of freedom in the whisper of the breeze against her bare arms, in the brisk slap of the cobblestones under her feet, in the man that led her through the darkness.

To keep her bearings, she trailed her hand along the brick wall lining the alley and murmured, "East, east," for that was the direction she thought they were heading. She was proved right when they came to the end of the wall and she recognized James Street ahead.

John stopped at the edge of the alley and held out his hand in warning. "Wait," he said softly, and she peered around his arm to see a watchman strolling past on the well-lit street. She held her breath till he turned the corner. "Now," John whispered, taking her hand.

They ran lightly across the street into the next alley. A light breeze followed them, and Jessica jumped and hardly suppressed a scream when scrap of newspaper wrapped itself around her legs. She stopped to pull it free, her grip on John's hand tightening to tell him to wait. He stopped and watched her, his eyes silver and unreadable in the darkness.

From the back garden of a house came a girlish giggle, and Jessica paused to wait for the expected masculine response. But John yanked her hand. "No time for that. This isn't a safe time to be out."

Another couple turns in these narrow backstreets and Jessica had completely lost her bearings. They were headed for Cavendish Square, she knew that, and she might have found her way in daylight, along the major streets. But the backs of houses and squares, she was learning, were not nearly so individual as their fronts. Brick wall gave way to stone, and occasionally to plank, but the little cobbled alleys varied mostly in the amount and type of rubbish heaped up along their borders. The stillness was broken sometimes by city noises: a lorry wagon clattered by, a drunken gentleman called out to a friend as he stumbled past their alley, a lonely cricket called out for a mate.

She was marvelling at the skeletal remains of a carriage when she sensed something moving behind it. As the man sprung out, John pulled her roughly against his side, his hand going to his pocket and emerging with a dagger flashing in the dimness. "Not tonight," he said, and she looked out over his arm to see a ragged man slink away down the alley.

"Was he going to rob us?" she asked when she got her breath back.

"No. He was going to try." Coolly he released her and sheathed the dagger. "Even Mayfair is dangerous after dark, you know."

"Well, I never actually been accosted this way, in or out of Mayfair. But I liked watching you turn him away. You didn't even have to hurt him." She looked back at the corner where the attacker had disappeared. "Most instructive. Perhaps you could get me a dagger like this?"

John glanced back at her, and she sensed him smiling. "You are wasted on Mayfair, do you know that?"

Warmed by this, she reflected that his compliments were as unconventional as they were sincere, and she cherished them. Oh, it might be pleasant to hear him praise her beauty and charm, but other men had done that. Not a one, she was sure, had even noticed what seemed to impress John the most—what she thought he might call her spirit and her quick mind.

And not one, she knew, would be quite as handy in guiding her through dark, dangerous corners of the world.

She slanted a look at him as they crossed another street. The streetlamp cast shadows on his intriguing face, sometimes so austere and sometimes, when he smiled, so appealing. She wished she knew more about his past, about the adventures that made him so handy with a knife, so casual under attack. She could ask him, she knew, and he might tell her a bit of the truth. But perhaps it was better to let him keep his secrets, and to just enjoy his mystery while she could. Then she could tell herself that however exciting he was, he was ultimately forbidden to her. Perhaps that was why he tantalized her so, because she knew she could never have him, and even if she had him, she could never hold him.

But that was because he was elusive, apart, alien, although not for the reasons her uncle endorsed—social class, birth. John might not understand the distinction, however, if he ever thought to consider it. "I meant to apologize for what my uncle said."

"Don't." He didn't look at her; he was staring ahead into the dark, perhaps watching for more assailants. "I have been expecting it anytime this past week. But it has given me an idea."

"What?"

"If he thinks you are in danger of running off with me, he might look with greater approval on one of your—your more eligible suitors."

She heard the irony dripping from those last words, but was too taken aback to laugh. She remembered Ada concocting the same scheme at the Devlyn ball, and responded with the same guilty ambivalence. "That's absurd. I wouldn't ever suggest such a plan."

"You're not suggesting it. I am."

His voice was easy, but he was striding ahead so that she couldn't see his face. "But he doesn't want me to marry *anyone.*"

"He's wavering. And he'll capitulate entirely if you stop letting him make the rules for you. Just make it clear you'll marry with or without his consent—to a man of your own choosing. He'll give in. Especially if he thinks that man might be me."

"John—"

"We'll do it. I can come to take you for drives, and then Friday to Vauxhall."

She finally caught up with him and took his arm to stop him. But he ignored her importuning hand, tugging her along down the alley. "I wanted to go there anyway, for it sounds to be an entertaining night of it. They're putting on some mishmash of Shakesperian Italianate scenes, done in an operatic mode. Your aunt will doubtlessly wish to chaperone you."

Jessica gave up trying to slow him down, instead letting go of his arm so she could reach down and pull up the strap of her sandal. It came loose, and she had to balance her foot on her other knee to work at the buckle. "But—but what if it becomes inconvenient for you?"

He stopped and retraced his steps, taking her elbow so that she wouldn't tumble over as she fastened her sandal. "Inconvenient? Taking you to Vauxhall? My time's not so precious as that."

"No, I mean, if your *friend* learns of this. Won't she object?"

As they resumed their quick pace, he gave her a sharp glance, started to speak, then stopped. Then, impatiently, he replied, "We are friends. We are not chained together. Neither of us would ever think to—" He broke off, looked away, added, "You needn't worry about that. She will not object."

This cryptic response to an essential question annoyed her. "Why wouldn't she object? Would you cut off her allowance if she did?"

"Her allowance? What allowance?"

"Don't men pay their mistresses an allowance?" She decided she liked it when he flushed like that under the ghostly light of a streetlamp—it made him seem less austere, more properly chastened. So she didn't relent, remembering what the poison-pen authors had said about her other suitors. "Don't they set them up in houses in Richmond and cottages by the shore? Buy them jewelry?"

"She has her own house. And a shore cottage too. Look, it's not that sort of connection."

"Oh?" She might have preferred this to be true, but his inability to look at her told her otherwise.

"I mean that—" he paused for a moment, and when he spoke again his voice once more had its cool assurance, "that some relationships shouldn't be commercial. I would help her if she needed it, but as long as she has paints and canvasses, she's content."

"She's an artist?" Jessica knew a blinding jealousy of this woman who needed only art and John Dryden to be content, and was fortunate enough to have both. "How lucky that you have a common interest."

"I told you, we are friends."

"And something more."

"It is none of your concern. I assure you, did she think I was of a mind to dispense with my freedom, she would be happy for me. *Friends,*" he said with stern emphasis, "want the best for each other."

"And you think dispensing with your freedom would be best for you?"

"*She* does. I don't.

"How can you be certain she doesn't hope you will marry her?"

"Because she's a nun."

Jessica stopped short in the middle of the alley. "A nun?" It came out a strangled squeak.

His grin now had just a slight malicious tilt. "Caught you there, didn't I, my curious one? You deserved that, for interrogating me this way."

"She's not a nun."

"No."

"But she doesn't want to marry you."

"She is widowed. She has no wish to marry again."

Why should she, Jessica thought cynically, when she gets to have a lover who cherishes his freedom too much to interfere with hers? It sounded . . . decadent. More decadent—more seductive—that those commercial transactions John scorned. And, an inner voice whispered, more fragile.

"You must send her a note warning her of this. Else she might hear it from another and—despite your certainty—be hurt."

"I must? Why?"

Jessica fancied that her expression looked properly prim, but to make sure she pursed her lips. "Because I can't go through with this courting scheme of yours if I think a lady might be hurt by it. We have to look out for each other, you know, we women."

The prospect of Jessica and this other woman in alliance obviously did not enthrall John. In fact, he looked appalled. "I think neither of you need any looking out for at all. She's not even in town."

"That makes no difference. Gossip travels on bird wings. You will write the note tonight then?"

John halted suddenly, and she thought she might have pushed him too far. Then she smelled the stench of decay over the usual garbage smells. She squinted to see what lay beyond on the floor of the dark alley, but after a moment decided she'd rather not know. "Wait here," he whispered, and went back the way they came.

So she stood there, shivering slightly, wrinkling her nose against the smell of death, watching his lean form move in and out of the shadows of the houses they had passed. Stopping under a tree that hung over the wall, he used the flashing silver dagger to cut off a sturdy forked branch. Then he came back and gently shoved her back. "It's just a dead dog. But it might be diseased. And there's not enough room here to get around it."

She steeled herself to watch, but could only see him pushing something into a rubbish pile with the fork of the branch. "You can come now."

Eyes forward, Jessica stepped gingerly through the path he had made. Once out of that alley into a well-kept lane, she took a deep breath of the cleaner air. "Thank you. But you didn't answer my question. You will write that letter tonight, to your—to your friend?"

John made an exasperated gesture with his hand, a hacking motion, as if he still had his dagger out. "You are the most tenacious woman when you have your mind set. This letter—should I bring it to you as proof first? Have you post it yourself?"

She considered this, for if she posted it herself she could discover this artist's identity. But a glance at his shadowed face persuaded her otherwise. "No need for that. I know I can trust your word."

"Thank you," he replied with heavy irony. "Then you will agree to my plan to persuade your uncle."

She murmured something affirmative, telling herself that she was surrendering because he was so determined, because his scheme was so clever. But unbidden came anticipation. For this to work, he must play the devoted suitor—and stay far away from his artist friend.

Fool, she scolded herself. He has just proved how resistant he is to attachment. Just as well, though; attachment wasn't her aim. She just wanted him near for a little while longer, to give herself a life's worth of danger in these few weeks. And then—well, she would have to be content with the memories.

Chapter Eleven

My father compounded with my mother
under the dragon's tail,
and my nativity was under Ursa Major,
So it follows that I am rough and lecherous.
'Sfoot! I should have been what
I am had the maidenliest star
in the firmament twinkled on my bastardizing.

King Lear, I, ii

John was striding ahead, and she had to run to keep
up. But before she could get out of breath, he stopped
in a particularly well-kept mews lane and pulled out his
keys. He unlocked a wooden gate and held up his hand
for her to wait while he checked the dark garden. "You
can come in now."

They walked down a path—flagstone, to judge by the
chill under her thin sandals—lined by a profligate array
of rose bushes. The night garden was sweet, heady, in-
toxicating, banishing the scent of death that had lingered on the edges of her memory. The path opened up
to a terrace, and beyond were the blank windows of a
set of French doors.

John led her past those, though, to an undistinguished

wooden door by the kitchen garden. "Where are we?" she asked as he used another key to open it.

"Devlyn House."

Oh. She didn't comment, however, except to whisper as they entered, "Are you certain no one's here?"

It was too dark in this back hall to see his smile, but she heard it in his voice. "I told you, the whole staff is in the country. I spent last night here, and heard only the resident ghost."

She didn't believe in ghosts, but she liked ghost stories. "And who is he?"

"She. A maidservant whining about having to get up before anyone else."

"Rather a disappointing ghost."

"Disappointed too. Imagine having nothing better to complain about in the hereafter—no murder, no abandonment, just tedium and travail." John struck a flint and lit the wall sconce, illuminating a backstairs hall opening into the kitchen. There he was much at home, getting a couple of mugs from the cupboard and filling them with water from the pump. "And she didn't even light the fire for me this morning, so I had to go out for my coffee. Here." He handed her the mug. "There's brandy in the study, but this'll do to quench your thirst."

She drank gratefully, then took his empty mug and rinsed them both out at the pump and replaced them. Lord Devlyn must not mind John's being here—unless John had stolen the keys, and she thought probably he had not—but there was no reason to leave evidence of their visit. "The index," she reminded him, as he seemed content for the moment to stay here in the vast kitchen and watch her, no matter how that unnerved her.

"The index. It's back in the study."

It was almost like one of the Gothics she and Ada used to invent at school. John took her through the dark halls, the light of his candle falling on the oddities of an empty house—a single boot left behind on the back-stairs, Holland covers over a suit of armor, a child's little doll sitting forlornly on a chair in the foyer. John stopped to pick the toy up, and at her quizzical look flushed and shoved it into his coat pocket. "Anastasia will be missing it," he explained. "I'll send it to her."

He opened the door to the study and then blew out his candle before letting her in. The only light came from the streetlamp just outside the windows, but that too was extinguished when John pulled the drapes shut.

They had been in darkness most of the evening, but somehow the quality was different now—more velvet, more seductive. She heard him coming closer and closed her eyes, waiting for him to touch her. But no. He had been the perfect gentleman all evening, taking her hand only to guide her, never once speaking to her in that low, thrilling tone that seemed to invite her desire. She opened her eyes as he lit the candle again. What use was the pretense of an illicit, impossible romance, if he decided so soon it could only be a pretense?

But in consolation, he beckoned her close, around the leather couch, behind the desk. There was a portrait of a tiara'd young lady—Princess Tatiana, she recognized—but John gave this no undue attention. He was more concerned, it seemed, with the frame, for he put his hands on either side as if testing the type and texture of the wood. Then he lifted it up and away from the wall, setting it gently on the floor. On the wall where the picture had been was a black metal door.

He looked back over his shoulder at Jessica. "Devlyn's

not one to buck tradition, you'll note. If there's a safe, there must needs be a portrait over it."

"He gave you a key to it?"

John unlocked the little door, turned the latch, and pulled it open. "Don't tell Monsignor Alavieri and my other rivals. This is where I keep acquisitions until I can move them to the vault at the Bank of England."

He rummaged around inside the dark safe, finally pulling out the sealed packet they found in the More cover. Then he closed the door but didn't replace the picture. "Here." He handed it to her, and she held it for a moment, staring at her mother's handwritten challenge, her father's reply, before sitting distractedly on the couch.

Setting the candle on the low table, John joined her there. When she only held the paper, he said dryly, "Jessica, I am trying to emulate your father's self-control, but it's not unlimited. If you don't open that in the next ten seconds, I will."

She nodded and handed it to him. He shook his head at her and broke the seal, giving it back to her to open. The writing was so hurried and blotted that she could hardly recognize it as her mother's. "La bibliothéque du Pierre St. Germaine, antiquaire."

Her voice gave out then, and John took her hand, pressing it gently. "I'll read it."

She was glad she didn't need to explain. It was just so complicated, anyway, that her mother had made this list of the St. Germaine treasures, perhaps even while the *sans culottes* were storming the chateau walls. And then, after taking such great pains to save the trunk, she had withheld this from her husband, and he had acquiesced. Out of love. Jessica supposed this was romantic—but then, she had never been much of a romantic.

Her thoughts were interrupted by John catching his breath. "You've found it?"

Wordlessly he held out the page, pointing at a single line. "Anthony Munday," she read. "Sieur T More. How do you know?"

John took a deep breath before he spoke. "Munday was a playwright who collaborated with Shakespeare. He was in the Lord Admiral's Players."

Foolishly, perhaps, she had hoped to see "Wm. Shakespeare" there. But she told herself it made no difference whose name was on the play, as long as Shakespeare's hand was inside. "You said it was about a riot."

"That fits." He was beginning to believe it, she realized. His voice was more certain, his breathing less ragged. "Thomas More was a sheriff at some point. He put down a Mayday riot, I think."

"It's true, then."

"Yes."

"And it's in the library. With Mr. Wiley."

"He's been there for a decade, and he hasn't touched it yet."

"That's not good enough," she said. "I want him out of there. If—oh, lord, if he knows about this—"

"He can't. He might suspect. But he's never found the index, never even thought to look, probably. Apparently he's willing to wait till the vault is open."

"It's too dangerous." She made an agonized gesture. "You must talk to my uncle, get him to send Wiley away—"

He caught her hands in his own and said in a gentle, reasonable tone, "I will do what I can. Now don't worry. I'm going to copy out the index, and leave the original in the safe here."

While he sat at the desk making his copy, Jessica was too restless to stay meekly on the couch. She paced around the room, squeezing her hands together until they ached. Would her father have been happy to learn what he had locked away? Would her mother have believed then that he had loved her? Would they regret it if their little game cost their daughter the collection and the treasure?

Somehow it was worse now, to know what she was on the brink of losing. She deserved the right to protect the collection, instead of turning it over to a man who couldn't be trusted.

She rubbed her temples, and started another circuit of the room, wishing she had light enough to read the titles on the bookshelves for diversion. At least she could make out the name on the brass plate under a small, eerily familiar portrait near the hearth. Nicholas Dane, the Viscount Devlyn.

This Devlyn wore the dress of an earlier generation, but except for that and his long hair drawn back in a queue, she might have thought it a picture of John. She could have turned around and looked at John, but instead, as a test, she closed her eyes and called up his face from memory. Oh, he lacked the signs of dissipation that marred the face in the portrait—John led a dangerous life, perhaps, but he was not dissolute; if anything, he was too controlled. And yet John somehow looked more exotic, alien, than this other man. But the resemblance was clear enough. She knew those reflective gray eyes, the relaxed but wary expression, the suggestion of wickedness on that hard elegant mouth.

Without thinking, she said, "You look very like your father."

His silence lasted long enough to tell her what a mistake she had made. Finally John said, "No, I don't. He was fair. My younger brother is more like him."

"I didn't mean—" But there was no way to erase her thoughtless comment.

"I know what you meant. You are not the first to make that mistake."

She turned to see his face hard and still, and thought, I have lost him. Worse, though, was the bleak expression in his eyes, that made her forget her own anguish. How often had he fought this battle? Too often.

"Oh, John," she said, half-laughing, "fathers are the very devil, aren't they?"

This at least had the effect of disorienting him. The bleak look left his eyes as he puzzled this over. All I need to do to win him, she remembered telling herself once, is to mystify him.

Eventually he shook his head ruefully. "Not mine. He was the very saint. Saint Thomas Curmudgeon. No wonder I went the opposite direction."

He was staring off into the distance, not at the portrait that so resembled him, not at that father but at the one who raised him.

"Why do you call him a saint?"

As if this awakened him, John picked up his quill. But instead of returning to his list, he answered her question. "Because—because he never disowned me. I can't tell you how much I did to provoke him. He used to thunder that I might think I was bound for perdition, but the only way I'd get there would be over his dead body. And not even then. By the time he died, I didn't want to go there any longer."

"Did he ever threaten to beat you, to keep you on the straight and narrow path?"

"Oh, he threatened me. It didn't work, because he would never make good on his threats. He never even denied me."

Quietly, Jessica came nearer to him, careful not to interrupt his unwonted candor. "Not once?"

"No. He never saw what you saw—what everyone saw. He would get angry at me, furious at me, but he never once made any sign—Finally I gave up trying to make him. He was tougher than I thought. Wouldn't give me up."

She wanted to touch him, to tell him how admirable she found this difficult loyalty. But as she approached the desk, he scrawled a few more words on his list, set down his quill, and capped the inkpot. "There," he said, rising to put the index in the safe. "We can try and decipher your mother's code for further surprises some other time. I'd better get you back home before dawn."

He slammed the safe door shut and replaced the princess's portrait, stepping back to make sure it was straight. "Have we got everything? Let's go."

This haste, she knew, must be designed to put back up the defenses she had just broken through. All right, she thought as she trailed him out of the house, time to roll out the big guns. She waited until they were in the little rose garden, then she took his arm. "Wait."

The moon had risen, and she could see the question in his eyes as he turned towards her. She rose on her tiptoes to touch his face and kiss him. She felt his sigh against her lips, the acquiescence of his mouth. Then he took her by the shoulders and put her away. "This is taking pretense too far."

She was so hurt that for a moment she didn't understand. Then she recalled his plan to pretend to be her suitor. "This is no pretense. There's no one to see it, for one thing."

"Just so. Perhaps you'd best save it for a more public occasion."

It was clear he was angry; what wasn't clear was why.

And so his straight back as he strode away from her was a goad to her own anger. "Now you just come back here, John Dryden, and explain yourself right now. Or I vow I shall not move one step from this garden." His steps slowed. Encouraged, she added, "The Devlyns will return and find me here, covered in snow, like Hermione's statue! And I will point my finger and croak, that villain did this to me!"

He stopped and retraced his steps to where she stood. "That's not how *A Winter's Tale* ends. Shakespeare didn't write Gothics, you know." He crossed his arms and regarded her ironically. "Have you ever noticed how frequently you resort to blackmail to get your way?"

"I must put my superior understanding of human nature to work for me somehow." She frowned forbiddingly—it was either that or let her triumph show—and said, "Now whatever did I do to make you take offense that way?"

He looked around the little garden as if bandits might spring out from behind the lilac bushes, and took out his circle of keys. "Let's at least walk while you extort me, shall we? If you must, you can always threaten to throw yourself under the wheels of a carriage."

"You haven't answered my question."

He unlocked the gate and held it open for her. In the alley, the moon was hidden by the buildings, so she couldn't see his face. No doubt that was why he had waited to reply. "I've had enough of noblewomen thinking of me as some diversion from their own kind."

"Diversion? What do you mean?"

"The peasant blood. Makes a man virile, you know."

The scathing tone of his voice indicated that he was quoting this. From whom, Jessica didn't want to imagine. But the implication that she might agree made her

furious. "That's absurd! I—I don't see you as a diversion! From what would you be diverting me?"

"From that elite ethereal poet of yours. I've heard all
about what in-breeding has done to the British peer—
made him effete and effeminate and weak-boned, unable to perform. That's what rough-hewn virile peasants
are meant to make up for."

It was so nonsensical that her anger vanished and she
almost laughed. But she couldn't let him go free so easily as that. "Well, I can't believe Damien's unable to
perform," she said fairly. "He's got a mistress. Surely he
wouldn't be spending all that money just for someone to
listen to his sonnets."

"Jessica . . ."

Her name sounded rather like a groan. She couldn't
see very well, but she thought he might have put his
hands to his temple as if he was in pain. Good. He deserved to suffer for such thoughts. "Besides, you don't
seem the least rough-hewn to me. Your manners are every bit as insolent as a prince's, and you must count
your moral authority somewhere up there with the
Archbishop of Canterbury's. If all peasants in England
were like you, we'd have been able to give the French
lessons in revolution!"

"I have never set myself up as a moral authority—"

"You just did! Accusing me of desiring to kiss you for
any reason beyond—well, desiring to kiss you! You have
forgotten, no doubt, that *you* committed this same
egregrious sin the other night, and I think I responded
much more appropriately! And, as for that peasant
virility—" She broke off, and stalked ahead. "Never
mind."

"Oh, no, please do go on. I wait with bated breath to
hear this. As for my peasant virility—"

"I have only your word that it exists. Your muscles

are impressive, it is true, and that tattoo on your wrist—" Out of the corner of her eye, she saw him tug down his cuff—"is rather manly, I suppose. But I wager the most effete of poets knows better than to respond to a kiss as if it were an insult."

"Jessica—"

Now there was laughter in his voice, but she chose to ignore it. "Indeed, you are so sensitive about this virility issue, I must wonder. Have you cause?"

In response he took her arm and drew her to him. "Usually, when my manhood's questioned, I resort to cutlasses. That tends to settle the argument. But in this case . . ."

Pressed against his chest this way, she could hardly find the breath to speak, but she said, "There are other ways, you know."

And just as he bent his head, she raised hers, so that their mouths met. This kiss wasn't tentative or one-sided, but a lingering exploration of the possibilities. John's rough hand was gentle on her cheek, his mouth softened in response to hers. She closed her eyes, letting him draw her closer, opening her mouth to his searching. It was dizzying, dazzling, impossible.

Finally he let her go. Warmth lingered where his body had touched, but the breeze cooled her. She lifted her hand to touch her lips; they were warm still, at least.

"Jessie—I mean no insult. But tell me, what is it you want?"

To drive all thoughts of that artist out of your mind. To have you to myself. To—But she could say none of that. "I just want—oh, we have such a short time. But I want something to remember. Don't you?"

He didn't answer. He only held out his hand to take hers, and looked up at the dark sky. "Pegasus is rising."

"Pardon me?"

"Pegasus. The constellation. It's been coming up about midnight this week. See? Look there, there to the east, over the trees."

Jessica peered where he pointed, but the horizon was lighter than the rest of the sky and she could make out only a few stars grouped in apparent randomness. "Is it supposed to look like a flying horse?"

"Yes. See the square? That's the body."

"You must have sharper eyes than I."

"I have to see to sail, you know. But it does help to know what I'm looking for. You know Ursa Major, certainly."

"Yes, but I've never figured out what it has to do with a bear, major or minor."

"You are relentlessly literal, aren't you? " He took her arm and turned her towards the west. "There's Ursa Major. Polaris—the North Star—is just above it."

She followed his pointing finger and nodded. "I see. That's the one you steer by."

"In the northern hemisphere. It doesn't move much, so it's easy to navigate by. Now draw a line down through that last star in Ursa's tail. That bright yellow one on the horizon is Arcturus. It's setting now. I think that's the star Shakespeare had in mind in *Merchant*—do you remember? You should, for it's addressed to you— 'Sit, Jessica: look how the floor of heaven is inlaid with patines of bright gold.' "

"Mmhmm." Arcturus looked no more yellow than any other star, but she knew if she said so he would accuse her of being literal again. Besides, she liked the feeling of his arm around her, familiar in its casual intimacy. Pressed against her side was the doll he had stuck in his pocket, the one he meant to post back to its little owner. To keep tears at bay, she said, "Doesn't it hurt your neck to gaze up like this?"

"You are so unromantic." He smiled down at her, shaking his head. "Come on. We have to find a hackney to get you back quickly."

In the carriage they shared a few languorous, lingering kisses. Jessica surrendered to the moment, leaning back, her eyes closed, her hands spread across his chest, her heart aching with longing. John cupped her cheek gently as he kissed her, his other hand resting lightly on her arm, his thumb making gentle circles on her bare skin, with the same seductive rhythm as his tongue around her lips. Just a little longer. Just a few more memories . . . then she would let him go.

As the carriage lurched to a halt, she opened her eyes. John was watching her mouth as he traced it with his finger. He looked up, and when she saw his eyes, she almost cried out at the sadness in them. "Hush," he said, closing her mouth with his finger. "You must go."

The hackney dropped them off a block from the house. As they approached the house, hand in hand, Jessica heard a low whistle. John raised his fingers to his mouth and whistled back. "It's one of my crew. Filby. I asked him to keep watch on the house."

"But there's someone already standing guard!"

"I don't trust Wiley to hire a reliable man. Off you go, now. I'll just check with Filby before I leave."

There was no last kiss, only the pressure of his hand on her arm and a quick smile. She walked to the house, looking back once to see him, silhouetted by the lamplight. He was so solitary. She had to remember that.

No tears, she reminded herself. Think of something else. She squinted at the block that was her home, trying to see if the new bars had already been installed on the nearest library window. Not yet. Unbidden came a plan—a good one, too good to wait on consultation with John. She tugged up her skirt and ran lightly along the side of the house. Then, under the window, she bent down, feeling along the walk. It was bordered with fist-sized stones, and she chose a likely one, and in one quick movement hurled it upward as hard as she could.

She started running even before she heard the pane shatter. Her sandals slipped on the paving stones, but she dug in and put her head down and dashed toward the street. Just as she leapt the last couple feet around the corner of the house, she collided with a hard figure. Instinctively her arms went around him. Her face pressed against his cheek, she breathed in the last scent of his shaving soap and thought she might stay here forever in his arms—if she hadn't just committed a felony.

His heart was pounding against her cheek. "Did I frighten you, John?"

"Frighten me? Devil a bit. You idiot!" He grabbed her arms and pulled her into the shadows. "What do you think you're doing? You should bless your luck. Filby said the other guard slipped away to the tavern. I just told him to scarper before he's hauled up for your crime—what are you thinking?"

She couldn't help tugging at his arm as he glared at her. "Now Uncle will listen. John, tell him—tell him," she said urgently. "That he must lock up the library and station guards. Two break-ins—he'll listen now."

"You're incorrigible." He kissed her hard on the mouth then thrust her away. "Go before they catch us both."

Chapter Twelve

> I hold the world but as the world;
> A stage where every man must play a part,
> And mine a sad one.
>
> *Merchant of Venice*, I, i

The next morning, Jessica was only halfway through her preparations when her maid whispered that Sir John Dryden had come to take her riding and was waiting in the drawing room. Jessica made no haste getting into her new blue riding habit, knowing that John would need time to seek out and convince her uncle that the library must be closed. Parham, despite his disdain, always expressed a grudging respect for John's acumen.

Even this morning at breakfast, he spoke of asking the Regent's consultant to recommend an artisan to restore the Parham Manor chapel's statuary. But almost immediately he had shot a glance at Jessica and told her perhaps she ought to invite young Damien to dinner again. John was right; those rejected suitors were looking more acceptable in contrast.

Leaving John alone with her uncle no longer seemed such a good idea. "Just braid it," Jessica said impatiently as Mimi started an elaborate coiffure. "I must get downstairs."

Downstairs, though, she hesitated on the last step. The door to the drawing room was half-open, and Mr. Wiley bent towards it, eavesdropping. Jessica held her breath to avoid alerting him to her presence, and in that silence she heard John's voice, carrying clearly into the hall.

"A broken window? Where was the guard?"

"Dead drunk. No one got in, I'm certain; Mr. Wiley heard the crash and spread the alarm. But I'm thinking you might be right, that a guard isn't enough. Even bars on the windows—"

"I'd suggest you close it up. Two incidents in less than a week—I think that's evidence of some conspiracy."

Jessica suppressed a chuckle at John's manipulation of the truth. There was a conspiracy, all right, but not the sort he meant Parham to believe. And it was a masterstroke. She could almost envision her uncle frowning, fretting over this supposed conspiracy.

"A conspiracy? But—but what would they want from a library?"

"You have thousands of pounds worth of rare books in that library—books that some colleagues of mine would sell their souls to attain. And as trustee, you're in a difficult position, Lord Parham. You can't get in and move the more valuable works to the Bank of England's vault, as I would suggest in other circumstances. You can only protect them as best you can in the few weeks remaining, so that no theft mars your tenure."

That was another clever tactic. Uncle Emory might not be the most conscientious of trustees, but he had a care for his reputation. "No, I shouldn't want anyone to think that I didn't do my duty by my brother. But what about Wiley?"

Mr. Wiley bent closer now, his hand on the door-knob.

"Wiley?" With a certain cruel carelessness, John said, "You won't need him if the library's locked up. Send him on a holiday."

Mr. Wiley made a single, contorted sound of rage at this, but his rigid form never moved.

"I can see to hiring guards—real guards, not lobcocks like that one who never noticed the intruder—and securing the library."

Parham said, "Yes, yes, perhaps that's a good idea, more guards at least. But—but just a moment, Dryden. What's in this for you?" His voice hardened. "Still have your eyes on the prize, don't you? Even after you promised to leave my niece well alone, here you are, taking her riding."

Jessica's heart sank. Her uncle just couldn't give off insulting John, even when accepting help from him. She couldn't blame John if he just walked out, abandoning the Parham Collection to its fate. But of course he wouldn't do that. That would mean giving up on that lost play, which had him in the grip of obsession. Just as well, Jessica told herself. She needed him for a little while longer, and she didn't care what kept him near.

And, as she predicted, he didn't walk out. He even sounded a bit bored with this constant suspicion. "I promised nothing. Jessica is of age; she may ride with me if she pleases. I assure you," John added, his voice all silken irony—did he know she was listening?—"your niece will not be corrupted by me. And my interest in the library is the same any booklover would have. I would hate to see the collection decimated by neglect or irresponsibility. That is more concern, I might add, than its librarian has shown."

Mr. Wiley's iron control finally snapped. He flung the

door open and stalked into the room, just as Parham was saying, "Oh, I will think about closing the library. For the time being, we'll go with guards around the clock. Dryden, you may see to the staffing, if you will."

Jessica slipped in just in time to see Wiley, his hand trembling, point at John. "Lord Parham, you are setting such a one above me? One who casts aspersions on *me* when he himself is scarce above reproach?"

John paled, but deliberately turned back to Parham. "I will take care of it. I should check the number of doors and windows, and the security of that vault. Jessica, I will have to forgo our ride. But we will still be set for Vauxhall tomorrow."

And with a formal bow, he left them, Wiley still breathless with rage, Parham with his brow knitted in a frown, Jessica with her hand out to stop him.

As soon as she could get away, she tracked him down in the storage room of the library. He was shining a light into the vault through the little slit, but looked up with a smile as she came up behind him. "Come here, Jessica. Tell me if all is still in its place."

There was a bit of constraint in his manner, but his smile was warm, and so she smiled back a bit uncertainly. She couldn't go on apologizing for her uncle and Mr. Wiley's snobbery; John must know after last night that she didn't share it. So she only edged a little closer to him in front of the door, trusting him to take advantage of it. And he did, putting his arm around her waist under the guise of positioning her to peer through the opening.

She leaned against him and obediently set her eye against the door. The bumpy shapes, darker than the inner darkness, were in their expected positions. She pulled back, blinking to restore her vision to normal. "Everything looks the same."

He put down the lamp and held out his hand to her, open, as if now that they were alone they could be as they were last night, friends—and something more. "I'm glad you have seen this view enough to know. It's rather like looking at stars, isn't it? You have to know what you are looking for in order to see it."

Jessica took his hand and studied it, touching the callouses on the palm, the slash—of a dagger?—across his lifeline to the tattoo on his wrist, turning it over to see the scarred knuckles, the clean but broken nails. It was the hand of a sailor, a working man, at odds with his gentlemanly dress.

He must have been thinking the same thing, for he closed his hand tight into a fist and pulled it away. "I suppose," he said, "we must be careful not to see only what we want to see—when we look into the darkness."

The next evening, before dinner, Jessica found her uncle in his study working on the estate books. She had made sure not to be alone with him for days now, worried that her anger might explode again and they might face a final break. She couldn't chance that now; she hadn't much in the way of loved ones, and couldn't afford to let another go.

So she reminded herself to avoid anger, accusations, apologies. This hadn't to do with her or with John or with Uncle really at all. But she owed it to—oh, to Shakespeare, she supposed, to do this, even if John had thought it would tip their hand to Mr. Wiley.

That John would not approve gave her a bit of disquiet. He was more experienced at this sort of thing than she was. But it was *her* discovery, and *her* collection, and *her* responsibility, and she knew what she had to do.

When she had her uncle's attention, she smoothed out the sheet from the wastebasket and set it on the desk before him. "This fell out of a book Mr. Wiley was carrying."

It was a small lie, the first of several she would have to tell. Another fortnight of this, Jessica thought, and she would be as blind as Mr. Wiley to the truth.

Her uncle looked down at the scrawled page without recognition. "Well, don't you think you ought to return it to him?"

"I was meaning to. But then—well, it's so curious. And it worried me. So I thought I'd show it to you, and ask what you think it means."

"Hmmph. I'm surprised you didn't take it to Dryden, did you want advice, since you seem to have a care for no one else."

"That's not true, Uncle! I only—" No apologies. She pushed it across the desk at him. "Look. It's Shakespeare's signature. Not the *real* signature," she added, guessing what his open-mouthed expression meant. "But a copy. A very good copy. It's so curious, don't you think? That Mr. Wiley would be copying out Shakespeare's signature?"

Uncle Emory made no move to touch the paper, instead staring hard at her. "What are you suggesting?"

Another lie. "Nothing, precisely. But—well, I worry that some might think that he—Mr. Wiley—might be following in William Ireland's path." And another lie.

"Ireland?"

"He was an antiquarian—or perhaps only the son of one, I forget. But he forged some papers and said that Shakespeare had written them, and he sold them to collectors. It was only a few decades ago, and sometimes his work still turns up."

She had staggered him, that much was clear. "You are accusing Mr. Wiley of forgery?"

"Not precisely." That much at least was true. "I don't

know. But I'd hate to think anyone else would find something like this, and trace it back here to the library, and think that—that Parham House was some sort of forgery factory."

It wasn't fair, and she knew it as soon as she saw the horror dawn on her uncle's face. He cared very much about his reputation, and even more about his family name. He grabbed up the page and held it close to his face, feeling for his spectacles with his other hand. Close study produced a grunt of agreement. "I see what you mean. Shakespeare. Can't have that."

"What do you mean to do?"

He lay down the page and stared down at it, and Jessica felt a stirring of guilt. Uncle Emory looked older suddenly, oppressed by duty. He said slowly, "This isn't any real evidence against him. It's not as if he's been caught with his hand in the ink."

"No. But if he is doing something wrong—"

He took off his spectacles and passed his hand over his eyes. "I think I shall just close the library, as Dryden suggested. Lock it up tight till July 23. No one in or out, not Wiley, not you, not even me."

"And then?"

"And then—well, it won't be my concern any longer."

Jessica had finally learned that pressing him only made him recalcitrant. So she didn't suggest that he fire Wiley outright. She looked down at her clasped hands and said, "Whatever you think is best, uncle."

He snorted at this. "Very meek, niece. Now what have you planned for this evening? I hear Damien Blake is back in town. Is he coming to dine?"

Jessica felt in her pocket for Damien's letter, which had just arrived along with a sonnet she hadn't had time to read. "No, Aunt and I are going to Vauxhall. With

John." She couldn't quite erase the defiance from that last phrase, so she added hastily, "If you'd like me to invite Damien to dinner tomorrow evening, I will, of course."

"If *I* would like? What have my preferences to do with Damien?"

It was a rhetorical question, and even if it wasn't, she didn't know how to answer it. So she said nothing.

"Invite him, then. He's not a bad boy, after all, is he? I suppose even Trevor would have sowed a few wild oats, had he the time."

Jessica rose to go, taking a quick glance up at the miniature of her cousin. She didn't tell her uncle that, from what she knew, Trevor had had time and more to sow oats. It was enough that Parham was softening his opposition to Damien, just as John said he would. It was enough—well, it had to be enough.

She stopped with her hand on the door. "You won't tell Mr. Wiley, will you? That I found that paper?"

"No, no. Best not say anything to him about it. We'll just close the library for the next few weeks because of these break-ins. No need to say more. I'll ask him to dine tomorrow with us, when young Damien comes. That will pacify him."

Jessica, remembering the hatred on Mr. Wiley's face as he looked at John, wasn't so certain that a dinner would mollify him. But she left it to her uncle to break the news and went to dress for the evening.

Her suspicion about Mr. Wiley's intransigence was borne out when John arrived to escort her and her aunt to Vauxhall. Uncle Emory entered the drawing room, the librarian stalking in behind him. She could tell at a glance that the interview was not going well. Even her uncle, who was not sensitive to mood, gave her a frantic glance as Mr. Wiley planted himself in the middle of the room.

Aunt Martha noticed the change in the room temperature also, and rose, holding her bouquet. "Come, Jessica, let us find a vase for these pretty flowers Sir John brought."

Jessica wasn't about to abandon John like that. "No, Aunt, you go ahead. I must ask Uncle about something before we leave."

Her aunt was too eager to exit to offer much of a protest, only murmuring her apologies as she left through the door John held for her. Once she was gone, though, no one spoke for an agonizing moment. Finally her uncle nodded to John.

"Ah, here you are, Dryden. I was just telling Mr. Wiley that you should see to securing the library until July 23—those bars for the windows, and substantial locks for the doors, and guards round the clock. What do you say?"

"I've already engaged the guards; they are in place at this moment. If you wish, I can take care of the rest tomorrow."

"Tomorrow? Good. Perhaps after that you can stay for—"

Jessica caught her uncle's eyes and shook her head vigorously. The prospect of John, Mr. Wiley, and Damien all to dinner was enough to dampen anyone's appetite. Lord Parham wasn't quick, but he did cut off that dangerous word "dinner," lamely substituting "a drink, to tell me what you've accomplished."

"As you wish."

John was at his most remote again, as he so often was in company, guarded, standing back near the door with his arms crossed. He didn't look at her, but Jessica knew

better than to take offense. She was an ally; he didn't
have to watch her.

Instead he watched Mr. Wiley, who stood silent and
still in the middle of the carpet. He shook his head when
Uncle Emory suggested they sit down, and so they all
kept standing in an awkward circle.

"You can take your holiday as usual in July, Mr.
Wiley."

No doubt her uncle meant this conciliatorily, but it
didn't work. The librarian's stillness broke in an abrupt
gesture of his arm. "And leave my library to this—to
this upstart?"

"It's not *your* library," Jessica said, but her protest was
drowned out by her uncle's hearty voice.

"Now, now, Mr. Wiley, no need for that. Dryden
works for the Regent, recall. He comes highly recom-
mended. The library will be quite safe with the mea-
sures he puts into effect."

"Will it be safe *from* him, that is what I ask."

As Parham repeated, "Now, now, Mr. Wiley," Jessica
stole a glance at John. He was still watching Mr. Wiley,
with the disinterested academic regard a natural scientist might give an insect. Don't look at him like that, she
wanted to plead. Don't you know it drives him mad?

But perhaps that was John's plan. If so, it was succeeding. Mr. Wiley drew himself up, ostentatiously ad-
dressing her uncle alone. "I will stay here. Stay in the
library."

"No." John never looked away from Mr. Wiley, but
his objection was directed at Lord Parham. "If the library is to be closed, it must be closed to all. I can't
vouch for the security of the holdings otherwise."

"You are right, Dryden. I regret, Mr. Wiley, that until
I can transfer the library, you too must be excluded. You

can, of course, retrieve your personal possessions from your office."

Jessica closed her eyes, sending out the fervent hope that John would not suggest that a guard accompany Mr. Wiley back to his office.

But she needn't have worried. John had no chance to speak. With a cold fury that seemed to erupt from deep within, Mr. Wiley said, "Lord Parham, is this what you intend? To trust this scoundrel with the Parham Collection?"

"Mr. Wiley!"

To Jessica, the insult sounded like just another shot across the bow in this secret battle, but her uncle was clearly shocked. He swallowed convulsively and found his voice again. "You go too far! You have defamed Dryden's honor!"

The librarian laughed bitterly. "He has none to defame. Or he would defend it, as a gentleman would! But no, he will not call me out."

John finally moved, uncrossing his arms and leaning casually against the door frame. His voice was almost peaceful. "No, Wiley, I shan't call you out."

Parham stirred uneasily. "It is your right. You needn't stand for insult."

"If I called out every man who insulted me—" John shook his head. "I should have no time to work. Anyway, this isn't a proper discussion to conduct in front of Miss Seton."

"That's right, take refuge behind her skirts, Dryden. You've already shown yourself a poltroon, after all. Your life is evidently worth more to you than your honor."

That insult broke through Jessica's determined calm. She started to protest, but John, never glancing her way, overrode her. "Not at all. *Your* life is worth more than that. My honor would be a paltry thing, wouldn't it, if I had to kill old men to keep it."

Wiley sucked in an outraged breath, then expelled it in a rush of words. "The excuse of a coward."

The word hung in the air even as Mr. Wiley rushed towards the door. Without comment John stepped back and let him by. When the door slammed behind the librarian, Parham drew a deep breath. "You would have been within your rights, Dryden. No man has to listen to that. I would have challenged him, had I been you."

There was a rebuke in that comment, but John only shrugged. "You are nearer his age. It would have been fairer—though I would have backed you, were I a betting man. His eyesight is faulty, can you tell? He can't focus with the left eye. Spent too long squinting in that dark office of his."

Parham was still uneasy. "Still, you ought to have taught him a lesson."

"I don't kill men to teach them a lesson."

"You are so sure you would win then?"

John regarded him with frank astonishment. "Lord Parham, perhaps you don't know what I have been doing these last decades. When I was fifteen, I was already a gun captain of an India-bound brig. I remember aiming a twelve-pounder at the main topmast of Malay pirates in the middle of a typhoon, and hitting it square enough to bring it down. I assure you, a man standing still at twelve paces poses no great challenge to me."

"You wouldn't have had to kill him."

"Well, I don't play at killing either, and I warrant I've seen more of it than he has. He wanted me to challenge him, or, more likely, he wanted me not to challenge him. I don't know why. But if—if being a gentleman means helping him commit suicide, I beg off. Jessica."

Jessica started. She had been hanging back, trying to

remain inconspicuous so that her uncle wouldn't order her out. "Yes?"

"Come see what I found for you."

As Jessica approached, she glanced back at her uncle. He was holding up his finger, as if he meant to make another comment. But then he shook his head. The issue of duelling was closed. Just as well. It was absurd to think of John shooting Mr. Wiley, however much he deserved it, or to believe that refusal to do so constituted cowardice. She had seen how quick John was with a dagger, and knew he must be just as handy with a pistol. Her uncle, of course, was probably too hidebound to consider that sometimes duelling would be the *dishonorable* action.

From his coat pocket, John brought a brown-paper wrapped parcel and handed it to her. The string was tied in an elaborate nautical knot, and after a moment or two of fumbling she gave it back. With a grin he pulled a loop and the knot fell apart. He tore off the paper to reveal a neat, quarto-sized volume bound in blue leather.

"*The Forced Marriage,*" Jessica read from the spine. "Oh, it's another play by Aphra Behn! Where did you find it?"

"Pulton's, down by Printer's Alley. Look at the frontispiece."

She opened the book to the first page. There, scrawled across it, was the name John Dryden. She knew a bit of disappointment, that he hadn't added some sentimental or provocative message above his signature. "Thank you, John. You might add the date there, you know."

"Add the date? Why? You don't think—Jessica, that's not my hand."

"You mean—you mean this is the *other* John Dryden's

copy? The poet's? Oh!" She turned back to the signature and traced it with her finger. "He was a friend of Mrs. Behn, wasn't he? Perhaps she gave this to him." She paged through it, searching for the annotations that were the mark of an enthusiastic reader. "Look, he's marked this passage." Heat rose in her cheeks as she scanned the page. "And I can imagine why. My word." She closed the book, glancing back at her uncle with a laugh, glad John was intuitive enough not to ask her to read it aloud. "Thank you. This will be quite an addition to my collection. Not the Parham, I mean. I've started my own little library."

"The Seton collection?"

"Oh, I like that. The Seton collection. It's rather eclectic, right now, because I haven't decided what my specialty will be. Perhaps it should be women writers. I've got several works by Frenchwomen—Marie de Pisan and Madelaine De Scudery. Do you know of any collectors who focus on that area?"

John's eyes narrowed as he considered the question. His remoteness was gone, along with any lingering tension from the confrontation with Mr. Wiley. Jessica bent her head to hide her smile and pretended to examine the book's binding. She was good at diverting him, at drawing him out. It took only a puzzle.

"None that I know. That would give you an advantage. If you chose an area such as early Caxton works, you'd have to compete for your acquisitions, which drives the price up considerably. And, truth to tell, it won't take you long to get a comprehensive selection, with so few women writers getting into print. To supplement it, you might look for collections of letters, or private diaries, which wouldn't be printed. I can keep a watch for you, if you like." John frowned thoughtfully and started counting off likely authors on his fingers.

"Hannah More—very recent, but that makes her first editions easy to locate."

"Elizabeth Inchbald."

"Anne Bradstreet, the American poet."

"Suzanne Centlivre."

"Aphra, of course. You might even find theatre promptbooks, since she came after the Great Fire. And—well, I might be able to locate with an odd poem or two by Queen Elizabeth—and they would be odd. She thought meter should submit to royal command."

Jessica declared laughingly, "I'd settle for her signature on an official document! Queen Elizabeth!"

They were so involved in planning the new Seton Collection of Continental and British Female Literature that Jessica almost forgot her uncle, sitting silent on the settee. Guiltily, she turned to him with a smile. "I'm sorry, Uncle. We must be boring you terribly."

Uncle Emory shook his head and rose. "No, no. You young people go on and converse. I'll just go tell your aunt that the altercation is over and she can come out now." At the door he paused and looked back, and she waited for him to speak the thoughts that were clouding his eyes. But he only repeated, in that oddly indulgent tone, "You young people go on. I'll leave the door open."

In the bustle of getting off to Vauxhall, Jessica gave little thought to her uncle's strange attitude. But when John got out of the carriage at the dock, she asked her aunt, "Is Uncle Emory ailing? He seemed so distracted when we left."

Peering out the window, Aunt Martha gathered up her shawl and reticule. "Oh, it's just that Mr. Wiley. He has been taking Parham aside and whispering to him, and upsetting him. Your uncle is a congenial man, you know, and he doesn't like such goings-on. But it will all

be over soon." She gave her niece's attire an assessing
regard, as if Jessica were yet a naughty child, then nodded her approval. "What a pleasant notion, going to
Vauxhall by boat! And it's a lovely night for it. Now you
remember to thank Sir John specially for arranging
this."

Jessica agreed meekly to mind her manners, and dismissed her uncle's distraction from her mind as they
journeyed to the dock. Their longboat was painted like
a Venetian gondola and poled by an old man in a
striped jersey and black hat with a red ribbon. "Apt,
isn't it," John commented, "since we'll be seeing scenes
from *Merchant of Venice* and *Romeo and Juliet*."

Even Aunt Martha enjoyed the short ride up the
Thames, exclaiming "How pretty!" when they rounded
the bend to see the gardens all lit up with lanterns, like
stars winking in the trees. On this "Italian night," the
dock was covered with a gaily striped awning in Medi-
terranean colors, and porters dressed in bright Borgia-
style doublet and hose leaped up to help the ladies out
of the boat.

"How do you say thank you in Italian?" Aunt Martha
whispered to John when they were all securely ashore.

"Just as you do in English." John tossed a half-crown
to each porter, then smiled down at Lady Parham.
"Grazie e buona sera will do very well."

Aunt Martha repeated this to the porters, conscien-
tiously trying to reproduce John's fluent pronunciation.
They grinned and ducked their heads, one replying,
"And bona sara to you, too, miladies."

Jessica was pleased to see her aunt trying so hard to
get into the fun of the evening, taking John's arm without a demur as they started down the Grand Walk and
making no sharp comments about the couples who kept
veering off into the shadows. She did, of course, remark,

"Vauxhall is rather thin of company, with everyone off in the country," an odd enough observation considering the hundreds of people strolling about the grounds.

But when she added, glancing about, "We needn't worry, need we, with Sir John here to protect us from the riffraff," Jessica wondered if her aunt was more anxious than she let on. She didn't get out much in company anymore, and disliked the dark.

Rather to Jessica's surprise, John kept the stream of conversation steady until the strange amalgamation of Shakespeare and Handel began. She would not have thought him at ease with an older lady, something of a dragon of society. But then, Aunt Martha was hardly forbidding tonight, even in her inevitable black dress, and she even managed to say no more than once or twice that she hadn't been here since before Waterloo.

There was something about Vauxhall that never failed to revive the spirit, some magic that made Jessica forget the artifice involved, rather as she chose to ignore the greasepaint and wigs on the actors pretending to be Shakespeare's creatures on the orchestra platform. While the footlights held the darkness at bay, casting a flickering illusion over the audience, it was easy to pretend that this was Verona or Venice, and that all the world was a stage in a starlit grove in a fragrant garden.

And with John beside her, pouring out champagne (though Aunt Martha archly protested), smiling that wicked smile whenever an actor in the expurgated *Merchant* referred to the character Jessica, it was easy to pretend that the evening would last forever.

Reality, however, encroached, in the unlikely guise of Damien Blake, who after what he termed an arduous search, entered their supper box. After a cursory greeting to her aunt and a nod to John, he sank down on his knees next to Jessica's chair. He was the very picture of a poet, his dark hair artistically disarranged, his cravat carefully casual, his eyes ardent.

"Your uncle told me I would find you here."

It was another indication that John's scheme was working. Uncle Emory wouldn't have directed Damien here if he wasn't looking with greater favor on his suit. Involuntarily Jessica glanced at John and found him regarding her with that ironic look she knew so well. But she hadn't time to speak to him, for Damien was pulling something from his pocket and declaiming.

"I shouldn't have come tonight, except I could wait no longer to present you the meager sum of my endeavors in the wild."

His flourishing presentation of the scroll of poems was marred only by Aunt Martha's remark, "You were in the wild, Damien? Oh, I thought you'd gone to Gloucestershire."

Damien inclined his head slightly at this, then laid the scroll on Jessica's lap. She thanked him, suppressing a worry that the picturesquely blotted ink on the cover would run off on her favorite silver gown. "How nice of you, Damien. And after you sent me that lovely sonnet too." John, she saw at a glance, had resumed his conversation with her aunt, and was ignoring Damien with every fibre of his being.

"How could I do less!" Damien possessed himself of her hand, exclaiming over it, "After all, you are my very inspiration, my muse, my reason for writing! Every night I would gaze up at the moon and dream of your perfect face, my very own Luna."

She wasn't sure she should be flattered to be called moon-faced, but she supposed she was being unromantic again. Still, a flush rose in her cheeks as she heard John murmur to her aunt, as if in response to a query,

"Oh, I like best Biron's line from *Love's Labour Lost*—you know:

'Taffeta phrases, silken terms precise,
Three-piled hyperboles, spruce affectation,
Figures pedantical.'

Particularly apt in these times of affectation and artifice."

Aunt Martha was nodding as if she agreed completely. "You are right, Sir John. Affectation is a curse of the day. Damien, dear, do get up. Your valet will chide you for mussing your trousers."

"That's true, Damien." Jessica detached her hand from his. "The farce is about to begin. You'd best get back to your box."

"My box? You know me better than that, Jessica," he chided, taking the empty seat next to her. He glanced with some disdain around the box John had hired, with its elaborate plasterwork and a blithe maypole mural by Francis Haydon. "I am standing in the pit, with the rest of the working men."

Once again Jessica's gaze flew to John's eyes, now she saw there a reflection of her own amusement. As the lights dimmed, she smiled at him, and sensed, as he smiled back, a slight lessening of tension in the straight line of his jaw and the set of his shoulders.

The farce was a short scene from an Italian *commedia delle' arte* of the sort popularized by Grimaldi. Jessica couldn't enjoy the clown capering on the stage, for Damien was whispering some sort of nonsense in her ear, and she could just feel John's tension again, crackling across the yard or so that separated them. This is what he wanted, she told herself resentfully—for Damien's suit to be renewed and accepted, so that she could inherit the collection and take possession of the lost play. That must be what she wanted too.

Irritably she shrugged, dislodging Damien's hand from her arm. To cap the ruin of the evening, she could hear her aunt's quiet weeping even over Damien's recitation of some love ode. Sighing, Jessica reached into her reticule and felt around the Aphra Behn book for a handkerchief.

But John was quicker, handing Lady Parham his own handkerchief and taking her hand. Fortunately the clown's billowing costume brushed one of the footlights and caught on fire. He exited hurriedly, pursued by the properties manager, who had pulled down a heavy drapery and was beating on the flames. The show must be over.

"I shall go." Damien rose, politely ignoring her weeping aunt. "I will call on you in the morning, Jessica, to see how you liked my verses."

Distractedly, Jessica nodded. Aunt Martha had quieted now, and was dabbing at her eyes with some embarrassment. "I am sorry, Sir John. It's just the clown. He reminded me of Trevor—you remember, don't you, Jessica, how Trevor used to laugh at the clowns at the fair?"

Jessica murmured something and patted her aunt's knee. It was inadequate, but then, everything was.

Aunt Martha drew a quavering sigh and tried to smile at John. "It's the small things, you know, that remind me."

"Oh, I know," John said unexpectedly. "I remember, after my father died, my mother could hardly abide the sight of strawberries. Poor Sophie—when she and my brother were just married, she prepared the most elaborate pie with the first strawberries, and she was so proud she presented it to Mother to cut after dinner. She didn't understand why Mother burst into tears and ran out of the room."

"She must have loved your father very much," Aunt Martha said, smiling, though the tears still glistened in her eyes.

"She did. And my father loved strawberries. He never would have run out on Sophie's artistry, you may be sure."

"And *you* may be sure, Sir John," Aunt Martha said, "that I know exactly how kind you are being to an old lady. And you shouldn't be, not with a young lady so close at hand."

"The young lady," Jessica said firmly, before John could say whatever it was that was causing that sardonic tilt to his mouth, "thinks it's time to get home. Too many late nights will age me fast."

As they gathered up their belongings, her aunt said, "Do say we will do this again next week, Sir John. I would so enjoy it, and I know Jessica will too."

John located her black shawl on the back of her chair and placed it on her shoulders. "Unfortunately, I must decline, Lady Parham. Tomorrow I will be occupied closing the library, and then I will be leaving town for a few days."

Jessica shot him a sharp glance as they left the box. He has said nothing about leaving town before Damien arrived. Her suspicions were proved correct when he said coolly, "I think Jessica, at least, will be too occupied with her poetry reading to have time for more outings."

Jealousy—was that the result of the success of his scheme? Whatever it was, Jessica knew he would give her no time to debate it, and no time to untangle this latest coil.

Chapter Thirteen

The sins of the father are to be laid upon
the children.

The Merchant of Venice, III, v

When he returned to his flat the next evening, John
found letters from his Weymouth agent and his younger
brother requesting his return. Good, he thought, folding
the letters away. Now that the library was locked up,
and Wiley locked out, John needed an excuse to get
away from town and away from the knot of emotions
he'd gotten himself tied in. Far away in Dorset he could
rest his weary mind and restore his tattered perspective.

He called to Arnie to pack a valise, then sat down at
his desk to send the necessary letters. On the third, after
starting "Dear Jessica," he hesitated and decided not to
list all the warnings he thought she might need to hear.
She was grown, and could take care of herself. She'd
been adroit enough, at least, in playing the card he had
dealt her when he suggested this courtship pretense. Already her uncle was becoming amenable to alternatives
to an unequal marriage.

Of course, that poet Blake was hardly one to negoti-
ate the channel just opened for him. He probably

wouldn't even notice the bouys marking his path. A spar applied to the side of his head might wake him up, but from his appearance, John doubted it. His eyes had that same moonstruck expression that distinguished the sainted Trevor, but Trevor at least had the excuse of being dead.

Damien Blake was just dead to reality. He never noticed the world had changed when he was off writing his sonnets. Jessica's liveliness—her life—would be wasted on him.

But that wasn't John's concern. He dashed off a quick note to say he would be back in a few days. Then he drew a savage line under his signature, and turned his mind to home.

The *Coronale* was still docked at Weymouth, and John planned to sleep aboard. But his brother greeted this intention with incredulity. "Rubbish. Why would you sleep in a hammock, when you can have a perfectly good bed right here?"

John rose from the table to pace across the tiny shop, repressing a shiver at the herbs hanging to dry in the window, the rope of garlic adorning the counter. "I've slept in a hammock most of my life. Besides, my cabin's as big as this room." And pleasanter, he almost added. But he closed his mouth tight over the words; against all sense, his younger brother loved this odiferous place.

"Well, I didn't mean you should sleep *here*, did I? I meant in the house. Sophie's expecting you, and the youngsters are speculating what you brought them from town." Dennis glanced down at the papers he kept rearranging, and added with careful neutrality, "Unless you're staying at the Keep, of course."

"No. If you think it won't put Sophie out—I expect

you'll give me our old room again." They'd shared a room for eleven years, there under the eaves of the old Tudor house on the edge of the village. Last year when John slept there, he'd found tacked to the wall the maps he'd drawn of the seven seas, back when they were only a vision to him. Sophie, bless her heart, knew how to decorate a room.

"Least I can do, considering—considering all you're doing for us." Dennis shuffled the papers again. "I didn't mean to ask you for this, you know. But Sophie insisted you wouldn't mind, even if—even if the shop was meant to be yours."

"Don't be a fool, Denny." John returned to the table, took his seat, held his hand out for the loan papers. He knew gratitude came hard to his brother, and didn't want to prolong the agony.

They'd never gotten on, not in all their lives. John was four years older, and spent most of his youth building sailboats to take out on the bay. For companionship and carpentry he had the socially superior but temperamentally similar Michael Dane, son of the local lord. Dennis he mostly ignored.

And by his twelfth birthday, John was sailing with the free-traders every moonless night.

He could only imagine the rows his parents had over him, on those nights while he was unloading brandy and silk from France and Dennis lay unsleeping in the room under the eaves. Sometimes Denny would still be awake when John crawled in the window after dawn. He was always a worrier, the conscientious one, the dutiful son; John was the black sheep, but withal, their father's favorite.

They both knew that, and both knew the injustice of it, that their father had always meant for John to take over the shop, though Dennis was the one who spent his childhood playing and then working behind the counter. He'd had to learn the medicinal formulas on his own, for his father refused to teach him. John hated the shop, hated the smells, the strings of herbs hanging over the cashbox, the diseased patrons, the confined space, hated the very idea of a shop. And only his avowal to close it down should he be unfortunate enough to inherit it forced his father, nearing death, to leave it to the more deserving son.

So Dennis could hardly be blamed for resenting his elder brother, and for chafing at the necessity to ask a favor, even so minor a one as a loan guarantee. John understood this, and regretted it, knowing that he'd always been too preoccupied playing the prodigal son to be much of a brother. As he scanned the clauses of the agreement, he said, "I'd've lent you the funds myself. I have no doubt that you will make it pay—you've done wonders already in the time you've had the shop."

Dennis nodded grudgingly as John signed his name. It was true; once his father's shade had departed, Dennis had started the modernization the old man had resisted for so long. He'd added a window to let in a bit of light, and installed a Bodley range in the back room for cooking up his potions, and now he meant to add a new room. "Well, business is up, that's clear. I might even have to hire a shop assistant so I can supervise the work on the new room. Sophie won't work for me, you know. Says I order her about enough as it is."

"A domestic tyrant. Just like Father."

Dennis's hands played restlessly over the plans for the new salesroom, and his gaze slid away from his brother towards the counter where their father used to stand. "Not yet. I haven't had enough experience at it. And Sophie'd never put up with it. Do you know," he added suddenly, "I imagine I'll be struck down by a thunderbolt for this, but lately I've realized that Father wasn't a very able businessman, for all he boasted of his acumen."

John was a bit taken aback, for he had always believed he'd inherited Tom Manning's self-professed flair for business. Perhaps he'd gotten it somewhere else after all. "No?"

"No. He never did a real inventory, that I can see, and he left the books all ahoo. And of course, half the village owed him for years worth of medicating, and here he forgave all debts in his will, so they came back to me demanding further credit, saying they'd as good as paid their bills off." He shook his head and folded away the agreement John handed him. "And he always, always preached thrift, and neither borrower nor lender be—well, he never borrowed, but he'd've been able to retire to Brighton had he collected what was owed. He hadn't the least notion of balancing the books, not if it meant dunning his neighbors. No, not any sort of businessman, not the modern sort, anyway."

John smiled wryly as he considered Tom Manning's other boasts. "I expect someday we'll discover he couldn't have thrashed us within an inch of our lives either, as he always threatened."

Indeed, their father never laid an angry hand on either son, no matter how one of them provoked him to it. John was reminded again of his comment that his father was something of a saint, if a particularly irritating and critical sort of saint.

He rose from the table and went to the door. The shop had always felt like a prison, but today, with his father's shade dimming the light from the window, it felt like a dungeon too. "He was a good man," John said. "Look, I've got to check with my first mate to see how the re-coppering took. I'll be back at dinnertime."

Dennis called after him, "Don't forget, Jack, you're in the country now. We dine at six, not midnight as you do in Town."

Dinner went well enough, though in this most familiar of dining rooms John kept expecting his brother to kick him under the table the way he used to, or slip salt into his pudding—Dennis had been a poisonous little brat, at times. But he'd come into his own as *pater familias*, sitting at the head of the table, carving the roast like a surgeon, pouring out wine with a hand far more generous than their father's.

And Sophie was far more socially adept than their mother. A schoolmaster's daughter, she had been brought up in the upper reaches of the middle class. Dennis had been lucky indeed to win her, for she could keep his books and scribe his correspondence and converse easily with all his customers from the princess on down. And she was a dazzling cook besides. The ripening of berries all along the coast had impelled her to dizzying heights tonight, and she blushed when John pronounced her Bakewell tart worthy of Carême.

Tommy and Lilly got to stay up a bit late to try out his gifts, little wind-up goblins from Germany, ghoulish enough in their lurching to delight any child. But as Dennis and Sophie took them off to bed, John felt the walls of the little parlor converge towards him. He called up the stairs that he was going for a ride, though he knew Dennis would probably take offense, presuming he was going to the Oak and Crown for a respite from family life.

Instead, by long habit John rode along the coastal road out of the village, watching the wind ripple across the bay. Though it was still light, all the fishing boats were docked, their sails furled and their masts standing lonely and brave above the harbor.

He reined in when he got to Traders' Point, scanning the horizon for a sail. There were none to be seen, but he knew better than to think that once he left the business, all the other Dorset free-traders had followed suit. Smuggling was too lucrative, and too seductive, to give up without a struggle. He'd had to be blackmailed into quitting himself, and still he missed it whenever the night was especially dark. Even now, he need only close his eyes to relive all those long lazy summer evenings spent out there halfway across the Channel, sitting crosslegged on the deck, tossing dice, drinking brandy out of the bottle, and keeping one eye out for the blockade ships and the excise boats. Waiting for dark.

John shaded his eyes and looked west across the bay. The sun was still glancing off the promontory of Portland Bill. The free-traders would be in hiding for another hour and forty minutes, by his estimate—too long to sit here, reminiscing about his misspent youth.

Around the bend from the point was the long avenue that led to Devlyn Keep, and without much volition he took it. The Keep was a precise brick Palladian house, an anomaly for more than a century here, where Portland stone was the usual material for manors. But an earlier viscount, besotted with his wife who was besotted with the architect Palladio, had torn down the stern old Keep and erected an Italian villa in its place.

There was some courage, he thought again, gazing up at the rotunda from the drive, in surviving despite such utter unsuitability. And there was beauty in it too. Books and sailing ships aside, all beauty needn't be functional.

But that reminded him of Wiley, and his useless, destructive obsession. There might be art in that, too, at least in the utter defiance of sense and tradition and evidence. No one else, not in two centuries, had ever conceived that Shakespeare might not be Shakespeare—no one else had ever dared.

He was still brooding on this when he located Devlyn on the south lawn, tape in hand, measuring out a cricket green in the fading light. John took out of his pocket the doll he had brought from London, and received the reassuring report that Anastasia had not perished for lack of it.

"She's just taken to crawling into our bed whenever she misses the doll." Devlyn held the doll out as if charging it with dereliction of duty. "This has been, you might imagine, rather a trying time on the marital front."

"Oh, I've something for young Jack too."

Devlyn wasn't so happy to see the cricket-ball-sized head, with its wizened face and sparse wiry hair. "For his collection of oddities, I take it?"

"It's not a real shrunken head. It's made of a coconut."

"Jack will be disappointed. Not to mention Tatiana."

"Well, I'll keep the truth to myself, if you will." John tossed it up and caught it again. "It is rather like, you know. I had a shipmate who had one of each sex."

Devlyn sent a gardener off towards the house bearing the gifts, the head held gingerly in two begrimed fingers. "We're in something of a building frenzy this summer. Come down and see the pier I built on the beach."

The new pier was a fine one, extending out fifty feet from the beach, with a sturdy iron rail and davits for several boats. John gave this new addition the attention it deserved, leaning over the rail to estimate the depth of the water. "I'd be able to bring the *Coronale* up here, if you'd cut a channel, you know."

"And what is it you plan to unload, if I cut a channel through?"

"Nothing too objectionable. Nothing to compare with what I used to haul up on the beach there, back in the olden days."

Devlyn was stomping a protruding nail in the boardwalk, but stopped to regard him suspiciously. "Did you really unload contraband on my beach?"

John only shrugged. He hadn't the heart to tell the truth, that while Devlyn had been off at war, this beach had been a major rendezvous for free-traders from two counties. Instead he leaned back against the rail and watched the sun get darker as it slid slowly towards the water. "Another sun gone forever."

Devlyn had found a hammer in a discarded toolbelt and was correcting all the carpenter's other mistakes. He paused in his pounding long enough to glance quizzically at John. "There'll be another tomorrow, you know." With the hammer, he gestured back in the other direction. "It'll appear on that horizon, oh, in ten hours or so. Haven't you ever noticed?"

"I've noticed that sarcasm doesn't become you. And it won't even be eight hours till sun-up. Someone who owns such a fine pier ought to keep better account of the sun times. And the tides too. And for God's sake, could you belay that infernal hammering?"

Devlyn frowned at this uncordial observation, as well he might, considering the fine Chambolles-Musigny he had brought along to christen the pier. But at least he replaced the hammer in the toolbelt and uncorked the wine. "What's ailing you?"

John took the glass and tasted the wine, and decided to forgive his friend for having no nautical training. "I am facing something of a moral dilemma."

"You are?"

Devlyn's all-too-evident surprise annoyed him and cut short John's impulse to confide. "I have them occasionally, you know. They come up every now and again, when I'm between throat slittings and embezzlings. Not that you're likely to recognize a dilemma, as you have gone through life unerringly doing only the right thing."

This got Devlyn's back up again, though he was too good a host to toss his guest over the railing into the surf. They stood there in silence while the clouds turned pink and orange. Devlyn was even better at withdrawing than he was, and stubborner besides, and would likely stand out here till sunup, too polite to go up to bed and too angry to say good night. John saw him looking purposefully at the hammer, and gave up. "I am about to ruin a man, and I don't know if I should warn him."

Devlyn picked up the wine bottle and refreshed both their glasses; it was as close to a signal of accord as he would give. "I'd say the moral dilemma would be— should you ruin him?"

"Ah," John said, "but I have no choice. He is doing great wrong."

He supposed he couldn't blame Devlyn for looking skeptical; Sir Galahad was not John's customary role. *"Incalcuable* wrong," he added.

After another sip or so, Devlyn accepted this. "Why do you want to warn him?"

"So that he can stop doing what he's doing."

"Is that what will happen if you warn him?"

It was this sort of interrogation he valued most from Devlyn—rational and analytical. "I'm not sure. I doubt it will stop him. He's obsessed with this."

"Then will warning him put you in danger?"

John envisioned Wiley, his sharp face and dim eyes, and shook his head. "I don't think so. He's not the violent sort, from what I can see. Just another dotty scholar."

"Right. Like that other—what's his name?—was just another devout priest."

"Alavieri. Oh, but he's different. He cut his eyeteeth on the Machiavelli journals. Hemlock is his favorite drink." John set his glass down on the rail and turned back to the sunset. The dying rays splashed red on the bluest part of the sea, then faded to pink. Fine day tomorrow, he thought. "This one—well, Wiley has hired a thug or two, though where he found them I can't think. Not the worldly sort, you know. And they haven't made any move towards me. He's more likely to confine his viciousness to pen and paper."

"So what damage can he do with pen and paper?"

Slowly John replied, "He might try to get me cashiered from the Royal Society. In fact, I don't doubt he's already started that."

"Will he succeed?"

He shrugged. "I hope not. I've been of more use than him to the Society, I know that much. He writes an occasional monograph about Bacon, but I'm the link to the Regent."

"Is he likely to damage your relationship with the Regent?"

"I can't see how. Wellesley and Castlereagh did their damnedest to discredit me when I worked for them, and they're both at Alavieri's level, when it comes to poisoning. The Regent thought it was amusing, defying his foreign secretaries like that. And Wiley hasn't any credit with the prince."

"What's the worst that can happen, then?"

John thought of the vault, securely locked up, the guards he'd stationed to watch the library, Jessica's eagle eye. "He might try to steal a document. I don't know if he'd be able to get to it. But he might do it anyway, eventually, no matter what I tell him. It's not beyond belief that he would destroy it, did he get his hands on it."

Devlyn probably didn't follow this tangle of possibilities. But he had been a colonel under Wellington, and knew how to summarize options. "So if you tell him what you intend, he likely won't stop what he's doing. Moreover, he might well try to damage your reputation, and it is not inconceivable that he might do injury to you or this document you value. And, of course, you will have lost whatever element of surprise you have right now. So your choice is clear: Do not warn him."

John was taken aback by this curt recommendation. "But you are giving me the pragmatical choice, not the moral one."

"The only moral dilemma is that first one, whether you are right to ruin him. The rest is mere pragmatics— what is the most efficient way to accomplish that. And the safest."

"But, as I told you, Wiley isn't much of a threat. He's—he's rather stupid, in that peculiarly scholarly way. Blinkered. He's caught in the grip of this obsession and thinks nothing of the consequences. He's already revealed all his secrets to me, without even noticing he was doing so."

"Then if he is stupid for making these revelations, what does that make you, if you warn him of your plans?"

John drew himself up straight. "I told you. I thought it made me moral."

Devlyn grinned and held out the wine bottle. "I can tell you haven't much practice at it. Morality doesn't mean martyrdom." He poured the rest of the wine into John's glass—he'd always been the generous sort,

Devlyn had. "Take my advice. Do what you have to do, but do it quietly."

"It sounds rather easier than I imagined," John said doubtfully. "I'd always presumed this would be painful, doing the right thing."

Devlyn laughed shortly and held the bottle upside down over the pier. Only a few drops fell to spot the planks, but that was christening enough. "It's not the deciding that's painful, but the imposition of the decision. I take it you won't be staying long, if you have such urgent business awaiting you in London."

John thought of Wiley, of his promise to Jessica, of the scene with Parham that awaited him. "I shan't be staying long, no. Just the night."

"Here, I hope."

"No," John answered absently, his mind on London. "I'm staying with my brother."

The silence was iron-hard, eloquent. John closed his eyes, but the setting sun blazed red under his eyelids. "Don't start, Devlyn. I am too weary for this."

But Devlyn ignored him. Staring off into the horizon, he said, "Do you know, my solicitor had a new will drawn up for me, since Anastasia's birth. It was the naming of a guardian for the children that stopped me. Naturally, I thought of you. But I didn't know if you would accept the commission."

John set his glass down on the top of the rail and rubbed his forehead with his fist. "You know I would be honored."

"Well, I didn't mean it to be an *honor*, for you to stand guardian to my children. A duty, more."

"Fine. A duty. We have been friends all our lives. That makes it duty enough, I suppose."

"No. I have other *friends*, you know, ones whose lives are more adaptable to childrearing than yours. But I wouldn't want them reared by a friend, when their uncle is available."

"Why are we having this conversation?" John said with exasperation. "We both know how it will end. I told you. Name me as guardian. If the worst happens, and I must, I will take good care of your children. Now have done, will you?"

"No, I won't have done. I thought we *had done* with this years ago, before Tatiana and I married."

John straightened and walked back towards the beach. When he felt the sand under his boots he stopped, but Devlyn remained a dozen feet back on the pier, leaning against the rail. The wind had lightened and the waves were only a whisper, so Devlyn's low voice cut across the distance. "But you couldn't acknowledge it. Couldn't live with it."

"Is that so hard for you to understand? I will not attach scandal to my mother's name. And I will not deny my father."

"For God's sake, John, they're long dead. And besides, you *are* denying your father."

With triumph as well as anger, John seized on this. "That's it, isn't it, for you? This father of yours—why do you think I would want to claim him?"

"You did once. When we were boys. You were the one who brought all this up."

The guilt stirred in him, even after so long. He had been a wild boy, and his father—his real father, the only one he had—was coming the tyrant, as might be expected. And, as might be expected, John had considered alternatives. "That was only because I didn't want the father I had. And there was some glamour in it, some notion of nobility." Sardonically, he added, "I learned better as I grew older, what real nobility is. And it has nothing to do with the sort of father you had."

"Our father's been dead these twenty years—"

"Not *our* father. You see, you insist on that tie. And I won't ever accept that. God! Have you forgotten? How can you forgive him? He left you destitute and alone like a stray dog. I remember stealing food for you, because I knew you'd never do it yourself, till my father found out and took to giving me shillings for you. Poor little Lord Michael, he used to say. Doesn't have a father—"

It was brutal, John realized when Devlyn sucked in his breath and stepped back, pressing against the rail. To remind the man of the boy he had been, an object of pity for his social inferiors—it wasn't fair, and yet it was true.

Then Devlyn forced a laugh, a harsh sound against the gentle surf. "How very like him you are. I never was. Never had that anger you had, that he had. I always forgave. He was a sailor too, do you remember? He used to take his yacht out every summer, until he lost it in a cardgame. You got that from him also. You just don't take your risks on cards."

"You're wrong. You're wrong. I have spent my life doing all I could not to be—No. I won't accept kinship like that."

"Oh, but you did. You've got his signet ring." There was quiet triumph in Devlyn's voice. "It was all he left, and you've got it on now."

"That's not why I took it, and you know it. I never meant to claim kinship with him. Here." John wrenched the ring off. "If it was his, it wasn't yours to give away."

Devlyn caught the ring as it spun through the air. He held it in his fist for a moment, then spun on his heel and hurled it into the water. For an instant it sparked blue in the dying light, then fell with a quiet splash and disappeared.

John reached out as if he could somehow grab it

back. But it was gone, fathoms deep in the dark water. "Michael—"

"God, that hurt." Devlyn's expression was hidden by the sudden dusk, but his tone was almost normal. "I must have thought myself trapped in a melodrama, to do that. But it's done. Good night."

And he strode up the beach path to his house without another word.

The princess was waiting for John in the stableyard, a slight figure in the dimness, a silk shawl trailing heedlessly from her arm. He dismissed the grooms with a jerk of his head; in her usual imperial disregard, Tatiana hadn't even noticed them skulking about, their ears aprick, their hands busy with small tasks.

She couldn't speak English quickly enough to suit, so she slipped into French, and even then sometimes words failed her and she had to make do with angry chops with her hands. But her intent was clear. She was fierce when she loved, and he knew how she loved her husband. "He asks so little—"

"He doesn't ask. He demands. And it's stupid, what he asks, it's trivial, it means nothing."

"It means something to him. And," she leaned forward and grabbed his wrist, "that matters to me. So you must do as he wants."

He wrenched his arm from her grasp and started to saddle his horse. "I know you are used to getting whatever you desire, princess. But this is not your affair. You will only complicate matters, with your high-handed ways."

"No. I will simplify matters." She shoved him out of the way with a small shoulder and efficiently unbuckled the stirrup he had just buckled. "You are not going till you hear what I say."

There was no use arguing with her, if he hoped to leave tonight. Resignedly he stepped back and crossed his arms over his chest. "Say on."

She wasn't expecting such a quick capitulation, and for a moment couldn't put the words together. Finally, she said, "You have another brother, someone bound to you by blood and not mere friendship. But Michael does not. You are all the family he has."

"But I have never wanted that. We were friends. That has been enough for me."

"But not for him. You have always known that, from the first. And you have used that, to suit your own purposes."

"That's not true! What I have, I've earned, my own way—and God knows, he's never thought it the right way."

"Oh, not that." With a wave of her hand she dismissed his ships, his commissions, his acquisitions. "No, you are too proud to use him that way, and you would have got all that regardless, I've no doubt. I mean that you kept him—oh, as a replacement. For that other family that wasn't like you, that never understood you, that you never really wanted. When you wanted understanding, camaraderie—fraternity—you would come to him. And then, when you'd had enough, you'd leave."

He bit back another angry denial, because something she said struck a chord of memory in him. He closed his eyes to the awareness in hers, and laughed bitterly. "I recall—on that voyage with you, when he was losing his heart, I saw it coming. He couldn't even help himself. He said he didn't, but he did. He wanted a family so badly. And I told him I never did, never wanted all that tangle that families bring. I should have been the one orphaned—even now, when I am, it is too tangled for me. But Michael—"

"Yes. He is not like you." The princess reached up to finger the buckle of the bridle, but the mare stirred, disturbed by the jerky motions of the princess's hand on her mane. Tatiana stopped and looked at her hand, then let it drop to her side. "He wants connection. He can't cut off as you do, not once he's committed. He can't leave it behind as you do."

"But I meant for you to do that. That is *your* job—to give him that family. To make him happy."

"Then I will."

All the pleading had vanished from her voice. He had never seen her so cold, so remote, not in all the years they had been friends. "As much as I love you, John, I think he is right now to end the debate. Perhaps it is only boyish sentimentality after all to want a brother. But he'll never be like you, nor like his father. He cannot come and go with his caring. I know he won't tell you—he is too much the gentleman. But I have no such scruples. He will do better without your friendship. So don't visit any more."

"Tatiana—"

He thought for a moment that her iron control would break, that she would give that tremulous smile and say, "Well, perhaps not." But instead she only nodded, stepped back from the saddle, and said with regal cool, "You may go."

Chapter Fourteen

And how can that be true love
which is falsely attempted?
Love is a familiar; love is a devil;
there is no evil angel but love.

Love's Labour Lost, I, ii

The guard at the library door snapped to attention when John came down the corridor. The brother of John's boatswain, Petrus was a powerful man whose coat gapped open to show a knife in his belt. "There you are, Cap'n. Been expecting you anytime. T'other one, the one with spectacles, just tried to pass me by."

"Wiley? The librarian? He was supposed to have left town."

"Well, he hasn't, that's for certain. Been here every morning since you left, trying to get in. Offered me fifty pounds, he did."

"Fifty pounds. Well, there'll be that much for you in bonus, then."

"No need for that, Cap'n." Petrus scuffed his foot against the sundusted parquet floor, absurdly abashed for a man of his bulk. "It's enough to have a position at all. Ha'en't any work at carpentry since I lost my hand."

"You kept the knifehand, and that's what I need from you. I don't mean for you to use it, you know. Just take the knife out for a polish next time Wiley comes up, will you?"

"Yessir. I've been sleeping here, you know, just down the hall there on that bench. Lord Parham said it was best. Not that the night man isn't a good man, but—"

"But fifty pounds is fifty pounds. Well, tell the night man he'll have it, and his skin still too, if Wiley's kept out of here till the twenty-third."

John brought out his ring of keys and unlocked the two new locks on the library door. So as not to cause suspicion, he ought to have someone with him as he went through the collection, but he didn't want to take Petrus from the door. He could send for Jessica, he supposed, but he wasn't in any mood to see her.

"Come inside here, will you, Petrus?"

He locked the door behind the guard. "Now stand over here in the entrance and watch me as I go back. I want to check on the vault, but I want you as a witness that I didn't take anything off the shelves."

Petrus shook his head, as if this was a jest. "You wouldn't do that, Captain. I know that."

John couldn't help but be pleased with this testimonial, however misguided it was. "Well, watch me anyway. Wiley's likely to complain if I'm back here alone."

The wax on the vault's locks was unbroken, and the bulky shapes inside seemed unmoved. John stared at the block that held the treasure and thought, only eighteen more days. Then I'll see it, and hold it in my hands—and hand it to Jessica.

And, if all went well in his interview with Parham today, she would be able to keep it.

The thought of how he was going to accomplish that brought the bile to his throat. He swallowed hard and went out to ask permission to pay his addresses to Jessica.

Fortunately, Parham was waiting in the drawing room, a room with space enough to pace in. Not that John meant to pace, or that, after so long as a sailor, he had developed a fear of enclosed spaces. But he needed some distance between him and Parham, the whole expanse of the Persian carpet perhaps, to disguise any tension he couldn't suppress.

Parham was all that was gracious, gesturing him towards a chair, offering him cigars and brandy. John refused the smoke but accepted the drink. As he waited for the familiar warmth to soothe his unfamiliarly frayed nerves, he noted that Parham was quite genial. The prospect of refusing another suitor no doubt put him in a fine mood.

In fact, Parham got the process going expeditiously. "I expect you want to speak to me about my niece."

"Yes." I should be standing, John thought distractedly, and rose. "I would like your permission to pay my addresses to your niece." That wasn't so hard. "I know I'm not the sort of husband you would wish for her." That was hard. The rest was easier, since he had written it down this morning and memorized it. "But my regard for her is so strong that I felt impelled to approach you, even knowing that you would not grant my request."

"You knew that already, did you?" Parham jerked his head towards the abandoned chair. "Sit down, young man. I don't like staring up at you. So why is it, do you think, that you're not good enough for my niece?"

Though he had expected nothing else, John knew a sharp sense of injustice. Not good enough, was he? If he hadn't a promise to fulfill, he might argue with that characterization. But it mattered naught. He might reject those values and this sort of people, but not before they rejected him.

So he resumed his seat, trying to damp down his anger. Let Parham have his fun. If it helped to secure Jessica's inheritance, John would enumerate what Parham already knew. "First there's my background. I've never made any secret that I was of the—" He started to say "lower classes," but then he remembered his mother and her two-story brick house, the carriage his father bought near the end of his life, the pride they took in those achievements. "Of the middle class."

"Yes, I recall. Apothecary, am I right? You grew up above the shop, did you?"

"No, we had a house and acreage outside the village. My father had a shop. My brother owns it now."

"Salt of the earth, your brother, I suppose?"

"Dennis? No. He's a businessman, not a farmer."

"I meant, a sturdy, stalwart, English sort."

"Well, yes, I suppose." He couldn't stay seated. No pacing, he told himself, so he walked to the window and opened the drapes. The sunlight was dense, filtered through the London soot, and warm against his face.

"I was wondering. You look foreign to me. Sound it a bit, too, but I suppose it's all that travelling you do. Glad to hear your family is British to the bone."

"Right. British to the bone." John pushed open the casement and let the air fill his lungs, buoying up more differences between him and the poet. "I work for a living. I expect to do so for the rest of my life."

"You look like you need some sort of occupation. Can't stay still for a moment, can you? Jessica's the same way. Tires me out just to watch her. You don't need to work, though, do you?"

John cranked the window closed again and leaned

back against the sill, turning back to look at Parham. There was no hostility in the man, but somehow that made the casual dismissal sting all the more. "I suppose not. I have seven ships carrying finished goods, mostly to the New World. There's enough in that to keep me. But—but I can't imagine giving up command of the *Coronale*. She's the one that carries the art I buy."

"The art you buy for the Regent."

"Among others."

"Unusual trade, that. Shipping art."

Since Parham had brought up that significant word, "trade," John had nothing more to add. But Parham cleared his throat and poured another glass of brandy. "I understand you had another trade too."

Self-abnegation must become easier with practice, because now the words came trippingly to John's tongue. "I was a free-trader for years. That's how I acquired the ships. The usual South coast trade—silk, brandy. Whiskey and wool going back. And art."

Parham held up his glass with a hint of pride. "This is smuggled cognac."

"I know. Out of Shelmerston, I wager." Anger made him cruel; he came over and picked up the decanter and held it up to the light. "You're being taken, you know. This isn't from Charente, but further south."

"What does that mean?"

"It's not real cognac." John set the decanter back on the table and restoppered it. "It's not bad brandy, but the grapes are from Bordeaux, I think."

This disspirited Parham so much he could hardly rouse himself to continue the inquisition. But sulkily he said, "I hear you had another profession too."

John stepped back, wary again. "What's that?"

"With the Foreign Office."

That wasn't generally known, even among John's friends and crew, none of whom were the sort to gossip. More likely it came from the FO, which had never been good at keeping secrets. "I had a letter of marque, letting me take enemy ships. But most of us got one, by hook or crook. Cut down on the competition from the other side of the Channel."

Parham laid a finger alongside his nose and nodded sagely. "I understand. Can't divulge national secrets. Very patriotic of you."

Irritated, John said, "I'm not patriotic. I told you, harassing the enemy is good business practice."

"But you weren't paid, now, were you? Not for the Foreign Office work."

John wasn't about to admit that he had anything to do with the Foreign Office, but he might have retorted that his payment was his freedom. Smuggling was punishable by deportation or hanging, and he liked both his homeland and his neck too much to turn down his government's commission. And there was the risk too—that was a form of payment. "I try to avoid associating with the British government as much as possible."

"But that's why you got the title, isn't it? For that patriotic work you won't admit you did."

This, at least, was one mistake he could correct. "No. I forgave a debt, that's all."

"Must have been quite a debt."

"It was."

"Kind of you. It's cruel, how whenever Prinny spends a bit of funds, those Radicals tie the pursestrings and try to foment revolution."

It wasn't just the Radicals, of course, who objected to Prinny's artistic extravagance. But John wasn't about to get into a debate on royal privileges. He just wanted out of this prison of a room. "As you say. At any rate, a new title hasn't any currency anyway, on the usual account books, no matter how it's acquired."

"Well, that new Duke of Wellington might disagree!" Parham laughed merrily at this, one hand on his chest. "A title's a title. In another generation, no one will remember why you got it. I've always suspected the first Baron Parham was raised for procuring Charles I some likely wenches."

"Have we done now?"

"Done? You're not finished, are you? No other objections to your suit?"

This was too much to abide. "Haven't you heard enough?" With heavy irony, John held up his hand and began counting off on his fingers. "One. Wrong class. Two. Wrong profession—that is, any profession at all. Three, criminal background. Four, havey-cavey wartime doings, real or imagined. That's all I've got."

"What about your irregular birth?"

John stilled his restless pacing, planting his feet firmly as if the carpet were the deck of a ship on treacherous seas. "My birth was perfectly regular. I survived, my mother survived."

"A bit early, weren't you?"

John had been expecting something of the sort, but this euphemism was simultaneously too delicate and too crude. "Say what you mean, Parham."

Parham flushed and looked down at his brandy glass. "Didn't mean to give you offense. Just heard your father was some lord."

"I told you. My father was an apothecary. Tom Manning. I care naught for any lord."

"Right. I understand." Parham added heartily, "Appreciate such loyalty. But—but Devlyn. The current one, not—not his father. The one married to the princess."

As far as apology went, it was the best John was likely to get. So he stopped halfway to the door. "What about him?"

"Do you get on well with him?"

"Devlyn?" John shoved that last encounter to the back of his mind. "We grew up together."

"You're friendly, then."

"What are you getting at?"

"The princess. Are you, ummm, *friends* with her too?"

It took a moment for the rage to subside enough for John to realize that Parham, in his clumsy way, was only angling for an introduction, not suggesting the unimaginable. "The princess occasionally gifts me with a bit of royal approval, I suppose."

"You see them in London, ever, the Devlyns?"

"Yes."

"Never met the princess, my wife and I. Don't run in those circles, and then, well, Lady Parham hasn't been getting about much. But to meet the pretty princess . . . she'd go out for that. Even to a ball, I think."

John sighed, thinking of Lady Parham and her lugubrious black gowns and her lasting lamentation. If anyone could cheer her, it would be Tatiana, she of the blinding smiles. "Perhaps when the Devlyns are next in Town, they'll give a party. The princess does love to give parties."

"And—" delicately Parham hitched his trouser legs up and leaned forward. "And Lady Parham will receive an invitation?"

Why John should be expected to cater so to the family that was set to reject him, he didn't know. But here he was, tangled up with these tenacious Setons. And it was a minor enough request, he supposed. "I will mention her name to the princess. Now can we get on with it? I've an appointment at two."

Parham straightened in outraged affront. "Wait just a minute, young man. I don't suppose you know much about this hand-seeking business, but I have been through it many times with Jessica's other suitors. You can't expect just to say your piece and go on to your other appointments. There's a certain ritual to these affairs. For instance, I haven't asked you yet why I shouldn't accuse you of fortune hunting."

"Fortune hunting?" Parham had enough reasons to prefer the poet. John wasn't about to start making them up. "No. I've got plenty of my own funds. There's a hundred thousand or so just in the ships and their cargo, and another hundred thousand probably in art. And stocks on the 'Change. I don't need to marry an heiress."

"Don't you want the Parham collection?"

"That's Jessica's. If your brother had a particle of sense, he would have left it to her outright. She'll do well by it, if she gets it."

"You'd like to advise her on it, though, wouldn't you?"

John kept a stubborn silence. Jessica and he had their own agreement; Parham didn't need to know about it.

"Come, Dryden, she's a bright girl, but she hasn't any experience. You'd like to counsel her, wouldn't you?"

"If she needs advice, I'll give it to her."

"You don't think that would be a trifle awkward, considering your feelings toward her?"

John turned away, but he could feel Parham's scrutiny on his back. "I'll learn to live with it."

"What are your feelings, by the way?"

There was a limit to duty, and he had fulfilled it. Parham had gotten his pleasure; Jessica no doubt would get her poet. John just wanted out. "My feelings are of the usual sort."

"Usual? That's all?"

Two more minutes, that's all he'd stay. John started counting off the seconds, watching the spasmodic little hand on the mantle clock. It said twenty-nine when he said thirty. Two seconds lost every minute; that would be two minutes every hour. A very poor chronometer—

"Dryden, are you paying attention? I said, I don't think your feelings are the usual sort at all."

"You needn't call me a liar on top of all the rest."

"Now, boy, take that scowl off your face. I'm not calling you a liar. A lover, that's all. You want to tell me, don't you, that if I refuse you you'll run off with her anyway. Even if she wouldn't agree—and she wouldn't. She can't afford my disapproval."

The two minutes up, John started for the door. But Parham's genial voice followed him. "I can sense these things, you know. Not many men would subject themselves to this kind of humiliation, you know, not a man with your kind of pride. There's a sacrifice involved there, don't you think I don't know it. You'd like to fling all my questions back in my face, wouldn't you, and just walk out. But you won't. Have to play it out, don't you? For her sake."

"No." John got his hand on the doorknob, but didn't turn it. He just stared at his scarred hand, fisted around it. "She deserves to inherit the library. You know that. It means the world to her. She's played by these rules of yours. Now it's time to let her win."

"You're right." Parham rose and approached him, nodding all the way. "All right, young man. You have my consent. You'd best get down and post those banns. If you do it right away, you can be wed before her birthday."

Anguish, injustice—these vanished into shock. He whirled around. "You mean—wait. What about the poet?"

"Blake?" Parham shook his head. "No. His feelings for my niece really are the usual sort, however he pretties them up in verse. And he knows her naught, does he, though he's known her all her life. Gives her sonnets, he does. You bring her old books. She ought to prefer the other, I suppose, but Jessica doesn't like to do as she ought. She wants the old books. You know her better."

"But—" It was all too much to take in, this hearty Parham clapping him on the back, this unrequested consent—well, not unrequested, but undreamed.

"No time to waste, lad. She's outside in the garden, I think. Go make your proposal to her. Not that she's likely to turn you down, with the collection at stake. But this is a ritual, and you have to play it out."

He kept hearing that as he walked to the garden— "Not that she's likely to turn you down, with the collection at stake." Parham had gone mad, of course, approving this marriage, but in that much he was correct. Jessica couldn't afford to refuse. And John wouldn't let her, were she mad enough to try.

The sunlight glancing off her hair was like a beacon, lighting his way to shore. He located her sitting on a blanket in the little arbor, frowning at a book—the Hannah More book, with Aphra inside. When she saw him she smiled, and he saw in her face relief mixed with trepidation. What was she worried about? She would get her wish, one of them anyway.

Mindful of eavesdroppers among the gardeners yanking weeds, he pulled her to her feet and out to a distant corner of the garden. In a low angry voice he explained that he had just met with Parham about their proposed marriage.

She sat down hard on a stone bench. "Proposed? John, I never meant for you to do that. You said you would—you would pretend to *court* me, not propose marriage. Why did you do that? It must have been horrid."

"It was. It was." Her confusion made him angry, if he needed any more excuse for that. "I thought you understood. I had to request your hand to force *his* hand. To force him to do better for you than this, if he cared at all for you."

"But you shouldn't have done it. I didn't want him to insult you again."

Pity was worse than the rest. "I complete my contracts, and I will complete this new one also." Furious now, he grabbed her hand. "I haven't a ring yet, but I'll get one this afternoon."

"A ring?" She shook her head, as if he had awakened her from a deep sleep, and focused all her attention on the hand that held hers. "Oh, I see. You've lost your ring."

Through gritted teeth, he said, "I didn't lose the ring. It's just gone. And I'm not talking of that ring anyway, but a betrothal ring. I'll post the banns this afternoon. You'll want St. George in Hanover Square, I make no doubt."

"You don't want—John, what are you saying?"

"I'm *saying*—" He broke off and took a deep breath to cool off his voice. "Your uncle approved my suit. God knows why. Lunacy runs in your family, I've always suspected. So we'll have to marry."

She went utterly still, and savagely he realized he'd made a hash of it, that she hadn't understood until just then that they would be marrying. "Do you realize what

I'm saying? Your uncle approved it. We'll marry. You'll get the collection."

"John, I didn't mean for this to happen, you know it."

"It happened. Accept it. You have no choice in the matter anyway. He's not going to approve the poet now."

"No choice?" She was still very quiet, still staring down at his hand. She rubbed with her thumb at the white circle on his ring finger, as if it were just paint and would come off with a bit of effort.

He jerked his hand away and rose. "No. I'm not going to be the cause of you losing your inheritance. And I'm not going to have it said that my behavior was less than that of a gentleman. I'll call on you tomorrow to get the arrangements started."

When he looked back from the garden path, she was still sitting there, her full mouth more mutinous now. But there was still that dazed look in her eyes, as if he'd struck her instead of proposed to her. He felt a stirring of guilt. She deserved better, he supposed, than all this. Tomorrow he would take time to make it up to her, to explain all the benefits of this arrangement, to assure her he'd do his best to make her happy.

But today he had to find a church and post the banns.

He was so preoccupied that he hardly heard the carriage lurch to a halt beside him. But he turned when he heard someone leap out of the hackney and call his name. He had just an instant to see the cool intent in the other man's eyes and reach for his knife. But an instant wasn't long enough. The assailant already had his truncheon lifted, so it was only a matter of bringing it down with sufficient force. And that the did, connecting smartly with John's head. John's last thought was regret

. . . that he hadn't turned back to conciliate Jessica, that she hadn't run after him to witness this, that he wouldn't get the banns posted this afternoon after all.

Chapter Fifteen

I have great comfort from this fellow;
Methinks he hath no drowning mark upon him;
His complexion is perfect gallows.
Stand fast, good fate, to his hanging!
. . . . If he be not borned to be hanged,
our case is miserable.

The Tempest, I, i

Suddenly it was morning, the sun appearing from the gray sea with an almost audible pop. Dawn came early and swift in the northern seas, John recalled, flexing his aching hands on the ship's wheel. Another night gone, another day begun, and London and Jessica were ever farther behind him.

Six days out of Chatham, the *Araminta* (a sloop, they called her, in that absurd argot of the Royal Navy; with her two masts, she was a brig by any other name) was being shoved slowly easterly, into the sun, by a wicked finger of a wind. Her captain wasn't much of a navigator, and the master had taken ill and been left behind in port, so there was little chance the sloop would be put through the complex maneuvers that might send it more truly northward.

John knew this route well, having made several trips to St. Petersburg on behalf of the Foreign Office, and he might have been able to plot a better course. But he was hardly going to volunteer to move them farther faster. In fact, he had spent the night making minute adjustments in his steering to slow the sloop's progress, navigating by the stars and the direction of the spray against his face. He might have been hanged for this, except the captain was an amiable dunce who didn't know enough about his vessel to know when it was being reined in.

But John would never get back to London at this rate. Ever since he had awakened four days ago in the sickbay, with an opium hangover and the clothes of a quartermaster named Jem Mercer, he had thought of nothing but Jessica, waiting there for him to come back and wed her. Now her birthday was less than a fortnight away and he was halfway to Denmark, filling the role of another man.

At least it was a slow progress, given the erratic and unreliable breezes here on the continental shelf that linked Britain to the rest of Europe. This was the shallowest of seas, with treacherous sandbanks and shoals even a hundred miles from land. John gazed ahead into the pale dawn, scanning for a chance to ground the sloop. But he knew he couldn't do it. He loved ships too much to deliberately damage one. He'd have to find another way home.

At eight bells, the dawn quiet was broken by the boatswain's piping and the thunder of feet as the starboard watch came on deck. Another quartermaster's mate came up behind him and checked the log, squinting to see the chalk marks in the early light. "Relieving you, Mercer. Easy night of it, I hope."

John had long since given up declaring that he wasn't Jem Mercer, able-bodied seaman and quartermaster's mate on transfer from the *Berendt*. A ship's company tolerated all sorts of eccentricities, and so they took little note of John's insistence that he commanded his own ship, or that he was an art dealer in London and not a quartermaster's mate at all. Occasionally a sailor would waggle a finger at his temple, pantomiming a lunatic, but no one even blinked at John's demand to be sent home immediately. This was the softest of walls, but as effective as brick in preventing his return.

"Easy enough. We've made about three knots steadily, but are a bit off-course, I think; you might bear a degree or two southerly. Shallow water, this."

"And chill." Genially, his replacement eased him aside and took over the wheel. "Go on below till breakfast, lad. And before you get into the hammock, you change into dry clothes, won't you? Wouldn't want you to take a chill from the spray."

It was annoying to be treated as a dimwit, but he supposed that he had invited it with his behavior early in the week, when the residue of concussion and rage had made him refuse even to eat. That had ended when he realized malnutrition could be a liability. Now he was eating again, but lightly. He hoarded the extra biscuits and salt-pork, hiding the bundle of food in an old cask, ready for the time he made his escape.

As the lowliest of the sailors crawled around him, holystoning the deck, John walked back across the stern, pulling his salt-wet shirt off over his head. Leaning on the rail, he gazed at the wake spreading out behind them like a bird's tail feathers. He imagined it leading all the way back to England, an unbroken line between him and Jessica.

"Lend a hand, mate," someone called from below. The captain's launch, its single sail furled tight, was tethered directly under the stern. A gunner's mate clung one-handed to the ropes a few feet down the hull, holding out a fishing net squirming with fish. John grabbed the net and hauled it aboard as the other sailor scrambled nimbly onto deck. "Best fishing waters in the north. We'll breakfast well this morning."

John watched him go below, then looked back at the launch, trailing behind in the middle of the wake. It was a capacious enough boat, meant for a four-man crew but sailable by one, as the fisherman had just proved. He turned and looked into the sun, calculating silently from the last reckoning of their position. They'd travelled two hundred thirty miles from home, give or take a league or so. It was a long, difficult voyage back, but John knew his strengths and thought he could do it. Captain Bligh, after all, sailed ten times that far in an open boat, across cannibal-infested waters.

It was just a matter of good luck and good sailing skills, and John knew he possessed at least one of those. He grabbed up his shirt and headed below decks to the tiny rectangle of floor reserved for his—or rather, Jem Mercer's—seachest. All around him the men of the larboard watch were slinging hammocks, ready for a few hours sleep before breakfast was piped in the forenoon watch. Turning his back to block their view, John grabbed up a change of clothes, a boat cloak, and a few other essentials and stuffed them in an oilcloth bag. It was only a matter of minutes before the boat crew pulled in the launch, so he did no more than retrieve his food hoard and sling a jug of water from a leather thong over his shoulder before returning to the stern.

The infernal noise of thirty men pumicing a deck drowned out the sound of John's escape. Dropping down into the boat, he undid the knots that connected it to the *Araminta*. He crouched down near the tiller, waiting till he saw the watch, high above on the mast, train his spyglass eastward. Then, as silently as he could, he fixed the oars and began rowing away from the ship.

He had pulled all the way out of the wake, away from the sloop's powerful draw, before the man on watch turned back. John knew to the instant when he had been spotted, and was ready for the pursuit when the cry of "On deck!" blazed over the distance. Abandoning any attempt at secrecy, he set the sail to take the best advantage of the fleeting breeze.

The sloop was small enough that turning about was the work of a few moments, and even as John added his rowing to the force granted by the wind, he knew it was futile. His luck was out, as it had been for a month or more. Still he kept rowing, stopping only to wipe the seawater out of his eyes or to work the tiller. He mostly kept his head down, concentrating on the arduous task. But when a shadow cut off the light of the rising sun, he looked up. The sloop bore down on him like a great seabird, canvas spread like wings and blocking the sun.

His muscles burned so much that he could only swing an oar at the boathook as it caught his prow. Over the roaring of blood in his ears, he could hear the cheers of his shipmates. He didn't know, and didn't care, if they cheered him or the marines who grabbed his aching arms and hauled him back on board.

The captain, that genial fool, was waiting at the rail when John was tossed aboard. He was doing his best to look like an Old Testament prophet of wrath, but his face didn't mold into wrathful lines. "Don't you know desertion's a hanging offense? I could have you flogged around the fleet!" There was a murmur from the assembled ship's company, of approval or disapproval even the captain didn't seem to know. "We punish on Tuesday. Shackle him until then."

One marine consoled John, as they dragged him

down the stairs, "Don't you be worriting none, mate. The captain's not a hanging sort. And if he means to punish you Tuesday, it won't be flogging around the fleet neither. We shan't catch up to the fleet till the Skagerrak at least. A dozen stripes, he might order you. But he's not the sort to hurt a poor loon like you."

A poor loon like you. John laughed weakly as he was left alone in the damp hold, the shackles chill and wet around his wrists and ankles. He supposed he should be grateful for the sympathy of his shipmates, and he was, especially when several appeared during the course of the next few hours to slip him a cup of grog or an ungnawed seabiscuit. It was just so ironic, that all his life he had lived on his wits, put all his pride into his sharp intellect—and now everyone thought him a lunatic.

And after a day or so, he decided he might become one. The hold was an unpleasant place, with water sloshing in whenever the sea got rough and the old timbers groaned, with rats the size of cats eying him speculatively, with the shackles and the salt wearing holes in his wrists. When his lamp sputtered out after a few hours, the darkness dug into his eyes as the damp dug into his bones. But he could live with that. He'd suffered nearly as much indignity as a boy in a China-bound privateering vessel.

No, it was the realization that he was indeed a fool that drove him nearly to despair. He had underestimated Wiley. And given his experience with other collectors, other obsessives, John should have known better. He had presumed that Wiley wasn't a killer, and so dismissed him as any kind of physical threat. He had presumed that his vast experience would protect him, but he had never imagined being so distracted by his emotions that he wouldn't hear an approaching attacker in time to parry him. It was a mental mistake, and he was being properly punished for it. The injustice of it was, though, that Jessica was being punished too, and she was blameless in this.

What would she do, when she realized he was gone? She would suspect right away that his pre-wedding absence was involuntary. Would she be valiant and foolish and confront Wiley? Or would she turn pragmatic and persuade her uncle to approve another marriage—to that poet, probably?

Such speculations were likely to drive him mad, so instead he spent the last night huddled in a boat cloak against the damp, thinking about flogging. They punished at noon, when the sun was high and blazing, the marine had told him. After six lashes, the captain would call a temporary halt to give the flogged man a few gulps of water. Then it would begin again.

In the utter darkness of the hold, he felt around on the floor for the battered tin jug that held his water ration. He plunged his hand into it, closing his fingers to catch the insects as the water ran through, then flinging them away into the darkness. He drank as much as he could swallow, choosing to blame the crawling sensation down his throat on the rancid taste.

Flogging could be no worse than this.

He had never been flogged, and never flogged either. But then, he'd never been in the Navy. Privateering crews were a practical lot, and sailed by choice, not conscription. To enforce appropriate behavior, the captain needed only to threaten to leave an unruly crewman at the next port of call without any prize money.

It wouldn't be so bad, he told himself as the marines returned Tuesday morning to take him above. A dozen stripes, that's all, the marine assured him again, pushing John's head down so he wouldn't hit the hatchway. He spoke loudly over the singing of the sails, "It won't hurt so much after the sixth or seventh lash, that's what I hear."

After days in the hold, the sun blazing off the water blinded John. Involuntarily his eyes closed to ward off the glare, and only the rough guidance of the marines got him across the deck to the gangway, where they unshackled his arms. Once the pain from his raw wrists faded, he forced open his eyes. The deck was crowded by both watches, ragged rows of his shipmates watching him with curiosity and sympathy and perhaps morbid enjoyment of his humiliation. The officers were there too, assembled behind the captain in his full-dress uniform: the sole lieutenant looking young and bored, the two little midshipmen each with a hand on his blade, just in case the marines couldn't handle the felon alone.

Before him was a metal grating, beside it the burly boatswain's mate fondling a cat-o'-nine-tails. John focused on the leather whip, counting the tails as the mate stroked each one. It was true, there were nine of them, thin and sharp and coated with something that looked like tar.

The boatswain's mate grinned at him, revealing two missing teeth. John narrowed his eyes against the light, focusing all his ill will on that mouth gaping in an insolent grin. The grin faltered, fell off, and the mate went back to combing his cat.

The captain of the marines raised his hand. The Navy had a ceremony for everything, John was learning, even for flogging a man. The ship's corporal shaded his eyes and read aloud from a sheet gripped hard against the wind's grasp. "Desertion. Theft of a boat."

"What say you to these charges, Mercer?"

John rubbed his wrist and said wearily, "I am not

Mercer. I am not of the Royal Navy, and thus I cannot be guilty of desertion."

The captain ignored this, as John knew he would. "He is in your division, Mr. Polter. Have you anything to say for him?"

The lieutenant, prodded by a midshipman's elbow, shook himself awake. "Sir, he's a good man at the wheel, notwithstanding his mental instability. Takes a good noon reckoning, and seems to know these waters well. I wouldn't want to lose him for long, what with the master left behind."

The captain nodded judiciously. "Good point, Mr. Polter. Just a dozen lashes, then, Barrett. And do make it quick. The hands will want their dinner."

John's personal marines seized him, one on each arm, and yanked his shirt off over his head. There was a roll of drums, the lonely whine of a pipe, as John's hands were bound to the grating with leather ropes. The marine shoved at his bared back, so that he was pressed face first against the hot metal. He closed his eyes, willing away the humiliation, the utter helplessness, the anticipation of worse. No, the pain didn't matter, it was the lack of control that agonized him. To be spreadeagled thus, his arms seized above him, his back naked, his shame plain to all his shipmates, while three hundred miles away his life was slipping away—it was too much to bear.

"One." There was a moment of utter stillness, except for the shipsong, and John dragged in a breath and squeezed his eyes shut and descended into those familiar sounds: the rush of the water against the side, the creak of the old oak boards, the croon of the sails filled with wind. One, he could hear, was flapping loose, and he had almost located it on his mind's sail plan when the whip whistled and snapped against his back.

Where is that sail? he thought, clenching his fists above as he felt the drip of blood down his spine. The forestaysail, that was the one.

"Two."

Mentally he caught the errant sail, fixed the corner back on its hank, surrendered to the familiar work and the blaze of the sun on his back. It didn't hurt so bad, a sunburn—

"Three." Another crack like a sail ripping, then the scrape like nails down his back. The old planks of the sloop were groaning, shivering beneath his bare feet. The rush of the water came more fervent, more resonant somehow. Something was wrong. He opened his eyes, raised his head, blinked to clear the sweat away, and stared enough through the grating at the sea ahead.

He knew this stretch of water. Dogger Bank. The shallowest part of the shallow North Sea, pale with the shifting of sand underneath. Sandbanks came and went, but there was usually one along this natural channel. "Captain," he said, in the normalest voice he could manage, "if you don't alter course three points to starboard, you'll ground her for certain."

"Four." But the boatswain's mate said this automatically, and no crack followed the doleful number.

The captain sprang to the rail beside John, staring wildly ahead. John clasped his hands together and closed his eyes, adding conversationally, "Rip the spine out of her, I wager, as swiftly as she's running."

"Helm!" cried the captain. "Starboard three points. All hands!"

The deck came to life, and John relaxed against the grating, imagining what he couldn't see, the men squirming up the ropes, grabbing the yards, stretching out for the sails. The sloop lurched hard to the right, the hull groaning in protest, and John was forced into the hot metal. He had a moment to imagine the ship foundering, him still lashed to the grating, before the marine appeared at his side. "Right good show, mate. Not a peep out of you. Captain said to take you down now."

Once freed, John leaned over the rail, fiercely ignoring the stinging on his back, rubbing at his wrist and assessing the color of the water. There were no other landmarks, so far out to sea, but the water was so clear he thought he could make out the individual shells pocking the white sand. "Get the lead going!" the captain called and a midshipman appeared at the rail to test the depth of the sea.

"By the deep seventeen, sir," came the call—plenty of room, but then the sloop lurched, and with a screech the spine scraped bottom.

"Let fall!" screamed the captain, and the last sails fell, and as they filled with wind the sloop was yanked off the bank, rocking hard and then settling safely into the deeper channel.

There was a collective exhale of relief, and the marine relaxed his tense posture and plucked John's shirt from the deck. "Captain wants to speak with you."

John pulled the shirt over his head, and when the rough linen stuck to his back he let himself feel for the first time the burning of salt on raw flesh. He could hardly force himself to approach the captain, who was directing operations from near the helm and greeted him happily. "Quick thinking there, Mercer. You know these waters?"

"Some."

"Well, you know your navigation, I'll give you that. Tell you what. I'll name you acting master. If you work out, I'll make it official in Riga. Now go see the surgeon about those stripes. Wouldn't want to lose another master to fever."

John managed to walk away before he gave way to weak laughter. He leaned against the mast, naming himself ten types of fool. He could have let the sloop run aground, and wait for a passing ship to tow them to the nearest shore. Then he could have deserted and gotten back to England in a few days. But no. He had to play the conscientious sailor and save the sloop's hull. Stupid. And now he was master, and instead of doing the sensible thing and heading southwest, assuring the captain all the way that the sun had reversed its path through the sky, he would probably find himself doing a capable job.

The ship's surgeon had ordered him to rest for two days. But by Thursday morning, even on the lower deck—John had refused, through some confused sense of principle, to move into the master's cabin—he could feel the heaviness in the air that presaged a major gale. After the surgeon changed the dressings on his back, John went up on deck. Absently answering the greetings of his shipmates, he went to the helm and checked the log. Then he went to the stern, watching the storm approach from the south across the strangely flat sea.

Even two hours after dawn, he couldn't find the sun in the sullen sky or trace the source of the weird silver light. The air was moist with heat, so still that the sails hung limply from their yards. The sky behind was an iron gray, black along the horizon, with a wavering sheen in between that meant a torrential rain a few leagues away. The storm approached like a panther, smooth and slow and coiled to leap.

And even after two decades at sea, the prospect sent liquid energy coursing through his veins.

Sending the helmsman below to rouse the captain, John took over the wheel, adjusting to the still unfamiliar starboard buck of the sloop's bow when it met a wave. The *Araminta* was old and set in her ways, with none of the sleek responsiveness he expected from his own vessels. Still, she could be handled, with the right touch at her helm.

The captain, still in his nightshirt, came up to check John's chart entries. He peered out at the coiled clouds and loudly proclaimed himself unworried. But he told the boatswain's mate to pipe the hands to breakfast early, so that they would be fed and full to fight the storm. "Won't be a bad one. Might even give us a bit of running room."

The captain's professed serenity was belied when he refused to go below to change and breakfast. Instead he haunted the deck, pacing back and forth and annoying John with his repeated and contradictory directions. John ignored most of them, letting the tension of the wheel in his hands guide his steering.

The approaching storm was sucking all the life from the air, so the sloop seemed to be skating forward just ahead of a vacuum. The air was so empty that John could clearly hear the uneasy mutters of his shipmates as they emerged onto the deck behind him.

The captain heard it too. "Belay that chatter!"

He didn't ask for advice, but John gave it anyway, in a low voice in case the captain didn't want to acknowledge it. "I'd shorten sail and put her about—take the force on the beam."

The captain gave him a disgusted look. "My orders are for Riga, not Ramsgate. We're already three days overdue, and this doesn't look to be much of a blow. It'll drive itself out in an hour or so, so we'll just take advantage of it to cover more sea. Should make up some time that way."

It was more daring a maneuver than John would have expected of this captain, more daring, in fact, than John himself would have attempted. Trying to outrun the storm could work for a faster ship. But the old, slow *Araminta* risked losing the race, and getting swamped by the high seas the storm brought along.

"She's not far enough ahead of the wind to do it safely." An ominous roll of thunder underlined John's protest. "The timbers won't stand for an hour's direct battering—she'll come apart."

The lieutenant, swinging down from the maintop with his spyglass under his arm, proved an unlikely ally. "He's right, sir, it's a moderate-sized blow, and gaining on us."

As the officers fell to arguing how much sail should be shortened, the first blast of wind caught the captain's nightshirt, lifting it above his waist. But John was too occupied keeping the wheel controlled to find the picture amusing. The howling that followed drowned out the shouts of the lieutenant and the stubborn replies of the captain—just as well, for the crew, up in the rigging taking in the sails, shouldn't have to hear their disagreement.

Suddenly the storm snuffed out the weak silver light, and the blow cast up a wall of waves that blocked John's view of the distant horizon, where safety lay. Strangely, there was no rain, only the spray kicked up by the force of the sloop hitting the storm.

For God's sake, put her about, John thought, putting all his weight into holding the wheel on course. But he didn't say it aloud. Too ingrained was the teaching of decades, that the captain had to prevail or discipline would be lost. They might be able to ride it out, if the timbers held and the masts didn't carry them over.

Like a shadow in the eerie darkness, the captain came up behind him, grabbing one of the wheel's oak spokes to test the resistance. The lieutenant was right alongside, his mouth working soundlessly as the wind ripped away his words. John kept his hands hard on the wheel, his gaze locked on the battering ram of a wave that had just curled up above them from starboard.

When it struck, the captain turned away with an almost comical expression of dismay. As the water swept over them, he reached out to grasp at John's shirt. Closing his mouth and eyes against the torrent, clinging to the wheel, John felt the fingernails scrape across his chest, the fist grip his lapel, the water close around him, dragging him down. Then the fabric gave way, and the pressure was gone, and the wheel was still solid and slick in his hands. The wave curled back into the sea, and the captain was gone.

In the momentary calm, the deck looked oddly peaceful, almost barren, washed clean of cordage and debris. John held tight to the bucking wheel and looked around for the other officers. The lieutenant had also vanished. The two little midshipmen were clinging to the mast and to each other, too frightened to stand unassisted.

John transferred his gaze to the rigging, where half a hundred men clung, waiting for an order. As another wave crashed into the stern, the little sloop trembled under his hands. The blood surged through his body as he felt her slide back, trying to escape the pounding. She would escape it, that much he could promise. He was hers; he was himself again.

He raised his voice to carry to the most distant of his

shipmates. "All hands to shorten sail! Strike down the topgallantmasts!"

He released one hand from the wheel to rub at the scratches on his chest, and called out the order to put the sloop about and head her into the storm.

Chapter Sixteen

If thou remember'st not the slightest folly
That ever did love make thee run into,
Thou hast not lov'd.

As You Like It, II, iv

Terra firma was all too firm under John's feet, after four days on a tiny sloop through two major gales. But it was English terra, at least, and so he tried to put a spring into his step as he shoved through the crowds at the dockyard. Finally his luck was in. It was morning, he was safe, and London, once a distant dream, was a mere thirty miles away—and Jessica's birthday was still to come.

"Dryden!"

Hearing his own name for the first time in a fortnight, John stopped short on the wooden path along the dock. It was his old colleague, Tressilian. They'd shared a berth on a Channel vessel when they were wild boys. But Tressilian had veered off course at some point and joined the Navy. Now the sun was glinting off his gold epaulettes, and even as John shook his hand he was thinking he hoped never to see another Naval uniform again.

Tressilian was eying John's own apparel. "You're off the *Araminta?*"

John yanked off the hat with its betraying ribbon. "It was something of an accident."

"Well, man, why didn't you tell me you were going Navy? You could have joined my company, and I'd've rated you master straightaway."

"I didn't *join*. I was pressed."

"Pressed?" Tressilian took the hat and peered inside, frowning at the "Jem Mercer" inscribed on the innerband. "We gave that up years ago, when the war was done. Don't have shiproom for all the seamen we've got."

"Well, I don't think it was the Navy that pressed me. What day is it, anyway?"

"Monday. Twentieth of July."

"Christ. Two weeks on that benighted brig. Tressilian, could you do me a service?"

Tressilian held out an open hand. "Anything, lad."

"I need to get to London immediately. I need—clothes. A horse." He knew Tressilian, one of the wealthiest men in the Navy, would keep a stable here. "Funds."

Without demur Tressilian started off down the dock towards a frigate whose mast was just being fitted with yards for a voyage. "Come on with me. My *Defiant*'s right here. I shouldn't help you, you know, seeing as how you've cost me a pony."

John shook the wool out of his head and trailed along, too tired to do more than ask, "How?"

"There was a bet in town on whether that heiress ran off with you or the poet." Tressilian climbed the steps to the gangplank and looked back ruefully at John. "Naturally, I laid down my bet on you, as a fellow sailor. Reckon I should have gone with poetry after all."

"Wait a minute!" John crossed over right behind Tressilian, instinctively adjusting to the sway of the gangplank. They almost collided as Tressilian stopped to salute the officer of the watch. The assembled company began one of those ridiculous welcoming ceremonies. Over the clash of the marines' weapons, John shouted, "What do you mean, she ran off with him?"

Tressilian gave a nod of dismissal to the line of officers and marines on the deck and led the way down the steps to his day cabin. With a light flooding in from the stern windows, this was as bright as on deck, and John sank gratefully down onto a settee warm from the sun. But he didn't let his head fall back onto the cushions, for if he relaxed his muscles, he knew he'd lose consciousness. And he hadn't time for that.

After a few instructions to his steward, Tressilian flung open a trunk. "Civilian clothes, you need, I make no doubt. We're of a size, I think." He pulled out an expensive shirt and a pair of breeches, added a riding coat and a cravat, and laid them out on the settee as precisely as any valet. Then he returned to the trunk. "You'll want riding boots, too, I expect." He tossed one back over his shoulder, muttering, "I know there's another one in here somewhere."

John caught the boot and set it aside, then pulled off his shirt and used the water in the basin to wash. Fortunately it was a quick job, as the last downpour had rinsed him quite clean. Shaving could wait. "For God's sake, Tressilian, tell me. Why do you say she ran off with anyone?"

"Well, you all three disappeared the same day. She must have run off with one of you, and if you've been on the *Araminta* for a fortnight—" Locating the second boot, he tossed it to John, who let it drop as he turned to grab a towel. "Jupiter, man, where'd you get those—"

Too late John remembered the stripes on his back, scabbed over now and painful only when he stretched. "Ran afoul of Navy discipline." He shot Tressilian a bitter glance. "I've sailed with the most ruthless privateers in the world, and never got whipped."

Tressilian made an apologetic sound and held up the fine lawn shirt so that John could insert his arms without too much pain. "Don't hold with flogging myself. I'd rather talk with the offenders. You know the sort of talk. More in sorrow than in anger. Disappointment and disillusion. After an hour or so, they're begging for the cat. At least it's quick, they say."

Courteously he turned his back, as if John might still somehow retain some modesty after two weeks spent in the crowded lower deck of a sloop. As John replaced his loose trousers with breeches, Tressilian glanced out the tall stern windows. "What did you do to her, anyway? The *Araminta*, I mean, not the heiress. That's her, isn't it, with that jury-rigged little bit of a mast, and those handkerchiefs for sails?"

"That's her. Couple late-season gales. Got smashed up a bit, and we had to bring her back." John fumbled at the buttons on the shirt—his fingers were rubbed raw by his time on the wheel—and was about to demand more news of Jessica when the door opened. The steward glanced cautiously at John and went off to whisper in the captain's ear, then vanished again.

The cravat was impossible to manage, and in his wornout state John found Tressilian's laughter almost too much. But he should have known better; Tressilian, for all his faults, hadn't a mean knot in his rigging. "Let me do that," he said kindly, and taking hold of the white linen, began crafting some elaborate knot. "That's a good jest on me," he added. "Thought you'd broken the *Araminta*, and here Brabant just told me you brought her

in safe and relatively sound. All the officers incapaci-
tated, were they? And you couldn't keep still, being a
commander yourself. Tell me how this came to be."

"Some other time. Just tie it, will you? I don't need to
impress the beaus on Bond Street! Now tell me all you
know about Jessica disappearing."

Tressilian finished the knot with a bit of a flourish
and stepped back. "A good fit, as I thought. The disappearing Miss Seton, hmm? When was it—a fortnight
ago, she scunnered—left some note, don't know what it
said. In the clubs it was thought she'd eloped, and since
you and the poet also vanished, well, you know how
these wagers get started."

"She's never come back?"

"I was in town day before yesterday, and she hadn't
returned." He watched John pull on the boots—a bit
loose, but very fine leather—and added sympathetically,
"My condolences, mate. I take it this little cruise wasn't
just a way to drown your sorrows?"

Viciously John stamped down on the floor to adjust
the boot. "No. Awfully convenient, wasn't it, though,
getting me out of town just then."

"You think the poet did it?" Tressilian considered
this, and finally shook his head. "Not likely. Hadn't it in
him. He'd be more likely to challenge you to a sonnet
contest."

"I don't think the poet did it. I think he's being heartily seasick on the Hong Kong route." He forestalled further questions with an imperious gesture. "Send your
steward for the horse, will you? And tell me, do you
know how to get a special license for marriage?"

This at least had the effect of halting Tressilian's speculations on the future of the *Araminta* and the whereabouts of the poet. "A special license? Well, no, I don't

know. I was married the proper way, by the bishop in Exeter Cathedral."

Only the sudden bleakness of his friend's expression prevented John from making some scathing comment about the noble way of wedding. Tressilian was scarce out of mourning, he reminded himself, and gentled his tone. "It's in London I'd get it, right?"

"My steward can tell you. He knows all about such havey-cavey matters as special licenses. Brabant!"

This font of all wicked wisdom, before being dispatched to the stable, revealed that a special license could be gotten from the archbishop's court at the Doctors' Common, south of St. Paul's. Five pounds would certainly cover the cost.

But after the steward left, Tressilian counted out fifty pounds and pressed it into John's hand. "You'd better be prepared for a price rise. Archbishops are forever picking pockets whatever way they can, and people desperate to wed are easy pickings."

John stuffed the money away into his coat pocket. "I don't know how to thank you. I'll pay you back when I get home."

"No need for that." Tressilian gave him an awkward cuff on the shoulder and shoved him out the door. "I'll be on my way to Copenhagen anyway. Consider it a wedding present. And a bit of thanks for saving His Majesty's sloop there. His Majesty probably won't get around to thanking you himself, and methinks you'd best leave the Admiralty in ignorance of your identity. Who knows what form their gratitude might take?"

It wasn't till John slipped between the closing doors of the Doctors' Common that he remembered his last visit to its high-arched halls, when he located the late Lord

Parham's will. That was the first mention he had seen of Jessica. The ecclesiastical clerk kept muttering, "We're closing, sir," as John studied the newly special license, assessing it for authenticity and accuracy. He hadn't seen one since he stood up for Devlyn at his hasty wedding to the princess, but this one looked just the same. He wrote Jessica's name in the space for bride, and his own as groom. Superstition, that was all. But it made it feel more likely, to link their names like this on an official document.

He hadn't yet accounted in his mind for Jessica's absence from town. She had not—he knew it in his heart—run off with the poet. If nothing else, Wiley would have prevented it, for as long as the poet was a rival to John, he was a threat to Wiley. Blake had most likely been abducted too, safely stowed away on some ship scheduled to be far away on July 23.

But he couldn't believe Wiley would do away with Jessica, though he knew even as he made the arguments he was trying to persuade himself she was safe. It would be too dangerous, too obvious—and unnecessary. With her prospective husbands out of the way, Jessica posed little threat to possession of the library.

As the doors of Doctors' Common were closed and locked behind him, John folded the license carefully and put it in his inner pocket. He wasn't a praying man, no more than any other seaman frequently on the brink of disaster, but he sent up a prayer that he'd have occasion to hand this license to a vicar and demand a wedding.

The Parham House butler was an unflappable sort. He didn't mention John's fortnight absence, or comment on the contrast between Weston coat and six days' worth of beard. He did admit that Miss Seton was not in town, Lady Parham was not receiving, and Lord Parham would see him in the drawing room.

Parham looked rather the worse for anxiety, his eyes shadowed, his brow creased with wear. John was ignobly glad to see that guilt had created such a visible effect. Parham deserved no better for having treated Jessica with such selfish neglect all these years.

He parried Parham's angry demands of his whereabouts for the last two weeks, saying only, "Wiley tried to remove me from competition. He didn't succeed. Where is he?"

Parham subsided into a sullen heap on the couch. "I don't know. He said he was going on holiday. I haven't seen him."

"And Jessica?"

"She left of her own accord, the servants said. Packed up her bag just after you spoke to her, and slipped out the back. She must have run off with Damien."

"I don't believe it." And he didn't, but even the barest chance of it was enough to start him pacing across the room to the window, there to look out on the singularly unedifying trees of Berkeley Square.

"Well, there's no other explanation, is there? She needn't have run off with you, for she had permission to wed you. And besides, here you are. And there's her note, also, that as much as admits it."

"Her note?"

Parham drew a folded sheet from his pocket and handed it over. From its creases ans smudges, John surmised that Parham had been tormenting himself with frequent readings for the last fortnight. And it was torment, enough, to see Jessica's flowing hand and frequent underscorings, and imagine her face in all its lively expressiveness.

"My dear Uncle,

"Despite my brave words, I cannot bring myself to marry where there is no Love. I learn I am as romantic as any shopgirl, after all. And, as Shakespeare said, *I am bewitched with the rogue's company. If the rascal have not given me medicines to make me love him, I'll be hanged.*"

Helpful to the last, she provided the reference— Henry IV, Part 1, II, ii—before closing with a promise to be careful and to return when she was more certain of her future.

"You see, she is saying she loves him."

"Loves who?"

"Blake. The rogue."

"Blake's not the rogue." John bit back the addition, *you old fool.* "I am. She loves me."

"Then why did she run to keep from marrying you?" There was a hint of triumph in Parham's expression; no doubt he saw this as an opportunity to pass the blame. "Especially considering the Parham Collection is at stake."

John folded the letter into its accustomed creases, and stared at it, running the already-memorized words through his mind. "I don't know. There's a trick in there, though, I know that much. Jessica delights in being mysterious."

"She does?" Parham shook his head. "Well, she's mystified me. I was certain she wanted that collection enough to marry you, but I guess I was wrong."

John took a deep breath and let it out slowly through his gritted teeth. "She wants to marry me. And not for the collection. I just have to find her, that's all."

Parham had regained a bit of his hauteur, and rose in dismissal. "Well, you'd best get on with it, Dryden. Her birthday's only three days away. And, unless you know something I don't, you've quite a search ahead of you."

John shot him an annoyed glance, but only suggested that he do his best to persuade the solicitors to postpone the transferral of the collection at least until the end of the day on July 23. No matter what, he promised, he would be back that day to see to the safety of the collection—and, he added silently, the St. Germaine treasure.

A check of the library's defenses, an uneasy night's rest, a clean shave, and a hearty breakfast did much to revive John, but little to solve the mystery of Jessica. He dispatched one of Arnie's nephews to canvass Mayfair hackney firms for any driver who remembered picking up a young blonde lady. But he had little hope that memories would hold after two weeks, even when coaxed with ready blunt.

A messenger to Damien Blake's rooms reported what John had suspected, that the poet never returned from a reading at a Southwark tavern. His parents were certain he had drowned himself in the Thames. That anxiety, at least, John could relieve. At his familiar desk, he penned a note to the marquis and marchioness, briefly explaining what had happened to him and what had likely befallen Damien.

When he gave it to Arnie to post, the manservant said hesitantly, "Was you wanting to see all your mail, sir? I put it in the basket there."

John knuckled his forehead, trying to force some sense in it. Two weeks worth of mail. He rifled through it, looking for familiar handwriting, but there was nothing addressed in Jessica's hand. Of course not. She wouldn't make it so easy on him.

More slowly he went back through the covers. There was a letter from his artist friend Caroline, full of gracious wishes for his happy marriage, "bogus or no." There might be the slightest bit of irony in that, but he couldn't take the time to decipher it. Nothing from the princess: A Romanov to the last, she wasn't about to forgive without prostration and imprisonment.

His sister-in-law Sophie had written her usual fortnightly note, reminding him to observe his father's birthday and reporting on village affairs. Dennis was much involved in building the new shoproom, and had only enough time to make up his chemicals and none to sell them to the public. Since Sophie would rather starve than take orders from her own husband, he had hired an assistant to handle the counter. A Female Assistant. One Who wasn't, You may be Certain, Exactly what She Appeared. John gave a moment's thought to whether Dennis had given Sophie any reason to emphasize that with underscoring—

Suddenly he felt in his coat pocket for the note Jessica had left for her uncle. He laid it side-by-side with Sophie's letter, and studied them together.

"I learn I am as romantic as any *shopgirl*, after all."

And there was that reference to medicine in the Shakespeare quote. It couldn't be. But it had to be. She had left no other clue—and Jessica, he knew, would leave clues.

He called to Arnie to pack his bag and order up his curricle. Jessica working for his brother—it didn't seem reasonable. But then, Jessica wasn't reasonable, not in the usual way, at least. She was ever challenging him, challenging his assumptions, going her own way, declaring them equals. It made as much sense as anything else, that she would see working in his brother's shop as another indication of equality—and another way to annoy and mystify him.

It was morning before he arrived in the village where he'd grown up, a brilliant Dorset morning, all the mist burned away from the surface of the bay. He pulled his hat down to shade his tired eyes from the glare of the sun off the water and drove his curricle and pair to the livery stable. Then he retraced the familiar path up High Street to the shop bearing the name Manning: Apothecary.

For once he didn't wince when he opened the door and heard the little bell tinkle a warning, and he didn't choke when he breathed in the familiar smell of camphor and herbs. In fact, the old prison of a shop seemed bathed in some iridescent radiance. And that glowing light was enough to outline the back of a young woman standing on a stool, her arms stretched up for a jar on a high shelf.

For fear of startling her, John didn't speak. But he gazed with immense pleasure at the fine ankles revealed when she hitched up her gray skirt to keep from tripping. "Just a minute, sir," she called out, grabbing the jar. "I'm just getting the arrowroot."

Her voice made him close his eyes with relief and the dissipation of tension. He heard her hop down from the stool, her shoes clattering on the oak floor.

"John."

It was only a whisper, but it echoed in his heart. He opened his eyes, and opened his arms.

Chapter Seventeen

Benedick: I do love nothing in the world so well as you.
          Is that not strange?
Beatrice: Love on; I will requite thee, Taming my wild
          heart to thy loving hand.

Much Ado About Nothing

Jessica took time only to set the jar on the counter before running into John's arms, into the warmth of his undeniable presence. For a moment she just rested there, her head on his chest, listening to his heart pound against the pulse in her temple. This was joy, wasn't it, as she'd never known, and he knew it too.

"John," she whispered into his shirt, "I could throttle you. What took you so long?"

"Took me so long? Took me—you little—"

His unwonted inarticulateness might have indicated guilt and remorse, but Jessica, leaning back against the support of his arms, saw something else entirely in his face. Fury.

She knew better than to give him time to express it. "Yes, you took too long! It's been seventeen days, for pity's sake. I finally gave up hope yesterday and bought a ticket on the noon mail coach, thinking at least I could be there to watch as Mr. Wiley took my collection and opened my trunk and stole my Shakespeare play and used it to persuade the whole world that Bacon wrote *Hamlet.*" She slanted a glance up at him: Still no remorse. "Another hour and you would have missed me, and I would have had to face Mr. Wiley all on my own. And then come back here and work for your tyrannical brother the rest of my days."

John's arms dragged her back to his rigid body. "If you knew what I've been through, you little termagent, you would be rejoicing that I managed to get here at all!"

"Well, I am rejoicing," she said fairly. "But it's been a difficult time for me, thinking that you didn't want me after all." She didn't want to think of the bleak nights alone in her inn room, the days she had to force herself to be cheerful so that no one would guess her heart was breaking. He was here, that was all that mattered. "Or that you were so stupid you couldn't figure out where I'd gone."

"It isn't as if you made it easy for me. Why didn't you tell me you were planning on scarpering? And why?"

"That would have been too easy. I had to know——"

"What?" That was only a whisper.

"That you cared enough to find me."

His arms tightened around her, until she thought she might faint for lack of breath. She wriggled against him to make a bit more space, and with a muttered oath he kissed her, his mouth hot and fierce against hers.

Finally, he let her go, all but one hand, which he held like a lifeline. "Well, now you know. I care more than enough. And——and I know you. I knew right away, that's why you ran off. To test me. To challenge me."

She felt bereft of his body, which had been so hard and still next to her. But there would be time for that later, after they had straightened everything out. So she only brought his hand up to her face, rubbing her cheek against his palm. "You needed a challenge to wake you up. You were so very insulting."

"I didn't mean to be. You know that. I—devil a bit, Jessica, you might have given me another day to explain. Not that it would have changed anything, what with Wiley's machinations."

"What do you mean, his machinations? When I left, he was going off on holiday to Tunbridge Wells."

He started laughing, and for awhile she thought he wouldn't be able to stop. He must be weary too, if he drove through the night—and she knew that's what he would have done. She thought he must have stopped at an inn this morning, for he was clean-shaven and his cravat was impeccably tied. But under his eyes were shadows of weariness.

Worried, she drew him over to the hard wooden bench that lined the wall under the shelf of ointments. When they were sitting side-by-side, her hands clasped in his, his laughter finally died and he laid his head back against the wall. She raised her hand to touch the faint remnant of a smile on his lips. "Tell me what is so funny."

"It's not funny. It's just that we should have known Wiley'd never concede defeat so easily. Sweetheart, he had me abducted and thrown aboard a Navy sloop. I woke up fifty leagues out in the North Sea. And no one—no one believed I had important business back in London."

It was too much to take in, that he had spent these last weeks helpless while she cursed his intransigence. "I'm sorry. I shouldn't have doubted you."

"I doubted myself, for awhile there. But as soon as I got back to London, I figured your puzzle out."

This Jessica found suspicious, considering how she had labored to set that puzzle up. "As soon as you got back? Surely it took you a bit of thought. I didn't mean for you to decipher it by lightning flashes."

"Well, your note to your uncle had all the clues, but it took a letter from my sister-in-law to show me how to interpret them. Sophie went on and on about this mysterious shop assistant Dennis had hired, and finally I found the key to the maze you made for me. I still don't know how she guessed though."

"I expect the princess was the one to guess. She came in here the first day I worked the counter, and recognized me straightaway. I made her promise not to tell you—" John looked ready to argue this, so she added quickly, "I told you, I didn't want to make it easy for you! I presumed, of course, that she would tell Lord Devlyn, and that he would write to you."

"He wouldn't. He would tell her that I wouldn't appreciate her meddling in my affairs."

"Men are so obstinate! I'm glad she was clever enough to tell Sophie, who must be less scrupulous about such things."

"So am I. I expect," John added thoughtfully, "that means the princess has forgiven me."

"Why was she angry at you?"

"Because men are so obstinate, as you said. Jessie, you know, I did this all wrong."

"You found me, at least, though you certainly didn't leave much time."

"No, I mean falling in love with you."

She looked up to see trouble clouding his eyes. A bit of her happiness dimmed. "That's not all wrong. It can't be. It feels too right to me."

"Idiot. I don't mean falling in love was wrong. But I didn't tell you that, did I? When I proposed."

All the joy came flooding back, and she could indulge in a bit of play. "I don't think you ever truly proposed. You declared that I was to marry you, whether I liked it or not, but I don't think that counts as a proposal. At least, it was unlike any proposal I've ever received."

He was grinning, a bit shamefaced, perhaps, but not as much as he ought to be. "I suppose it lacked a bit of passion."

"Oh, no, it had plenty of passion. None addressed towards me, unfortunately. More directed at the injustices of the world which had led you to this disastrous development." Even after three weeks, and these last precious moments, she couldn't quite keep the bitterness out of her voice. "The most insulting part of it, of course, was that you seemed to think that I would be resistant to the prospect of marrying you."

His assessing gaze took in their prosaic surroundings, then focused on her gray shopgirl's frock and dark blue apron. "Not such an unwarranted suspicion, considering that you fled the city to avoid our wedding."

"Not to avoid the wedding. To—" She couldn't explain precisely, so she was relieved when he smiled and brought her hand to his lips.

"To test me. Well, I suppose I deserved it, considering what a cock-up I made of the proposal. Will you let me try again?"

Graciously she nodded, and to her surprise he went down on one knee before her, like the veriest cavalier, and took her hand in his hard grasp. "Doubtlessly you've noticed, my darling, that my devotion to you has grown to something more fervent, more fierce, something that can only be called—dare I name it?—love. Your beauty, your spirit, your quick intelligence—all this has won my admiration and my ardor. I will not know happiness until you say that you will be mine."

He seemed to be waiting for some response, and with a smile tugging at her mouth, she gave him one. "That is much better. One of the best I have heard. Not quite as elegant as Damien's—he did his in tercets, like Dante—but much improved."

He rose and yanked her to her feet, crushing her to him. "Say you'll marry me, or I'll not answer for the consequences."

Breathlessly, she whispered, "Yes," and lifted her head to kiss him.

The bell on the door tinkled, but for the first time in two weeks she was too occupied to pay it any mind. She pulled an inch away from John's mouth, just long enough to murmur, "I shall be with you in a moment," to the entering customer, before returning to the kiss.

"John?"

Even with her back to the door, Jessica recognized this disbelieving voice as that of her employer, Mr. Dennis Manning. She would have told him to go away, except that she recalled with a bit of guilt that she had been planning to vanish without giving him notice in an hour or so. So she just ignored him, and noted with pleasure, as John murmured love words into her ear, that this was a consensus decision.

She should have known, however, that Mr. Manning wasn't one who took well to being ignored. A square hand took hold of John's shoulder and pulled him away from her. She managed to retain John's hand, though, and together they faced the intruder, wearing, no doubt, identical expressions of annoyance.

Her employer, however, only looked astounded. Not for the first time, Jessica noted with some relief that John did not in the least resemble his stolid, stubborn brother, in feature or character. Dennis gazed blankly from one to the other, pausing to stare at their clasped hands.

"John, what on earth do you think you're doing?"

"Seducing your shop assistant." John turned away from him, bringing Jessica's hand to his lips and looking deep into her eyes. "Now be a good lad and go away and let me finish. It's all right," he added, "we're betrothed."

"Wait!"

Jessica ignored him, but John wasn't so stubborn. He sighed and raised his head to regard his brother. "What?"

"Think of what Father would say. Lord, I can hear him saying it now—'What are you doing, Dennis, letting your brother scandalize the customers by seducing your shop assistant right there in the middle of the shop?'" Disgruntledly he added, "Wouldn't you know he'd blame me."

Jessica closed her eyes, leaning against John's chest. "Perhaps this will surprise you, but he labors under the impression that your father haunts the shop. And, you might as well know it, the ghost does not approve of female shop assistants."

"And Mother," Dennis broke in, "wouldn't approve of you marrying one either. She expected you to do better than that."

Jessica felt John's chest throb with laughter and raised her head to kiss him again. She decided she would never get enough of that, of the absolute freedom to kiss him, even if it did cause employers and ghosts to squawk with outrage.

"She's just pretending to be a shopgirl," John said, between kisses. "She's really an heiress."

"An heiress?" This at least had the effect of silencing Dennis. In fact, he was so silent that Jessica became worried that he had expired from holding his breath too long. When she sneaked a glance over her shoulder, though, she saw that he was glaring at her.

"An heiress, and you asked for a rise in pay? That takes cheek, I'd say!"

"And now she's going to leave you without giving notice."

"When?"

John detached himself far enough to reach for his watch. "Immediately. We must be married and back to London by tomorrow morning."

"Can we do it, John? Have you got a license?"

"A special license. Now we just need a vicar."

They were too engrossed in exchanging smiles at this prospect to notice Dennis, but eventually his throat rumblings turned into a statement. "Well, if you must marry, you must. Mother wouldn't be happy to see it done by special license, but I suppose that's what you must do with an heiress—snabble her before she changes her mind."

"She's not changing her mind."

Jessica nodded firmly, and Dennis sighed.

"Then I suppose I should come with you to the church to stand up with you."

John glanced at Jessica, then at Dennis, and after an awkward pause, replied, "Thank you, Denny, but I think that's a duty for my elder brother."

For a moment there was silence. Then Dennis, with more grace than Jessica would ever have expected of him, said, "I expect you're right. I'll go for the vicar. He might require a bit of persuading, considering this is one of the days he communes with God out on the fishing pond."

Once he had gone, Jessica let John hold her in tender silence. But finally she had to ask, "Do you think that

we should wait till after tomorrow to wed? Just so that
we will always know that we married for love, and not
the collection?"

John groaned. "No more tests, Jessica. We love each
other. We will share a life of adventure and achievement—
and start by thwarting Wiley's attempt to slander Shakespeare. After a century or so together, if I haven't made
you happy, then—then I will have failed the test. But give
me until then, will you?"

"A century?" It sounded rather too seductive to bear.
"I suppose I can wait that long—if I spend every day
with you."

They might have sat in the old apothecary shop all
morning, holding hands and talking of the future, if
Sophie and the princess hadn't arrived to take her up to
the Keep to dress. Jessica went unwillingly, telling John
she'd just as soon be married in her gray shopgirl frock,
but that was enough to make the other women gasp and
drag her out the door into the dusty sunlit street.

"You must dress for the occasion, dearest." The princess took the coachman's hand and climbed the steps of
the carriage, saying over her shoulder, "We are of a size,
so you may make yourself free of my wardrobe."

Jessica's resistance faltered as she recalled the deli-
cious gown the princess had worn at that fateful ball six
weeks ago. She saw her face reflected in the carriage
window and realized that the gray dress made her look
rather washed out. "Well, if you don't mind . . . I suppose John would prefer me to look dazzling."

"Yes, he would," Sophie assured her, giving her a bit
of a shove up the carriage steps. "Men do prefer a dazzling bride. Gives them a memory to cherish when
you're nine months gone with child." With a happy sigh,
she settled next to Jessica on the upholstered seat and
gazed around her. "What a commodious coach," she

said to the princess, who had taken the seat opposite. "Thank you for inviting me along, your highness."

"Oh, no thanks are due! And do call me Tatiana. We are all going to be sisters, after all. Oh!" The princess covered her mouth with her hand, like a small child who had uttered a naughty word. Her expression was so comic that both Jessica and Sophie burst out laughing, and soon, they were all whispering between chuckles as the carriage lurched up the long avenue.

"It's obvious enough. They are next to twins, John and Devlyn," Jessica said, holding onto the handgrip to keep from falling against Sophie.

"But if you'd known Mrs. Manning—" Sophie rolled her eyes. "The most *proper* lady you ever imagined! She was shocked when I let little Tommy run about bare-bottomed, and he was but a year then! I just can't imagine *how* she ever managed it!"

The princess gave a shrug of Gallic sophistication. "Well, I suspect that the late Lord Devlyn, for all his faults, was nearly irresistible. In fact, I know Michael worries that he will someday encounter other half-siblings, none quite so congenial as our darling John. Aren't you glad," she said to Jessica, "that the sins of the father seem to have bypassed these two sons? Not that John hasn't his share of sins, but profligacy with women isn't one of them."

"I'm relieved to hear that. I think I'm likely to be the jealous sort, given the opportunity," Jessica observed, but hadn't time to elaborate before the carriage stopped and the coachman yanked open the door and bowed them out.

The princess's wardrobe took up an acre or two of a dressing room, and Jessica, who ordinarily cared little for apparel, was transfixed by the array of colors and fabrics on display. Tatiana and Sophie held a whispered consultation amidst the gowns, and emerged from it with a consensus choice, an ivory blush dress with tiny puffy sleeves and a cascade of lace on the silk bodice. The princess held it up against Jessica's chest. "It's perfect for a bride, and I've never worn it—I've never been able to blush. I think it will do very well."

And indeed, it made Jessica look both fragile and splendid, rather like Shakespeare's fairy queen Titania. She knew John would have loved her did she resemble a gnome, but it was a pleasure to see his eyes glow silver when she met him in the little chapel attached to Devlyn Keep. He wore borrowed finery too, a morning coat, a satin waistcoat, crisp white linen shimmering with colored light from the stained-glass windows. He stood with his brothers near the altar, looking for all the world like a pagan prince renouncing his ancient gods for the love of her.

She wanted to tell him he need renounce nothing, that she wanted him pagan and all. She wanted to touch him, to trace the exotic lines of his face—but the vicar was entering, muttering under his breath as he fumbled behind his neck with the fastening of his clerical collar.

So Jessica only stood next to her pagan, bending her head and smiling when he stealthily took her hand and hid the contact between their bodies. Very soon, his hand promised her, they would be alone, and they would be married, and no one in the world could keep them apart.

There was just a moment when her joy muted, when she glanced back at Devlyn and the princess and Mr. and Mrs. Manning—John's family—and longed to see her own family there too. But she supposed it was enough that her uncle had consented to the wedding, finally putting her happiness above his grief. Somehow he—and Aunt Martha too—must have seen that John, for all his apparent faults, was the one she had to love.

But the vicar wasn't so ready to let the past go. He shook his head until the sun danced off his shining pate. "Miss Seton, are you certain this is what you want to do? You must not know all there is to know about this groom of yours." The reverend shot an accusatory glance at John, who tried but failed to look innocent. "He wasn't always a baronet, you know. In fact, he was other things, far more disreputable."

Jessica regarded him with a hauteur the princess might have envied. "I know exactly the sort of man he is, and I wouldn't have him any other way."

She thought she heard a sigh of relief from behind her, where her two future sisters-in-law sat. John only pressed her hand and smiled down at her as the vicar made a minute study of the special license. "I suppose it's in order. We don't get many of these here in Dorset, you know. *Most* couples post their banns ahead of time, for they have nothing to fear and nothing to hide. And they haven't any reason not to place their own names on the license, the ones they received at their christening."

No doubt this was an acquaintance of longstanding; indeed, Jessica thought perhaps this old vicar had christened John so many years ago. Probably John had bitten him during the ritual, and the vicar had never forgiven it.

At any rate, the ironic glint in John's eyes indicated that he was about to say something. Devlyn forestalled whatever it was, stepping forward so that he blocked the vicar's view of the disreputable groom. "Thank you, Mr. Tooley. Let's get on with it then. Do we need anything else?"

"A ring," the vicar said, a bit sullenly.

Beside her, John closed his eyes as if in pain.

"You didn't forget the ring." Though Devlyn's voice was perfectly level, something in the way he gazed at the flowers on the altar suggested that he was about to laugh.

Unexpectedly the princess spoke up from the first pew. "Of course he forgot a ring, darling. I'm surprised he remembered to bring his head with him, as distracted as he must have been when he left London. Fortunately, I thought of that, and checked my jewel box before we came down. Here."

She interposed herself between Jessica and John, indicating with a nod that they were to hold out their hands. As if doling out candy to children, she said, "One for you, John, and one for you, Jessica. A matched set. Aren't they lovely?"

They were, actually, a slender twist of gold in John's hand, crowned with sapphires circling a diamond, and a wider twisted band for Jessica to trade for the other. "But these must be worth a fortune!"

"Not at all!" The princess closed Jessica's hand around the man's ring. "Oh, they are valuable. But they aren't part of the crown jewels, just some bits that my mother's great-granduncle left behind when he disappeared. That was Fyodor Romanov—"

"The Butcher?" Devlyn broke in, adroitly catching the ring John tossed him and putting it away in his pocket.

"Oh, no. This was Fyodor the Intriguer. If he'd been the Butcher, he would never have disappeared." She flashed a blinding smile at John. "I tried to use them for our wedding, but Michael said he'd rather have his finger ripped off than wear a Romanov ring. I knew you wouldn't be so scrupulous. In fact," she added, slipping back between them to retake her seat, "you will appreciate them, both of you being so very *Byzantine*. Now, Mr. Tooley, do let us get on with it. The bride has another ceremony to attend tomorrow in London."

Jessica was about to object that few men wore rings these days, but then she saw the glint of gold on Lord Devlyn's left hand and thought that perhaps the princess had the right of it after all. There was no harm in alerting other women ahead of time that a man was unavailable, especially a man who might well have inherited his father's irresistible quality.

And so, with a clear conscience, Jessica was able to repeat the vicar's reluctant words, "With this ring, I thee wed."

John's most fervent vow was the next one, "With my body I thee worship." Jessica looked up to see that disorienting flash of desire in his eyes, and though her heart tumbled in confusion, she smiled at him. It was a marriage of true minds, she knew that, but bodies could worship too.

Twelve hours later, though, as dusk fell around them and John showed no signs of tiring, Jessica realized that he had forgotten all about that vow. A bridegroom in the grip of an obsession was a most frustrating companion.

As they approached an inn yard bright with lanterns, she put her hand on his gripping the reins, and tugged at it. He murmured something to calm the startled horses, and reined them in just before the inn drive. "What is it, sweetheart?"

"John, do let's stop for the night. Or at least *part* of the night."

"But, Jessie, we must be in London as early as we can

in the morning, before Wiley can get his hands on the play! You know that."

"All I know is this is my wedding night, and I am spending it squinting into the darkness at a horse!" She didn't mean to sound plaintive, but weariness and frustration had taken a toll on her self-control. John's curricle was well-sprung, and she found his lean form beside her a welcome support, but not nearly so welcome as it would be in a bed.

She raised her hand to touch his face. She could hardly see him in the dark, but under her fingers his jaw was tense with the conflict she had posed for him. He was vulnerable, and she knew just how to take advantage of it. She edged a little closer so that their legs touched from hip to knee, trailed her fingers to his mouth, and gentled her voice. "We are already past Basingstoke. We can leave before the first light, and be to Berkeley Square by nine. You said my uncle would delay the transfer—we will be there in plenty of time."

He closed his teeth gently on her thumb, then pulled her hand away only to tug it back so that he could kiss her knuckles. "It's just that I've had little rest this past week. I think if I close my eyes, I will sleep the clock round."

She leaned closer, so that her lips were only a fraction of an inch from his. "I think I can contrive some way to keep you awake."

"Another test?" His kiss brushed her mouth longingly then drew away. "This is one I hope I can help you pass."

Chapter Eighteen

Soul of the Age!
The Applause, delight! the wonder of our stage!
My Shakespeare, rise.

> Ben Jonson, "To the Memory of My Beloved,
> The Author, Mr. William Shakespeare"

She didn't pass the test. It was a valiant effort, but they fell asleep just before dawn, still tangled together. John woke an hour later, when the full morning light streamed through the window. He knew a moment of panic, then forced it down as he calculated from the sun's angle that it wasn't yet five o'clock. He subsided again next to Jessica, his chest pressed against her naked back, his mouth against the sweet curve of her neck.

There was some simple, profound wonder in this, that he could wake up beside her, see her nakedness glowing golden in the morning light, and know that this moment would be his every day of his life. And it was only that knowledge, that after another night he would have this moment again, that got him up and washed and shaved before she woke.

He pulled on his breeches, though he knew they would prove only an inadequate guard against temptation. Breakfast ordered from a chambermaid in the hall-way, John returned to sit on the bed beside his wife. Even as he bent to kiss her cheek, he regretted the necessity of awakening her. It was for her own good, he reminded himself, and the good of the collection, and the good of English literature. Were the stakes less exalted, he would crawl back into bed with her and let the sun run away with time.

Instead, he waited till her eyes opened and closed and finally opened again. In their drowsy blue depths he saw incomprehension, surprise, and finally remembrance. "John," she whispered.

"Happy birthday, my darling. I wish I'd had time to find something to give you."

"You have. My happiness—" She frowned, and used his arm to leverage herself into a sitting position. The sheet fell to her waist, but she didn't seem to notice. He did. "And my collection. Is it very late?"

"No. We have time." He had come prepared to wake her up. He gave her a drink of water, then took a cool damp cloth from the basin on the washstand and applied it to her sleep-flushed face, then down along her shoulders and arms. When he drew it back up her side, she seized it, color rising in her cheeks, and said with asperity, "I shall see to the rest myself. And I think I can manage to dress myself too, if you can locate my—my undergarments."

So he turned to find her shift tangled in the bed-clothes. She touched the healing slashes on his back with a gentle finger. "I'm sorry they hurt you."

"Believe me, the anticipation was worse than the reality. And solitary confinement was worse than either."

He rolled the silk garment up and fitted the neckline over her head, helping her find the sleeves with each arm. There was a moment's remorse when her breasts disappeared from view, but he reminded himself that they were married for life, and he would surely see them again.

She wriggled the shift into place around her hips—a surprisingly erotic process, one that he would like to see done in reverse—and slanted one of those inquisitive glances at him. "You do hate confinement, don't you? You said you didn't want marriage, because it would restrict your freedom. I took a shirt out of your bag for you last night, by the way, to let the wrinkles hang out."

It was a most wifely sort of comment, and John cherished it, though he regretted its premise that their wedding night was truly over. He found the clean shirt hanging on the bedpost and pulled it on. "That was when I thought I couldn't marry you. When I was truly confined, the freedom I craved was to come back to you."

"I suppose it isn't *solitary* confinement, if we share it together."

"It isn't confinement at all. We are choosing to share our lives, aren't we?"

She sighed happily, coming into his arms, warm and inviting and all too appealing. "What a lovely thought. All of our lives to share. Starting today."

They lingered that way, not speaking except with kisses, until a knock signalled the arrival of their breakfast. Reluctantly he released her and rose to retrieve the tray of food from the hallway. She took advantage of his distraction to dash into the dressing room to finish washing and dressing, and he was reduced to applying jam to toast and speculating whether she would sugar her coffee or salt her eggs. This morning he would find out; for tomorrow's breakfast he would know.

When she emerged dressed for the day, he could tell from her shadowed expression that she too was contemplating the immediate future. She ate sparingly and abstractedly, stirring her coffee long after the sugar lump had dissolved. "I hope my uncle persuades the solicitors to wait until we arrive before they try to transfer the library. They will wait, don't you think?"

"We will be there by nine. If I know solicitors, they will just be finishing their breakfast then. And we will present our marriage lines—" He felt in the pocket of his coat, and the crackle of paper assured him they were still there—"and your uncle will present his consent, and they will have no choice but to turn over the collection to you."

He made sure to smile as he said it, so that he sounded more confident than he felt. They had made the mistake of underestimating Wiley once, and so now John was prepared for anything. He searched through his bag and brought out another document. "Here, sweetheart, keep this with you today. I had Devlyn write up an affidavit that he witnessed our marriage. That at least should stall them if something happens to the official paper."

Obligingly she took the page and glanced at it before fetching her gold-chained reticule. "What could happen to our marriage lines?"

"I don't know. But in my experience, if there's an important document about, it's sure to vanish just when it becomes essential." He watched her maneuver the affidavit into the book that filled most of her valise-shaped reticule. When she finally accomplished this task, she looked up suspiciously at him.

"Why are you laughing?"

"I am just wondering how I managed to get a wife who brings along something to read on her wedding night."

She settled the reticule's chain on her shoulder and

replied coolly, "I always bring something to read, to ward off boredom and wasted hours."

The reticule, slipping down her arm, banged into him as he caught her up in an embrace. He pushed it back up on her shoulder and then trailed kisses up her neck till he reached her ear. "By the time I'm done with you, my love, you'll have forgotten how to read. But I don't think you'll consider them *wasted hours.*"

Once they emerged into the daylight, John and Jessica crossed the final forty-five miles in a bare three hours, thanks to the fresh horses he had arranged at every post stop. But when they ran up the stairs into Parham House, never pausing to gratify the butler's curiosity, they found that Alfred Wiley had been even more beforehand.

Though it lacked a few minutes till nine, they heard an unprecedented amount of noise emerging from the reading room of the library. Petrus, John's chief guard, was blocking the door, but stepped aside with some relief. "Almost lost hope for you, Captain. They been arguing out in the hallway, and Lord Parham finally agreed to let them into this room. No further, though. And I ain't let nobody leave." He pointed back the way they came. "Don't know if you saw him, but Wilbur's out by the door to the main hall. And I got another man stationed outside the house, just in case."

John let Jessica slip into the room, but stayed to give some last directions to the guard. "I don't know if Wiley will try to take anything with him. But don't let him leave without searching him thoroughly, no matter how he protests. And no one else enters, is that clear? He might be planning to pass something to a confederate."

Petrus nodded and planted himself in the doorway, his broad back blocking the exit.

The reading room was crowded with bodies; he located Jessica's right away. She was tugging at her uncle's sleeve, but Parham was too preoccupied to notice her. He stood before the great vestry table, making his case for a postponement like the most accomplished barrister. "We don't know if my niece has fulfilled the requirements of the trust, and until we do, we would remiss in making any transfer. She must marry *by* July 23, and in this case I think it fair to assume that 'by' means 'by the end of.' And the end of July 23—" he pulled out his watch with a flourish and consulted it "is yet fifteen hours removed."

Three solicitors, distinguishable by their old-fashioned bagwigs, sat in a line behind the table exchanging judicious nods as they listened to this. In front of them was a wooden casket of papers, with a hefty ring of keys on top. Their clerk, a scrawny young man with too-long hair, stood behind them with an inkpot and quill, looking bored.

With enormous relief, John saw Wiley squeezed between the table corner and the wall, trying without much success to shout Lord Parham down. Their eyes met, and Wiley's widened with shock—evidence enough of his involvement in John's disappearance. His expression changed from surprise to despair, and John knew he was witnessing the death of a man's hopes.

So be it. He stepped forward, pulling out the all-important document that proved Jessica's right to the Parham collection. "Lord Parham."

This succeeded where Jessica's increasingly vehement tugs had failed. Parham's voice faltered and he turned. "Dryden! And—" He glanced down at his arm, and for the first time noticed his niece. "And Jessica! You are here! And—and wed?"

"Yesterday."

Wiley made a grab for the licence, but John yanked it away and handed it to the solicitor in the center. "Lord Parham is here to give evidence to his consent."

"Just a moment, now, young man. We must examine this more closely."

In unison, the solicitors reached into their breast pockets for spectacles. John glanced over to make sure Jessica still held her reticule, with its confirmatory affidavit, then kept his gaze locked on the marriage lines lying on the table. The assault he expected came, Wiley's hand snaking out under the solicitors' faces.

"Let me see that."

"Not on your life." John planted his fist on the marriage license and slowly, sullenly, Wiley withdrew his hand.

"Our marriage is entirely official," Jessica put in defiantly, as the central solicitor picked up the license to peer at it. John waited for her to add that it had been duly consummated also. But she must have felt his amusement, for she turned to him with a challenging glance that suggested such revelations were the husband's job.

Apparently consummation wasn't an issue; the vicar's signature was. It was an angry, incomprehensible scrawl, only halfway set on the appropriate line, and the solicitor on the end claimed it didn't say Jeremiah Tooley after all, but Joseph O'Toole, and no one named O'Toole could be an Anglican vicar. John resolved that the supply of Burgundy wine to the vicar's table would be cut off immediately, and had almost decided to resume his childhood pastime of stomping melons from the vicarage garden, when Lord Parham resumed his barrister act at an even higher volume.

"Even if this is an O'Toole," he proclaimed, "and a Papist priest to boot, it matters naught. Clergy is clergy! Surely Mr. Wiley can't claim that every Papist couple in Britain lives in sin?"

"Mr. Wiley?" With a whispered gasp, Jessica escaped from John's side and through the door to the main collection room.

John cursed his new wife's predilection for independent action. But a glance at the wooden casket of papers told him what she hadn't taken the time to explain. The ring of keys had vanished, and with it the magician-handed librarian. With a muttered oath, he jerked at Parham's arm, then took off after Jessica before he could determine if her uncle understood his warning.

John wasn't quick enough, however. By the time he raced up the stairs and along the mezzanine to reach the back storage room, the door to the vault was open and the trunk pulled out into the middle of the floor. Over to the left, Jessica was over by the window, half-hidden by the corner of the long worktable. She struggled in the grasp of the solicitor's clerk, who had his hand clamped over her mouth and her arm wrenched behind her.

In two steps, John crossed the room and seized the clerk by the neck, his fingers tightening on the meager set of bones. "Let her go or I'll kill you."

"No, no, Captain Dryden." Mr. Wiley came out of the vault, a pistol in his hand. He pointed it at Jessica's chest. "Let *him* go, or I'll kill *her.*"

Immediately John loosed his hands and stepped back, every sense on alert for an opening. He thought he saw one when the clerk, coughing, let go of Jessica's arm so that he could rub at his neck. But Mr. Wiley's aim was still sure, and the clerk's hand still covered her mouth. Above it, her eyes were wild as she looked from the pistol to John.

Mr. Wiley smiled. "I gather, Captain Dryden, that I've found something that matters more to you than whatever we'll find in that trunk. I shan't forget that."

"I shan't forget this either, Wiley. You can't expect to survive this. The others will be along in a moment."

"Oh, I don't know if they will find us in time. Parham has never been back here, nor the solicitors, and it's not easy to find. But no matter what, my work will survive. I've filed a copy of my monograph with the Royal Society's secretary, who will open it in one week, whether I live or die."

"Don't do it. You will just ruin yourself, don't you know that? It's naught but folly, what you believe."

John might have been arguing with a saint, so unworldy was the gaze turned on him. The eyes were almost unfocused behind the thick lenses, the voice abstract. But the hand that aimed the gun at Jessica never wavered. "You will know it's not folly when the St. Germaine trunk reveals its treasure. Let her go, Meeker. She knows better than to shout as long as I hold this pistol."

The clerk let her go, and Jessica shook her head frantically, loosing her golden hair from its braid. She scrubbed at her mouth with her palm and shot a venomous look at Meeker. "I hope your hand falls off," she told him.

Always defiant, Jessica moved slowly away from the window towards John. Wiley didn't protest, but kept the gun trained on her and the table between himself and them. Never looking away from him, John held out his hand. Jessica took it, then almost immediately let it go. They needed the contact, both of them, but not the confinement, if they were to escape this trap of Wiley's devising.

Following Wiley's gentle-voiced directions, Meeker shut the door and wedged a chair under the knob. John exchanged a despairing glance with Jessica. Now the storage room would be less noticeable than ever, a closed door hidden away in the stacks of shelves, in the gloomy heights above the remotest room. If he knew Parham, their rescuers would be headed in the opposite direction.

Meeker took the key ring and, stooping, found one that fit the padlock on the black leather trunk. With a snap it sprung open, and he pushed up the lid. "Now what, guv'nor?"

Wiley kept the gun trained on Jessica, but backed up a few feet so that he could see over the lid of the trunk.

"Show me what's in it. Take out each item and read out to me what it is. Then hold it up so I can see it."

Meeker did as he was bid, reading off the titles of a half-dozen volumes that earlier John would have given an arm to possess. But now all he could concentrate on was that gun, pointed at Jessica. He had to draw it to himself somehow, to give her a chance to escape. The door was just behind them, and help not far beyond that. Meeker might chase her, but in a fair fight, John would lay odds she could lay the clerk out—and he was determined to give her the chance.

Finally Meeker read out in a bored voice, "Sir T-H More. By Anthony Munday." He held up a gray pasteboard box about the size of a folio volume.

John felt Jessica standing tense and silent beside him, and blessed her stoicism. That part of him that still cared about such things went still, hoping that Wiley would wave the box over to the pile of unimportant treasures.

But Wiley smiled peacefully. "That's it. Bring it to me."

John said rapidly, "Wait, Meeker. Whatever he's paying you, I'll triple it. Bring it to me." Wiley would forget about Jessica then, if John had hold of the prize.

But Meeker rose to his feet and started towards the librarian. Desperate, John said, "I assure you, I have far more funds than he does."

"Right. But he has the gun."

"Smart lad," Wiley said as the clerk approached him. "Now open up the box and put it on the table there, in the sunlight."

When that was accomplished, Wiley, gun still at the ready, edged over to the table. His gaze flicked back and forth between the box and Jessica, but his voice never varied from its gentle tone. "Undo the wrapper, Meeker. No, don't rip it. Don't you understand, this might hold the key to the great conundrum—it might be beyond price. Turn the pages, Meeker, one by one."

John couldn't see the handwriting on the turning pages, but he could smell the dusty dampness of the old paper. And he could see the expression on Wiley's face flicker from inquiry to concern to, finally, sorrow.

Jessica saw it too. "You were right, John. It must be in Shakespeare's hand." There was no triumph in her voice.

"No!" Wiley shook his head sharply. "Not in that hand. Not in Bacon's either. But this means nothing, that some actors—who knows who they might be—penned a few pages of indifferent verse."

"That's right," Jessica said eagerly. "It means nothing. It could have been any of the actors in that company. So you can just leave it there on the table, and no one will care in the least."

Wiley seemed to give this some consideration, tilting

his head to the side and studying her, then the book. Then he shook his head. "No. Others might be more gullible, don't you think? Best to relieve them of the temptation to leap to the wrong conclusion. Meeker."

The clerk had been lounging against the table, staring down at the box lid as if it were the treasure and not just its container. But at this he snapped to attention. "What do you want, guv'nor?"

"Is that lamp still in the vault? Go fetch it, if you please." With one hand, Wiley replaced the book in the box and closed it up; with the other, he kept the gun steady.

John waited, every muscle tensed and ready, until the clerk was inside the vault. Then he hissed, "Go!" to Jessica and hurled across the table towards Wiley, his only intention to interpose himself between her and the pistol.

He took him by surprise, enough so that Wiley had only time to raise the gun towards John's head. He hadn't the instant needed to aim the gun and get off a shot. Fortunately, the old blunderbuss of a pistol didn't go off even when the collision with John's forehead sent it spinning across the floor. Unfortunately, Meeker heard the commotion and emerged from the vault, lamp in hand, just in time to hook the skidding gun with his foot.

Even worse, instead of running towards the door, Jessica—insubordinate to the last—ducked under the table, evaded the falling bodies, and grabbed up the pasteboard box. Dazed from his collision with Wiley's gun, John pushed away from the table, only to see her dash past Meeker and into the vault.

At least she managed to get the door slammed before Meeker set down the lamp and, holding the gun gingerly, came up to help Wiley to his feet. "Here you go,

Mr. Wiley," he said imperturbably. "Gun. Lamp. I'll go get the girl."

John started after him, but the blood pouring from the cut on his forehead blinded him momentarily. By the time he blotted the blood with his handkerchief, Wiley had recovered, bringing the gun up and declaring, "I've got it aimed at your back, Dryden. Meeker, man, just open the door and pull her out!"

The clerk grunted and applied his meager shoulder to the oak and iron door without effect. He straightened up and peered through the little slit. "I can't, guv'nor. She's got something wedged in there. And I can't see nothing either."

"Jessie," John said, in some despair, envisioning her standing there in the dark, clutching the pasteboard box, without any chance of escape.

Wiley raised his voice. "It must be gloomy in there, Miss Seton, and stuffy too. You can't escape, and soon the air will grow close, and you will start to feel faint. You will have to come out eventually, so please don't make us wait." When his only response was a stubborn silence, he gentled his tone. "I do so deplore violence, my dear. Please don't make me use it against your new husband. What a terrible birthday gift his dead body would be!"

The door opened, and Jessica emerged, defeat written in the bend of her golden head and the slump of her slender body. Without looking up, she held out the box. Meeker grabbed it, and said brightly, "You want me to burn it, guv'nor?"

"What a likely lad you are, Meeker. Yes. Get the wastebasket there, from under the table."

As Meeker bent to comply, Jessica came, head bowed, to John's side, and silently passed him a lacy handkerchief. He blotted up the blood from his forehead, wishing she would have stayed back out of the range of the gun. But at least now he could take her hand and try to squeeze some sympathy into it. As bad as he felt, she must feel worse, for this was her mother's treasure that Meeker was holding over the open lamp and setting afire.

When the box was ablaze, Meeker let it drop into the wastebasket. The thump of its weight against the metal echoed in John's mind, and involuntarily he reached out his hand towards it. But Wiley turned the gun towards Jessica, and John let his arm drop back to his side, holding his breath so that he did not breathe in the smoke of his dying dream.

They all watched in silence as the flames shot up above the top of the wastebasket. When they subsided again, and finally went out, Meeker kicked at the basket. A last wisp of smoke curled up and dissipated in the uncaring air. "Naught but ashes left, guv'nor."

"Good. Here." Wiley brought a purse from his pocket and tossed it to Meeker. As he caught it, the clink of coin on coin grated in the silence. "Go on now, get out. And not a word of this to anyone, or there will be no more commissions for you."

The clerk stuffed the purse into his shirtfront and, wrenching the chair out from under the doorknob, called out a merry farewell and departed. The smoky air followed him, curling out the door like an insubstantial snake.

Wiley sighed and shook his head. "A most accomplished accomplice, don't you think? Oh, Miss Seton," he added, smiling at her, "I forgot to bid you a happy birthday. I mean, Lady Dryden. I am sorry that we will not be working together here in the library. But it is not to be." He drew a sealed page out of his pocket and dropped it on the table. "My letter of resignation."

Finally he turned to Dryden. "I know you will not neglect to read my monograph. It will be in the next Journal of the Royal Society, I have no doubt. You will find it most ingenious. No one will ever regard Francis Bacon in quite the same light, once my evidence is revealed."

On top of the letter, he laid his pistol. At the door, he stopped and looked back. "I told you I deplored violence. It is true. I could never have shot you, Lady Dryden." He paused, his hand on the door. "I do not think I could, at any rate. How fortunate for us all, that I didn't have to test my resolve."

John released Jessica's hand and walked to the table to check the pistol. It was primed and loaded. He listened to Wiley's footsteps on the staircase and hefted the pistol in the palm of his hand. Then he placed it back on the table. Vengeance was not worth a human life, any more than honor was.

Next to the gun, he set the wastebasket. "Naught but ashes left," he repeated, running his bloody fingers through the debris. There were still coals enough to burn him, but he didn't care. He held up his hands so Jessica could see his ash-coated fingers.

But instead of weeping, as he certainly would do if he weren't a man, she was smiling. "Get the lamp," she whispered, and gave him a shove towards the table.

Uncomprehending, he did as she bade. She took his lamenting hand and drew him into the vault, closing the door behind him and wedging a piece of wooden crating in the bolthole. Then she sat cross-legged on the floor, tucking her skirt under her. She patted the place beside her as if inviting him to join her at a picnic. "Come sit with me, John. I have a surprise for you."

He set the lamp down and dropped down beside her, suddenly weary in every muscle. "Tell me. Quickly."

Jessica tugged the gold chain of her reticle off her shoulder and passed the bag to him. "Open it."

He took a deep breath of the hot air and brushed his hands off on his breeches. Then he withdrew the book from the reticule. It was folio-sized, wrapped in cheap parchment apparently torn from an even older book. Across the front of the wrapper was written in spidery, faded ink, "The Booke of Sir Thomas Moore."

With shaking hands he unwrapped the book and opened it on his lap. He glanced at the first pages only long enough to see ink slashes across a few passages, presumably by the same man who also inscribed some comments in the margin. Later John might go back and read those, but now, he sucked the blood and ash off his index finger and, taking care not to tear the fragile paper, paged through the first couple scenes. Finally, on the eighth folio, he saw it. "There."

Jessica, still smiling her secret smile, bent to read where his finger stabbed, and murmured her appreciation. In a voice that sounded reverent even in his own ears, John explained, "He was younger when he wrote this, and stronger than when he made his will. But do you see? Look at the end flourishes on the 'e.'"

"It is very like. The final 'h' too—that is very familiar to me."

He wanted to stop and assemble all those swimming, slithering letters into words that combined to form some meaning. But he could only stare at the open page and then at Jessica's radiant face. There was a smudge of ash on her cheek; he made it even worse trying to rub it off. "Jessie, love, how did you do it?"

"I substituted another folio."

He looked around him at the shelves that lined the vault, at the treasures they hadn't had time to discover.

"Not— not one of the First Folios? No—no, it's all right. There are other First Folios."

"Not one of the First Folios. It was dark as pitch in here, John! I couldn't have laid my hands on it even had I no ready substitute." She picked up her reticule and opened it, showing him that, except for a comb and a tiny coin purse, it was empty.

"Your book. The one you brought in case you were bored."

"Yes. It was the Hannah More-Aphra Behn hybrid my mother had built. I took it to Dorset with me, to remind me of that night in the library. It was a folio also, and much the same weight."

"You came out with your head down, looking as if you were walking to the gallows! I thought—"

"What you were supposed to think. That my heart was breaking. And I was shaking like a leaf inside, afraid that in the dark I hadn't gotten the lid back on right, or that Wiley would feel a difference in the weight. But he never even touched it. I think he feared he would lose his courage, did he take it into his hands again."

There was a crash outside on the stairwell, a faint voice calling "Jessica!" But they were too busy to respond, alternating between kisses and reverent glimpses at the distinctive crabbed script on the three pages. Finally, when the lamp started smoking, John wrapped the book back up and returned it to Jessica's reticule, which he laid in her lap. He rose and held out his hand to help her up.

"You know," he admitted, pulling her close to nuzzle at her dusty ear, "you have more potential for derring-do than I would have imagined. That was—brilliant." He released her so that he could pull out the wedge of wood and open the vault door. Cooler air rushed in and snuffed out the lamp. "In fact," he said, taking her hand to lead her out into the open, "I think you were splendid."

"Do you?"

Her bright face turned up to him like a flower in the sunlight. He sighed and bent to kiss her again. At this rate, they would never make it out of the library. "I can't wait to take you to Rome. There's a man I want you to meet, a Monsignor Alavieri."

"The curator for the Vatican? The one who wrote the essay on ethical behavior in book collecting?"

"That's the one. He's a thousand stories to tell, and a thousand volumes to show us. He has a collection of forgeries I have been meaning to visit. It will add immeasurably to your education, I think. We can spend all winter there, and come back in the spring."

Still holding hands, they left the storeroom. Their brief interlude was over. Lord Parham, halfway up the stairs, called out, "There you are, Jessica! Don't you worry, sweet! We caught Wiley and his henchman, trying to slip out the door." In his haste to reach her, he tripped over a pile of books left on the step and regained his balance only by grabbing the railing with both hands. But his beaming face was evidence that he wasn't hurt. "Now that I've located you safe and sound—well, not sound, in fact, you both look the very devil—I'll just go back and make certain he hasn't persuaded the solicitors to release him."

"That's good, uncle." Jessica sat down on the top step, watching him thread his way through the stacks of books. John saw a sigh lift and lower her bosom, as she surveyed her new domain. It looked even worse for wear after Parham's search through the shelves. "Oh, John," she said, "don't you think we'd best postpone this wedding trip? In six months or so, we might bring some order to this chaos."

John sat down beside her and put an imperative hand under her chin, turning her gaze away from the mess. He looked into her eyes, watching the glow start up in their depths and radiate out to him. Then, gently, firmly, he said, "No, Jessie, it's waited twenty years, it can wait another few months. I'll have a colleague come in and see to tidying it up. We can put Sir Thomas in the vault in the Bank of England so we won't worry about it as we disport ourselves in Rome." We can sail on the *Coronale,* he thought; Jessica will appreciate her beauty. "Wait till you see the Vatican library! The Salone Sistina is the most extraordinary display room— the frescoes are as lovely as the artifacts."

He added a few more kisses, on the theory that a distracted woman was less likely to be obstinate. At least it quieted her objections. She subsided into his arms, and he leaned back against the wall, closing his eyes, wondering if they could walk as far as Jessica's bedroom without collapsing. Best not to try.

Jessica murmured something indistinct, and he roused himself enough to ask her to repeat it. More clearly she said, "I have always wanted to see Rome. And the Vatican Library. Papa used to marvel at its holdings, especially the Borgia collection. And you say Monsignor Alavieri is a friend of yours?"

"Something like that." With his eyes still closed, John envisioned Alavieri as he had seen him last, generous, warmhearted, tragic. "Just one thing you must remember when you meet him, sweetheart. He might be a bit—distrait if he hears about this latest discovery of ours. In fact," he added, in a tone that offered no judgment, "I'd be very surprised if he didn't decide to kill me."

Jessica lifted her head from his chest. "Really?"

"It is his way, you see."

She drew herself up, resolve mixed with ashes on her face, and said coolly, "Just let him try."

He traced the outline of her stubborn mouth with a gentle, dirty finger, marveling at the intensity of his desire for her—for all of her. "Ah, Jessie, my very own, the Borgias themselves would quail before us. What a team we will make, the two of us!"

Historical Note:

The character of Alfred Wiley is inspired by the Rev. James Wilmot, an Oxfordshire vicar who in 1780 started a search for books and papers that Shakespeare might have owned. Finding none, he concluded that the great plays had not been written by the man from Stratford-on-Avon, who must have been illiterate. Wilmot named Bacon as the leading candidate for the position of playwright. Frightened by his own theory, he burned his notes and confided in only a few people. It was another seventy years before others began questioning the identity of the author of the Shakespeare plays.

In reality, the play *Sir Thomas More* had been banned during Elizabethan times as subversive and thus was apparently never duplicated or performed. Its manuscript surfaced in the early nineteenth century in the Harleian Collection and is now in the British Museum. The script has been written in several hands, one of which was in the 1860s tentatively identified as Shakespeare's. From the 1920s, scholars have generally accepted that Shakespeare wrote three pages of that play. It is the only extant literary work known to be in Shakespeare's hand.

I am naturally taking a few liberties in placing the

manuscript in the St. Germaine trunk. But I am not inventing the manuscript, or the idea of Bacon-as-Shakespeare: They were both in England, however unnoticed, at the time of my story. That Alavieri and John identify it as Shakespeare's work so early is the biggest fiddle with the facts. I presume their theory was scoffed at for fifty years, but their expertise proved impeccable in the end!

ZEBRA REGENCIES
ARE
THE TALK OF THE TON!

A REFORMED RAKE (4499, $3.99)
by Jeanne Savery

After governess Harriet Cole helped her young charge flee to France—and the designs of a despicable suitor, more trouble soon arrived in the person of a London rake. Sir Frederick Carrington insisted on providing safe escort back to England. Harriet deemed Carrington more dangerous than any band of brigands, but secretly relished matching wits with him. But after being taken in his arms for a tender kiss, she found herself wondering—*could* a lady find love with an irresistible rogue?

A SCANDALOUS PROPOSAL (4504, $4.99)
by Teresa DesJardien

After only two weeks into the London season, Lady Pamela Premington has already received her first offer of marriage. If only it hadn't come from the *ton's* most notorious rake, Lord Marchmont. Pamela had already set her sights on the distinguished Lieutenant Penford, who had the heroism and honor that made him the ideal match. Now she had to keep from falling under the spell of the seductive Lord so she could pursue the man more worthy of her love. Or was he?

A LADY'S CHAMPION (4535, $3.99)
by Janice Bennett

Miss Daphne, art mistress of the Selwood Academy for Young Ladies, greeted the notion of ghosts haunting the academy with skepticism. However, to avoid rumors frightening off students, she found herself turning to Mr. Adrian Carstairs, sent by her uncle to be her "protector" against the "ghosts." Although, Daphne would accept no interference in her life, she *would* accept aid in exposing any spectral spirits. What she never expected was for Adrian to expose the secret wishes of her hidden heart . . .

CHARITY'S GAMBIT (4537, $3.99)
by Marcy Stewart

Charity Abercrombie reluctantly embarks on a London season in hopes of making a suitable match. However she cannot forget the mysterious Dominic Castille—and the kiss they shared—when he fell from a tree as she strolled through the woods. Charity does not know that the dark and dashing captain harbors a dangerous secret that will ensnare them both in its web—leaving Charity to risk certain ruin and losing the man she so passionately loves . . .